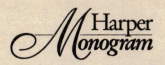

Harper
Monogram

W9-AGB-607

Miranda

⊰ SUSAN WIGGS ⊱

HarperPaperbacks
A Division of HarperCollinsPublishers

HarperPaperbacks *A Division of* HarperCollins*Publishers*
10 East 53rd Street, New York, N.Y. 10022

Cover and stepback illustrations by John Ennis

First printing: August 1996

Printed in the United States of America

HarperPaperbacks, HarperMonogram, and colophon are trademarks of HarperCollins*Publishers*

❖ 10 9 8 7 6 5 4 3 2 1

A vital yet invisible person in the publishing process
is the editor of a book.
My editor is one of the most clever and creative
women I've ever met. Add to that a sense of humor,
a deep appreciation for history
(not to mention men in kilts),
and a healthy respect for a writer's vision and voice,
and you have the perfect partner in publishing.
To my friend and editor, Carolyn Marino.
This one's for you.

ACKNOWLEDGMENTS

Special thanks to Barb, Betty, Joyce, Debbie, Alice, and Christina—for reading and believing.

Also, thanks to the members of the GEnie® RomEx electronic bulletin board—your help with research was illuminating and hilarious. And for the record, any mistakes or liberties found herein should be blamed on alien mutant swine who took over my body.

He's got nothing left to fight with. He's exhausted.
He'll crawl under a bed and hide.
—TALLEYRAND

Every man has his own threshold of impossibility.
—NAPOLEON BONAPARTE

Prologue

London
June 1814

The writing paper held the scent of violets, and that was the first clue.

The difficult cipher, based on a momentous day in the life of Napoleon Bonaparte, became clear after study. The key was not his birthday, after all, but an event far more significant: the date the defeated emperor went into exile on the Isle of Elba—4 May 1814. And that was the second clue.

The Allies believed the wars were finally over. At last a Bourbon king again sat upon the throne of France. Bonaparte would never return to seize power.

But the sender of the message disagreed.

M—
The hour of glory approaches. The crowned despots of Europe and their butchering battle

commanders will all arrive in England before the end of summer.

They believe they have come to celebrate a lasting peace. Only you and I know their true destiny.

The final solution lies within our grasp, thanks to Miranda Stonecypher. Once we learn her secret, she must die. Else half the men of England will be after Miranda.

La Couleuvre

The hand holding the message clenched into a fist, crumpled the perfumed paper, and hurled it into the hearth fire.

1

*How weak and powerless I am in this whirlwind of
plotting and treachery.*
—Empress Marie-Louise,
second wife of Napoleon Bonaparte

London
June 1814

In the beginning, there was a single point of
light. It narrowed to the tiniest tip of a needle, piercing in its intensity, cold and white as the brightest
star. She went toward it, a dreamer compelled by a
quest of the soul. Closer, closer she drew, the light
her only guide along the inexorable journey. Closer,
closer. She was almost there; soon she would be able
to reach forward, to tumble into the light. . . .

The pinprick grew and exploded into searing, shattering pain. A cry started in her chest and rose
through her, emerging ragged and desperate from her
mouth.

A fog of noxious sulfur corrupted the air. She could see the yellow-tinged cloud in the deadly flashes erupting all around her. The menacing whine of flying rockets screamed in her ears. A bomb soared and careened against the roof beams of the warehouse.

She stood amid hellfire and brimstone, confused yet feeling oddly unafraid. She had bruises on her body, and her wrists were burned by the rope that had bound her. Perhaps knowing she was doomed, knowing the matter of her own death was now out of her hands, banished the fear. Gripped by a peculiar, numb tranquillity, she watched a wooden crate catch fire.

Eerily beautiful flames flared with a dreamlike slowness, licking along the edges of the crate and then climbing to the boxes stacked above it.

A single word was stamped on the face of each box: EXPLOSIVES.

Even as a sense of peril registered, she knew with a strange feeling of detachment that it was too late to run. A second later, the crates and boxes exploded, bursting outward from a force within.

She felt pain, but from a distance. The force of the explosion hurled her backward. She waited for the impact of the wall, something to stop her, but the wall had disappeared. Just for a moment she was flying, flying into the black night.

She landed against a mound of baled cotton piled in an alleyway adjacent to the warehouse. The breath left her in a *whoosh*. She lay still, with the pain dancing madly, like a dervish, in her head.

The fireworks soared, turning night to day, angry lightning bolts in the sky. She began to realize, with dawning wonder, that she had done the impossible. She had survived. Perhaps, after all, she might live.

If she wished to.

Then a new flash cleaved the night. A plume of fire and smoke erupted in the alley. She could feel the roar of heat in her face. The flames reached for her, golden talons stretching closer, touching off the bales, sealing off her escape route. She tasted death again, its nearness, its allure whispered in her ear with a breath of fire.

Still unafraid, she started to surrender. Some part of her rejoiced. It was over. At last, all over. No one had won. All was lost.

A ball of fire rolled toward her, hungry, angry. Trapped in the alley, she slid deeper and deeper into submission, welcoming the end. But some tenacious hesitancy niggled at her, some sense that she was not ready yet. Someone needed her.

She staggered to her feet, swaying, the brick wall too hot to touch. Unfinished business. Benignly she noted that the bodice of her dress had been torn and then hastily repaired with a curved dressmaker's pin.

Unfinished business. Her mind groped for the nature of that business, but smoke filled her lungs, and thoughts skittered away.

Concentrate, she told herself, closing her eyes. And she began to open up, to let in the unthinkable, and it almost surfaced. Then her awakening sense of reason snapped shut like a closing mantrap.

"Lass!" a voice called. It sounded faint, but she realized it was because the explosions had deafened her. "Give me your hand!" the stranger yelled.

She opened her eyes. Turned toward the deep, urgent voice. Through a veil of fire she saw him, tall and broad, a fluid, racing shadow backlit by shooting stars.

"Lass," he shouted again, "you've got to come away from there now, while there's still time."

She couldn't move, couldn't speak, could only stare as the blaze rose higher around him. He was wonderful, an archangel of shadow and light, bursting through the curtain of flame. Gloved hands snatched her up as if she were a poppet doll.

She tucked her face into the shelter of a huge shoulder. The frock coat reeked of sulfur and smoke and sweat. She felt the jarring thud of his footsteps as he ducked his head and spirited her away from the exploding building.

Shouts and whistles echoed through the streets. A brigade was already strung along down to the wharf, passing buckets frantically from the river.

He set her on her feet in the recessed doorway of a brick building, gripped her shoulders, and leaned down to peer into her face. "What in God's name were you doing there? Are you all right?"

Dust and ash clogged her throat and mouth. Her vision was blurred by cinders and tears. She could not see his features, could make out only the shape of her savior against the roaring light of the fire behind him.

"Lass!" He gave her a gentle shake.

She managed to nod, to croak, "I am not badly hurt."

The shadow man swung off his frock coat, draped it around her shoulders. She had a swift impression of a broad chest, powerful arms. Safe. She would feel safe in those arms. She desperately needed to feel safe.

"Aye, then," he said. "Take care you don't—"

"Help! Help me!" The cry pierced through the bellow of flames and the crash of falling timbers. High in a tenement across the way stood a boy, just a little child, waving from a window. The roof above him had caught fire. So had the stairwell below him.

Her rescuer uttered a foreign word; it sounded like a curse. Before he even spoke or moved, she knew he would leave, and she felt an inexplicable sense of grief and yearning.

Stay with me, she wanted to plead. She longed to draw him into the light, to look at his face, to know the man who had snatched her from death.

Yet she felt no surprise when he shoved her toward a red-faced man overseeing the brigade. "Are you the watchman?" her savior asked.

"Aye, on patrol I was, and found myself in hell."

"Look after this one," he said, indicating her with a nod of his dark head. "I'll go for the lad."

"Christ, you'll die trying," the watchman said. "There's no way to get to the child."

But the man was gone, rushing toward the flames, disappearing into the burning building. The watchman pulled her to the end of the alley, where people were starting to gather.

A kaleidoscope of horrors wheeled around her. She saw the walking wounded, people with blackened burns and bleeding cuts, their faces lacerated by flying debris. Shredded paper made a snowstorm of confetti that flurried through the night sky. A woman ran past, cradling a child in her arms. A man walked by, his face as blank as a sleepwalker's. From the front, he appeared unscathed, his starched shirt and cravat perfectly white. Then, making no sound, he pitched forward and landed facedown at her feet. In the back, his clothes had been burned and shredded away. Smoke rose from his blistered flesh.

She bent to help him, scooping water from a bucket onto his skin. He screamed and shuddered, choked out a prayer, fell silent. She gestured frantically to two men who were bearing off the wounded on litters made of bedsheets and rough blankets. While they moved the victim onto the litter, she chanced a look at the tenement. The stranger who had helped her was now climbing the burning stairs toward the child. For a big man, he moved swiftly, gracefully, as if accustomed to performing with great competence during a disaster. He snatched up the boy. For a fraction of a second, he simply stood and clasped the child to his chest, holding the small form as if it were infinitely precious. An orange glow formed a halo around them so that they were beautiful together, bejeweled in flickering light.

Ah, she knew what the child must be feeling. Those all-powerful arms enveloping her, bearing her to safety.

She had just decided that he *was* an angel when the stairs collapsed. She half expected him to sprout wings and fly. A whimsical notion, a fleeting hope. Both the man and the child plummeted into a pit of burning timber. Sparks gushed upward from the broken skeleton of the building.

Choking with sobs that tasted of sulfur and soot, she tried to go to them. A wall of flame obscured them from view.

Someone grabbed her roughly, drew her back. "Too late," the watchman said. "You're needed here."

She heard someone else shout, "Miss, over here! Help us with this one!"

She struggled with the watchman, but he held her fast, shoving her to her knees beside a man with something metal embedded in his leg. "Concern yourself with the living, for chrissakes," the watchman ordered.

The eyes of the wounded man pleaded with her. She had no choice but to stay with him.

Moving like a dreamwalker, she survived the night, helping, grieving, casting glances down the alleyway and hoping against hope that the tall man would come out, unscathed, with the little boy in his arms.

She had no sense of the passing of time, but rain began to fall as dawn tinged the sky. People raised grateful, smoke-blackened faces, welcoming the rain, letting it deal a final death blow to the fire they had battled all night.

The watchman found her as she was offering sips of water to a shaken old man. She looked at the blackened remains of the tenement. He shook his head. "There were no other survivors, miss. I tried to stop him, but . . ." He lifted his shoulders in a helpless shrug. "You'd best be finding your way home."

Home. She mouthed the word. No sound came out.

"Your family'll be asking after you."

She stared at the harsh, weary face, the small, speculating eyes. Despair trickled through her, drizzling like the rain.

"Miss?" He cocked his head. His singed brows drew together. "Shall I send for someone?"

She felt a great well of emptiness open up within her. Heard a silent scream inside her soul. And finally forced herself to face the truth she had avoided all night.

She had no memory, no notion at all of who she was, no knowledge of what she had been doing in the warehouse.

Or why someone would want her dead.

The thought chilled her, but she knew she was the reason for the disaster, knew it just as certainly as if the devil himself had whispered it in her ear.

She gave a strangled cry and put her hand to her dry, raw throat. Her fingers encountered a metal object there, something round, suspended from a thin chain.

A silver locket. She pulled it from her bodice and squinted at it through smarting eyes. Something was engraved on the locket. A word. Someone's name. *Her* name.

Miranda.

Ian MacVane stared out the window of his fashionable Hanover Square house, watching a piece of torn silk blowing on the breeze and feeling a cold sense of doom.

"You didna tell me there was a girl involved," he said in a low, furious voice. Its tone was even deeper than usual because of the smoke and fumes he had inhaled from the warehouse explosion.

His visitor followed his gaze to the window. Heavy velvet draperies framed a view of elm and cherry trees, elegantly understated wrought-iron fences in front of handsome houses. A blue-eyed stare sharpened on the bit of blowing silk.

"What do you suppose that is, flying about like an infernal kite? A piece of someone's parade flag or aerial balloon, no doubt. London is simply *crawling* with dignitaries this summer. One can hardly take a chaise down Regent Street without stumbling upon a Prussian prince or a grand duke or some war hero draped with decorations."

The speaker turned to face Ian where he lounged on the bed, naked from the waist up. "These are interesting times we live in, darling, are they not?"

Ian glared at Lady Frances Higgenbottom. "The

girl," he repeated. "You didna tell me the traitor was a girl."

Lady Frances sighed. She took out her silk fan and idly waved it in front of her round, beautiful face. "If I had mentioned a girl, you might have gone and had a fit of scruples and possibly refused to help us. We are charged with safeguarding all the crowned heads of Europe while they're in London. That duty must come first."

Ian shifted on the satin sheets, wincing as the fabric brushed his burned shoulder and back. He told himself to be grateful to be alive at all. God knows he had wished for death in that moment when he'd looked down, realized that he had climbed to such a great height to fetch the child.

More than death, more than heated battle, even more than the past locked up tight in his heart, Ian MacVane feared heights.

The fall should have killed him, but somehow both he and the lad had managed to survive. He remembered being dragged to safety on a length of sailcloth. Gingerly he lowered the sheet farther so the fabric wouldn't chafe him.

Lady Frances fell so still that her golden ringlets stopped bobbing. "Good Lord, MacVane. *Must* you be so damnably alluring? The fate of Europe is at stake, and all I can think of is your body."

"You don't even like me, Frances."

"Whatever gave you that idea?"

A wry smile curved his mouth. "I think it was the time you made me fight a duel with an unloaded pistol, or perhaps your sending me by unarmed tender to deliver a message during a naval battle. I began to suspect—" Ian stopped himself, for she had done it again. Twisted the conversation away from the point he was trying to make. It was one of her many talents, and one that made her so effective in her secret role as chief spymaster of the Foreign Office.

"The lass," he said grimly. "I'm still waiting for an answer."

Frances snapped her fan shut and slapped it against the palm of her gloved hand. "You would have balked. Or gotten—heaven forbid—passionately entangled."

He narrowed his eyes at her, giving her the full force of an icy glare. "When have I ever gotten passionately entangled?"

She rubbed her hands up and down her arms as if the room had grown chilly. "God, MacVane. You're as cold as a Highland winter. I've always wondered why."

There was a reason, but Frances was the last person he would tell. She knew far too much already.

She went to a cherrywood butler's table and poured sherry from a crystal decanter. Ian studied each dainty, deceptive movement. Her costume was a confection of pink silk and frills, with little pink top-boots showing beneath the scalloped hem of her skirt. To anyone but the most astute observer, she was an empty-headed miss with no more on her mind than a plumed cap. The one concession to her true vocation was a tiny black lily stamped on the heel of her left boot.

She tasted the sherry and regarded Ian with a half smile. "We had been watching Miranda Stonecypher for some time—along with her father, Gideon. She is presumed to know very little." Frances's sweet, kiss-me-you-fool mouth twisted into an ironic smile. "Even less now."

"Bitch." Ian blew out a sigh and flung his forearm

over his brow, scowling out the window again. The scrap of silk had caught in the branch of an elm tree, fluttering red and royal blue on the summer breeze.

He squeezed his eyes shut, trying not to see the wounded with their bleeding faces and wide, wondering eyes, the eyes of innocents caught in the maelstrom of the explosion, eyes that asked the one unanswerable question: *Why?*

Ian himself had wondered that, all those years ago, back when he had been innocent, when he had been a victim.

"Everyone who is anyone is coming to London this summer," Frances continued, ignoring his insult. "There will be an assassination attempt, an elaborate one. So far, that is all we know. Our task is to find out the rest, and then keep it from happening."

"Go on," he said through gritted teeth.

"There's nothing more to report." She took a dainty sip of sherry. "Traitors are a dangerous lot, MacVane. They often turn upon their own." She paused dramatically. He caught her meaning.

"So it wasna you nor any of your agents who set off the explosion?"

Her nostrils flared. "I'll pretend you never asked me that, MacVane. Innocent people could have died last night, damn your eyes. As it happened, the only casualty was the traitor."

"You just said the woman knew very little," Ian pointed out.

She glanced at herself in the mirror over the washstand and primped. "As we know, looks can be deceiving." She cleared her throat. "The demise of a woman is a regrettable thing. But in this case, it is serendipitous and will—at least for a time—disrupt the plans of Bonaparte's conspirators."

Ian thought for a long time. His bed was unspeakably comfortable, his home luxurious, and a delicious luncheon was set out on a tray. No one would blame him for spending the day in idleness, nursing his wounds and resting.

Damn. The notion tempted him.

And so it was all the more excruciating for him to brace his arms on the mattress and lever himself up. He swung his legs to the floor.

Lady Frances squealed and clapped her hands over her eyes. "MacVane! My virtue!"

He had to laugh at that. "Virtue is surely the least of your worries, Fanny. Don't fret, I won't tell your precious Lucas you were here."

"He is not *my* Lucas," she retorted. "Yet."

He stuffed his legs into buckskin breeches and swore with the pain as he drew on his freshly polished Hessians.

She peeked through her splayed fingers. A tiny gasp slipped from her.

"You're cheating, love," he said with a wink, but he couldn't resist flexing his chest muscles.

Her fingers snapped shut. "You're insolent. And what the devil do you think you're doing?"

He swore louder now, in English and Gaelic both. "Putting on my shirt. Which is not a comfortable operation given the condition of my shoulder."

"You shouldn't have gone into that tenement, MacVane. But I'm not surprised you'd insist on playing the hero."

"Saving a child from certain death is not heroic," he told her. "Merely human."

"Then you should have let some other human risk it. I *need* you. Whatever became of the child, anyway?"

A loud crash sounded from somewhere belowstairs, followed by the patter of running feet and a childish giggle. Ian bit back a grin. "Does that answer your question, my lady?"

"God, MacVane! We've got enough troubles without becoming an orphan asylum."

"Then adopt the little mite, and he'll be an orphan no more. You'd make such a charming *maman.*"

She borrowed one of his choice oaths, and the word sounded incongruous coming out of her cupid's-bow mouth. Then she said, "Are you decent yet?"

He let out a bark of a laugh. "Fanny, my dear, I have *never* been decent. That's what you like about me."

She dropped her hands to plant them on her dainty waist. "So?"

"She didna die, Fanny."

Her sweet red mouth formed an O. "What?"

"The girl. She survived the explosion. I had no idea she was the one or I would not have misplaced her."

"But that's imposs—"

"How would you know?" he snapped. "Unless you ordered her killed." He watched her closely. "Och, I didna mean that, Fanny. For all that you are, you've never resorted to murder."

"Yet," she reminded him, fixing him with a lethal glare. "So where are you going?"

"I'm surprised you haven't guessed yet." He selected a waistcoat from the clothes press. It was made of tweedy Lowlander stuff, but he had no time to be selective. He donned the waistcoat and said, "I'm going after Miranda."

Leave me alone. I am looking into hell.
—King George III,
during an episode of madness

Miranda stood beneath an imposing gray stone lintel. A pair of statues with mouths agape and staring eyes glared down at her, and she recognized them—Cibber's statues of Madness and Melancholy. She looked at the words engraved in the stained granite: *Bethlehem Hospital.*

Her heart drummed against her breastbone. Reeling with dread, she turned to her escort, the watchman who had been with her at the fire. "This is Bedlam."

"Aye, miss."

"It's a hospital for people who are mad."

He moved closer to her, put his hand on her arm. She supposed it was meant to comfort, but instead she felt nervous, trapped.

"Miss," he said, "at least you'll have a roof over your head, a meal—"

"I'm not mad."

His hand tightened on her arm. "You say you don't know who you are, where you live, who your family are."

The black gulf of emptiness invaded her again, as it had each time she'd tried to remember *before*. Before the night, before the fire, before the terror and the insanity.

She stared at the ground, studying the cobbled street and the sparrows and rock doves poking at crumbs. London Wall. It wasn't a wall, but a roadway at the edge of Moorfields. How was it that she knew the name of this street if she could not even name herself?

The heavy door of the entranceway creaked open on iron hinges. She found herself looking at a beefy man with a mustache that swept from ear to ear.

She shouldered back her weariness, lifted her chin. "I don't belong here." Despite the show of resolve, she staggered, on the brink of exhaustion, and her vision swam. "I belong in . . . in . . ." Her chest squeezed with dread. "In hell," she said before she could stop herself. "Just not here," she finished weakly.

The warden exchanged a fleeting look with the watchman behind her, and she felt their unspoken exchange: *Mad as a March hare.*

"That's what they all say," the warden remarked in a bland voice. "Does she need restraints?"

Restraints. They would chain her like an animal.

She took a step back. Bumped into the watchman. Strong hands grabbed her shoulders.

"Sir!" she choked out. "Unhand me! I do not belong here, and I certainly don't need re—"

"You did well this time, Northrup. Got here before Dr. Beckworth makes his rounds."

"He oughtn't to complain, the stupid cit. The gate fees pay his wages," Northrup said. His hand snaked into her hair. He pulled, forcing her head up. "Such a pretty piece will be a nice addition to the menagerie."

"I'll be able to charge the gawkers double. They like the pretty ones."

"Arrangement!" Miranda echoed. "You mean I am to be sold like a monkey to a zoo?"

The warden lifted a bushy eyebrow. "A show of spirit is always welcome. She'll be an interesting specimen."

"This is criminal!" she shouted. "Kidnapping!"

The warden captured her wrists in one hand and brought them up high behind her. A wrenching pain seared her elbows and shoulders. She could smell his sweaty body, could feel the heat of his breath on the back of his neck. Could hear the clink of coins in the small cloth purse he gave the watchman.

Outrage gripped her in a choke hold. The man who was supposed to be helping her—a man she had trusted—had sold her to a madhouse.

The watchman slipped away, ambling down the fog-shrouded lane.

Miranda shuddered out a long sigh. "Please, sir," she said, affecting a small, meek voice. "It has been a rather long, eventful night for me, and I am quite exhausted. Truly, I need no restraining whatever."

He laughed unpleasantly. "So you'll make it easy on both yourself and old Larkin?"

She swallowed. Her throat still burned from the smoke. Her mind held nothing but emptiness—and fear. "Certainly, Mr. Larkin," she forced out through dry lips.

The hard grip eased. She rotated her aching shoulders. Think think think . . .

The man called Larkin opened the door wider. The sharp smells of lye soap and urine gusted out, along with the roars and wails of the inmates.

Miranda ran.

Bunching her tattered skirts in one hand, she plunged down the lane. Her feet, laced into sturdy brown leather boots she did not remember putting on the previous morning, clattered over the uneven cobblestones.

With the curses of the warden ringing through the rows of close-set buildings, she ran blindly. She had no idea where she was going except *away.*

Away. The thought pounded in her head, counterpoint to the rhythm of her running feet.

Away, away, away.

Why are we going away again, Papa? And why must we leave in the middle of the night, without even saying good-bye?

It was a very old memory, incomplete, a vague impression of a slender man in a shabby coat, a warm hand closed around her small, cold one.

"Stop, thief!" the warden bellowed. His big voice roused a few sleepy-looking pedestrians as they walked along the street. Here and there, shutters opened and heads poked out.

"Stop her!" Larkin called again. "Stop her, I say!"

Miranda plunged on. She had a fleeting impression of inquisitive glances, but no one seemed inclined to stand in her way. There was, she decided, some small advantage to having one's face and clothing soiled with black soot. No one wanted to touch her.

Don't touch me don't touch me don't— Another memory, this one dark and disturbing. She was almost grateful when it evaporated like the fog.

She careened around a corner, nearly colliding with a costermonger's cart. The coster swore. Loose onions and potatoes spilled out, filling the narrow lane. She hesitated, then tried to leap past the cart.

Brutal hands dug into her shoulders. She turned to see Larkin's face, red with fury.

"That's the last time you'll run from me, my fine lady fair," he said, huffing with exertion. Even as she fought him, he hooked his leg behind her knees and forced her to the hard ground. He settled his weight on her, filling his fist with a handful of hair and giving it a cruel twist. "You want to earn your keep on your back, eh?" His eyes were small and hazel in color, hot and hungry. "I can arrange that."

Miranda screamed.

Lucas Chesney grew impatient, waiting for Miranda. She had never been late before. He plucked a gold watch—one of the few items he had yet to pawn—from his pocket and thumbed it open, just to make sure.

Yes, it was half noon. She was late. Was she still angry about their ridiculous quarrel? What a barbarian he'd been, ripping her dress like that.

He paced, noting his surroundings with idle curiosity. The clutter of low buildings was dominated by soot-blackened churches, St. Mary-le-Strand, St. Clement Danes, St. Brides. The area near Blackfriars Bridge was not quite a slum, though it had its share of press gangs and flash houses. Some of the residences still possessed a smidgen of old-fashioned charm in their sandstone edifices and boxy gardens, but the neighborhood was clearly a place for people of less than modest means.

The perfect spot for you, old chap. Lucas slammed a door on the thought. He could not allow himself to dwell on the state of disaster known as the Chesney family fortune. He was Lucas Chesney, Viscount Lisle, heir to the duke of Montrond, and he had a reputation to uphold.

Even if that reputation hung on the flimsiest string of lies and excuses since the Whigs had dominated Parliament.

The crumbling neighborhood had one distinct advantage, Lucas observed. No one here knew him.

No one except Miranda.

As always, his heart beat faster at the thought of her. A beauty, she had no particular use for her appearance. Though brilliant, she did not use her cleverness as a verbal lash, to cut and belittle people. While her radical views worried him, he had no doubt that in time she would temper her opinions. She was a delicious enigma, sometimes sweet-natured in a distracted, absentminded fashion, other times fiery and tempestuous.

She was fascinating, funny, and passionate. Dazzlingly beautiful. She had but a single flaw. It was the one matter that haunted Lucas, troubled his dreams at night and made him feverish to find some solution.

Miss Miranda Stonecypher was penniless.

She made money and possessions seem unimportant, but Lucas loved his family and felt compelled to provide for them. Ever since the hunting accident that had left his father bedridden and staring mad, Lucas had taken on all the duties and debts of his office. And perhaps, he thought with a surge of hope, perhaps he had found an answer at last.

He had recently made the fortunate acquaintance of a—what was Mr. Addingham? A benefactor?

Lucas shook his head and laughed at himself. Silas Addingham was a ruthless social climber who had more money than shame. He wanted an entrée into polite society. Lucas could give it to him.

For a price.

He had tried to explain it to her the previous night, just before their row. Addingham's money would enable Lucas to marry Miranda at last. To bring their relationship out in the open instead of sneaking around, hoping they wouldn't get caught.

Eager to patch things up after their quarrel, he did something he had never done before. He went to her lodgings.

Lucas stood outside Number Seven Stamford Street. He knew only that Miranda lived here with her crack-brained father and a servant called Midge.

Feeling conspicuous, he rang the bell pull, then waited on the stoop. The air was filled with the smells of cooking and rubbish, the occasional laughter of children and shouts from watermen on the river.

When no one answered, he rang again. Not being able to introduce Miranda to his family, to his friends, had always brought him a faint sense of shame. It would be a relief to be open now.

He laughed to himself, picturing the look on Lady Frances Higgenbottom's face when he appeared in public with Miranda.

Lady Frances, as lovely as she was wealthy, had been after Lucas for years. Though her relentless pursuit flattered his manly pride, he had long since grown weary of her shallow, tiresome ways. She swore that only by marrying her could Lucas save his family's estate from the auctioneer's hammer. But he had found another way. He had found Silas Addingham.

There was no response to his second ring. Lucas pushed open the door.

"Hello!" he called out. The smell of sulfur hung in the air. Miranda and her infernal experiments. She was always dabbling in some chemical reaction or other, trying to generate nitrous gases or hydrogen. Once they were wed he would delight in giving her a new outlet for her inventiveness—their marriage bed.

As he mounted a flight of creaky, uncarpeted stairs, he became aware of a subtler scent—acrid, hot, and rusty.

Blood.

Lucas took the stairs two at a time, calling Miranda's name. He emerged into a dim sitting room that reeked like an abattoir. The last time he had smelled death this sharply had been in a field hospital in Spain.

He forced away the nightmare memory of his soldiering days and went searching through the flat. It was a ghastly quest marked by a thickening trail of blood, overturned furniture, broken lamp chimneys, scattered papers.

He came to a tiny room with a single bedstead, the coverlet trailing along the floor.

A muffled moan issued from beneath the frayed cloth.

Lucas plunged to his knees. "Miranda!" With a shaking hand, he moved the blanket aside. A death-pale face stared up at him. The odor of fresh blood slammed through him.

And Lucas felt a shameful flood of relief, for the face of the dying woman was not Miranda's.

"You must be Midge," he said gently. "I am Lucas, a special friend of Miranda."

The woman's crusted lips moved. He bent forward to hear.

"'Randa . . . has no friends," the servant whispered.

Lucas's heart constricted. "She has one," he said. "She has me."

A bloodied hand clutched his sleeve. "They took her. And . . . Gideon."

Lucas squeezed his eyes shut. Somehow he had known from the moment he'd set foot in this house. Damn! He should never have let her storm off in anger last night.

"Who?" he forced out as grief and rage and panic tore into him. "Please. For Miranda's sake, you must tell me. Who did this?"

She spoke again, her voice fainter than ever. "Vi . . . Violet." The word was more sigh than speech.

Despite a pounding sense of urgency, Lucas could not leave her. He held her for what seemed a long time. Her hand, icy cold on his sleeve, went slack and dropped. A rattling sound he remembered from the field hospital filled the silence.

He felt strangely calm as he relinquished his hold on Midge, poor Midge, whom he had never known. He put her head on a pillow and settled the coverlet around her as if she were a child being tucked in for the night. For eternity.

Then, still seized by an eerie serenity, he went through the apartment, seeking clues.

The problem was, someone had been here before him. Someone had ripped out desk drawers and rifled through papers and books. Someone had taken three innocent lives and cut them short.

He must contact the authorities. He would do so anonymously, of course, taking care that his name not be connected with this whole unsavory affair.

As he left, he passed through the vestibule. On a peg behind the door hung Miranda's plain blue wool shawl. He pictured her in it, strolling along with him, gesturing as she spoke, her eyes brighter than stars as she gazed up at him.

He snatched up the shawl and buried his face in the soft wool. It smelled of Miranda and memories.

He had been too damned late to save her.

Ah, God, Miranda. I'm so sorry.

The dam broke. Lucas Chesney, Viscount Lisle, hero of the Peninsular Wars, sank to the floor and sobbed.

Miranda forced herself to stop screaming as Larkin yanked her to her feet and dragged her back to Bedlam. "I have a wealthy family," she said. Her voice had taken on a surprisingly cultivated tone.

"Have you, then?" Larkin asked cynically. "I thought you didn't remember."

"Perhaps I do, perhaps I don't," she said in a singsong voice. "The question is, will you risk it?"

Larkin paused at the entranceway to the hospital. "Risk—"

She barked out a laugh. "Your decision, Mr. Larkin. Are a few moments of fleeting lust worth losing a handsome reward?"

He studied her for a long moment, his mustache twitching. "You're a skinny, filthy wretch anyway," he muttered. Then he hauled her through a corridor with cracked plaster walls, stopping at a wide, barred door. "Your home away from home, milady," he spat.

He shoved her into the women's gallery. She pressed a fist to her mouth to stifle another scream. A high fanlight let in streams of the afternoon sun. Dirty straw covered the floor. The plaster walls were crumbling and weeping with moisture. And everywhere, in every nook and cranny, on each rickety bench or moldering pallet, some dangling from manacles and leg irons, were the insane.

A few of them looked up when she entered. Most continued their mindless rocking and moaning, some screeching or muttering to themselves. One had plucked out the hair on the left side of her head. Another sang a tuneless, repetitive melody. But for the most part, the women lay as unresponsive as corpses.

"Hey, warden!" A buxom woman with bad teeth and jet black hair sidled toward them. "What have you there? A new jade ornament?"

"Stand aside, Gwen, she's none of your affair."

Ignoring him, Gwen put her face very close to Miranda's. "'Neath all that dirt and soot, she looks a bit too fine for the likes of you, Larkin." Gwen lifted an eyebrow. "What say you to that, mistress?"

A spark of outrage flared to life inside Miranda. She jerked her arm from Larkin's grasp. "What I *say*, Mistress Gwen, is that any woman in this room is too fine for the likes of Warden Larkin."

In the stunned silence that ensued, more women lifted their faces toward Miranda, like broken blossoms seeking the sun. Gwen let out a laugh of delight, braying loudly until the warden backhanded her across the mouth.

She barely flinched. A group of women ambled closer, baring their teeth. Sweat broke out on Larkin's brow. He took a coiled leather lash from his belt. A few inmates shrank back, but still more advanced.

Barking an oath, Larkin stepped outside, slammed the door, and shot the bolt home. Gwen laughed again, and others joined her, their shouts of mirth no longer eerie, but strangely joyful.

Miranda stood with her back to the wall of iron bars and stared. When at last she found her voice, she asked, "Why did you do that, all of you? Why did you defend me?"

Gwen clasped Miranda's hands in hers. "Because of what you said, girl. About us all being too fine for Larkin."

"I spoke no more than the truth."

"Aye. But no one's ever said it before."

The explosion was four days past and Miranda's trail was growing cold. Ian MacVane had inquired at churches, poorhouses, bawdy houses, almonries. He had paid bribes to wharfside idlers and ships' masters, to innkeepers and stablers, all to no avail.

His superiors were growing more insistent by the hour. Frances had been shocked to learn the young woman had survived the explosion, and she was frantic to speak to her—or so she said. But Ian knew instinctively that Frances was not particular. She merely wanted the girl found—alive or dead.

Frustrated, he stalked through the ransacked house in Stamford Street for the tenth time. Curses trailed like a black banner in his wake.

Four days, and he was no closer to finding her than he had been after the night of the disaster.

And to think he had held her in his arms!

The thought haunted him. He remembered how fragile she had felt, remembered the fright and confusion in her eyes. The urge to protect her had been powerful. He should have heeded his instincts rather than entrusting her to the watchman.

"You should hae listened to the voice in your noggin rather than shunting her off on that peeler," Duffie said, shouldering open the door and stepping inside. "You knew that, did you not?"

Ian glared at his assistant, Angus McDuff. "Not before you did, it seems. Truly, you give me the willies." Duffie had an uncanny gift for reading a man's thoughts. "If I were the superstitious sort, I'd call you a devil's imp and banish you to the Outer Hebrides."

"The London peelers are as corrupt as the criminals themselves," Duffie said. "It takes no great gift to figure that out."

"Aren't you supposed to be looking after Robbie?"

"The lad's fast asleep in the coach, bless his wee heart," Duffie said with fondness. His bristly, graying beard outlined the bow shape of his broad smile. "At the moment, you need me more."

They stood together in thoughtful silence, surveying the place that had been the home of Miranda Stonecypher.

It was a modest suite of rooms with scuffed plank floors, threadbare upholstery, and papers crammed on shelves or strewn about. Black smears of dried blood marred the walls and floors.

Books were piled on every available surface. The topics ranged from works on moral philosophy to scientific tracts on physics and cosmography.

Had Miranda read them, or had they been her father's? The Englishwomen Ian knew did not trouble themselves to read anything more challenging than *La Belle Assemblée*. God forbid they should actually have to *think*.

By far the most disquieting item in the room was a painting over the mantel. It was a reproduction of *The Nightmare* by Fuseli, Swiss painter and darling of the radicals. A sleeping woman, clad in a gauzy night rail, reclined on a draped bed. On her bosom perched a creature with a burning gaze and a wicked leer, and in the background loomed a horse with glassy eyes and flaring nostrils.

"Now that," Duffie said, "gives me the willies."

"Be certain Robbie doesna see it." Ian turned away from the picture. The room was in a shambles, destroyed by the murderers and then rifled by officers from Bow Street who had been alerted by an anonymous citizen.

Ian grinned humorlessly. Lady Frances hated the Runners. This was not the first time they had interfered in her work.

He and McDuff picked through the rubble that was left. A half-written letter responding to a lender's dun for money. Greek symbols sketching out some mathematical formula. A mundane list in a more feminine hand: *foolscap, ink, silk thread . . .*

In a carpetbag he found a stocking to be mended, along with an unfinished needlework project depicting a spray of forget-me-nots around an old-fashioned tower house. The caption read, "One father is more than a hundred schoolmasters." A faint floral scent clung to the bag. Ian dropped it and raked a hand through his hair.

He knew nothing about this woman.

Except that she read wonderful books and liked dangerous paintings and loved her father.

And that when he'd held her, he had felt a reluctant stirring in his heart.

"Och, I dinna believe my eyes," Duffie exclaimed.

"What do you mean?" Ian asked in annoyance.

"The great MacVane of the Highlands actually felt something other than hatred and rage. Ah, dinna deny it. I saw it in your pretty face. You care about the lass, don't you?" Duffie gave a sly wink.

Ian clutched the back of a wooden chair and glared down at his gloved hands. The gloves spared him from seeing the stump of his finger, from remembering the past.

"She's a puzzlement, Duffie. There was something . . . not right about her that night."

"People dinna generally appear their best following a massive explosion," Duffie observed helpfully.

"It was more than just panic and confusion. It was—" Ian nearly strangled on his own words as a blinding flash of memory cleaved his thoughts. Just for a moment, he was in another place, another time. . . .

Burning buildings, thick smoke, people running to and fro. And his mother, unable to stand what they had done to her, had that same look in her eyes. That look of madness. . . .

"Madness, you say?" Duffie asked.

"Did I say that?"

"Well, if people were to perceive the poor lass to be mad, then . . ."

Duffie and Ian looked at each other. At the same time, they snapped their fingers and spoke the same thought.

"Bedlam."

3

Marriage is for life. If I were in your place, I should tie my sheets to a window and be off.
— Queen Maria Carolina of Naples,
grandmother of Empress Marie Louise

Ian disliked Dr. Beckworth on sight. It had taken a small fortune in bribes to get this far into the horror chamber that was Bedlam, and now Beckworth stood in the middle of his office, the implacable guardian at the threshold.

"What do you mean, you willna take my coin?" Ian demanded.

"I am a man of ethics as well as science, sir. I do not take bribes." Above a boiled collar, he lifted his chin to a haughty angle.

"Would you consider a grant in the name of charity, then?"

Beckworth tightened his mouth until it resembled a sphincter. "Please."

"I merely want to see Miss Stonecypher."

Beckworth's hands gripped the lapels of his frock coat. "Stonecypher."

Ian cursed himself for showing a card to his opponent. He needed to play them closer to the chest. "There, you see. The poor lass has been here four days and you haven't even found out her family name."

Beckworth sat down behind a writing table. He fingered a quill stuck in the inkwell, staring at the feathers, turning it this way and that. "It's very irregular. I can speak of this case with no one save the girl's family. . . ."

"She has no family," Ian said. Then, gambling all, he added, "Except me."

The doctor lifted a monocle to one eye. "You are related to Miss, er . . . "

"Stonecypher."

"Stonecypher." Beckworth tasted the unusual name again.

"I am betrothed to her," Ian assured him. Lying had always come easily to Ian. He had learned it at an early age and considered it one of the most fundamental of survival tactics. *Please, sir, I canna work today. My cough is infectious. . . .*

"Why didn't you explain that right from the start?" Beckworth asked.

He's as suspicious as I am, Ian thought. "Perhaps, like you, I prefer to guard my privacy."

"Ah." Beckworth tucked the monocle into the pocket of his waistcoat and took a deep breath. "Have you any proof of this betrothal?"

"I do." Ian levered himself up out of his chair and paced the office. He ducked his head beneath the lime-washed ceiling beams. He stopped in front of the table and slammed his palms down on the surface.

Beckworth flinched.

Ian leaned forward and said, "Aye, I have proof, but she's locked up like some moonstruck lunatic, damn your eyes!"

"She can't remember anything," Beckworth blurted out, then clamped his mouth shut, clearly angry at himself for having divulged Miranda's condition.

This, Ian realized, was no gamble after all. She would not recognize him, but that, of course, would all be part and parcel of her affliction.

"I want to see her," Ian stated. "Now."

Beckworth hesitated. Ian subjected him to the coldest, most menacing stare he could summon. The stare worked. The doctor stood. "Follow me."

Moments later, Ian wondered if Beckworth was leading him along a circuitous route just to punish him. They passed through a long gallery lined with barred cells. Dank shadows hung in the unlighted corners. Sleek rats scurried in and out through cracks in the walls. A babble of nonsense talk, moans, and tuneless singing joined with the foul stench to make the air almost unbreathable.

Fashionable people with handkerchiefs pressed to their noses strolled along, stopping to gape at the inmates. It was a common recreation to buy a ticket to view the insane. Ian, who had looked madness in the face, found the practice more disgusting than anything he could see behind bars.

"Oh, look at that one," a lady exclaimed, giggling and pointing. "What is he doing with his—"

"Surely he is thinking of you," Ian whispered in her ear as he passed behind the woman.

She gave a little shriek. She and her gentleman friend hurried out.

A cleric clutching a prayer book nodded mournfully as he passed. Several inmates reached through the bars, grasping at the air as if it represented free-dom itself. Ian fought the urge to run, far and swiftly, away from this place that evoked such uncanny reminders of his past.

This was different, he told himself. Perhaps *this* woman could be saved. He despised the idea that the girl with the large brown eyes had been trapped in this place for four days. If she wasn't insane before, she surely was now.

When Beckworth brought him to a large, barred common room for female inmates, Ian spied her immediately. She sat on a wooden stool in a flood of sunlight that streamed through a high window. On a bench in front of her, a chess board was scratched into the wooden surface, small light and dark stones serving as chessmen.

She wore an unbleached muslin gown, plain and much mended, and her abundant brown hair was tied back with a bit of string. Her face looked clean but weary, her complexion smoother and richer than the heart of a rose.

In her lap, propped on her knees, she held a bro-ken piece of slate. She was reciting aloud to a group of uncannily attentive women. "'It is time to affect a revolution in female manners—a time to restore to them their lost dignity—and make them, as part of the human species, labour by reforming themselves, to reform the world.'"

Ian was familiar with the writings of Mary Wollstonecraft. He had discovered a set of treatises by the female zealot while waiting out a long calm during a sea voyage. But hearing Miranda recite the words aloud, with such conviction, and to such rapt women, was stirring indeed. "You said she had no memory," he whispered to Beckworth.

"She has perfect recall of general knowledge. It's really quite astonishing. Yet she has no recollection of personal matters." Beckworth motioned him into the common room.

"Och, 'tis Bonny Prince Charlie!" An elderly woman, her hair a dirty gray mop, scuttled over and dipped a curtsy to Ian. "I'd know ye anywhere, laddie," she said in a thick Highland brogue. "Ah, the midnight hair, the eyes of blue. Been waiting for you to return since me granny's time, we have." She gave him a toothless smile and remained there, one knee on the floor, quivering slightly, clearly unable to move.

Ian flushed and glanced back at Beckworth, who stood just inside the door. The doctor stared straight ahead. Ian had no choice but to hold out his hand and help the old woman up.

"And a fine gentleman you are, sire, and always have been," she declared. She turned to address the ladies. "Well, what are ye waiting for? 'Tis our own rightful prince come back to us, just like I told ye he would. And he's a ghostie, he is. 'Tis why he stays so young and bonny."

A few of the women, their faces blank, inclined their heads. Ian's ears heated. He cleared his throat. "It is a high honor to meet you, but I am not Bonny Prince Charlie. Regrettably, he died some years ag—"

"Weesht!" The old women held a finger to her lips. "We ken. You're in disguise, eh?" She tugged at his waistcoat. "I thought there was a purpose to that MacLean tartan."

He nodded in exasperation. "I am here to see Miranda."

Some of the women began to hiss and whisper among themselves. Ian cleared his throat again. "You are . . . dismissed."

The old woman backed away, bowing as she retreated to another part of the room. Most of the others—those who were not chained or bound—went with her. Miranda looked up anxiously.

There was one thing Ian had not remembered from the night of the fire. And that was how stunningly beautiful she was.

Even like this, in a plain shapeless gown, her hair and face unadorned, she was like the moon. Pale skin, sable hair, a study in light and dark. He felt something unexpected and ecstatic in the center of himself as he looked at her. She had a sort of heart-catching innocence that sat ill with his sense of who she was, what she was capable of.

"Hello, Dr. Beckworth," she said in a soft, cultured voice. Then she looked at Ian, the huge brown eyes showing—not surprisingly—no recognition at all. "Good day to you, sir." Then she frowned.

"Is something wrong?" Beckworth asked.

"No. For a moment I thought . . ." She waved her hand distractedly. "It was nothing."

"My dear," Beckworth said, his meddlesome manner irritating, at least to Ian. "Do you recognize this man?"

"Hello, Miranda," Ian said softly. He lowered himself so their gazes were level and sent her his kindest smile. "It's a high relief to find you at last." Another of his well-honed skills was the intimate whisper. Women succumbed to it almost too easily, tumbling into his arms in fits of ecstasy. He waited for Miranda to melt.

Instead she cocked her head to one side and asked, "Do you play chess?"

He blinked. "Chess."

She frowned in concentration at the chess board. "It seems that I do. Perhaps too well. Each time I play myself, it ends in stalemate."

"This gentleman claims he knows you," Beckworth said. "He says you were betrothed."

She caught her breath. "To be married?" She stared at Ian with new, keen interest.

"That's right, love," Ian said, amazed that he felt guilty deceiving her. According to Fanny, this woman was a deadly traitor and the key to a hideous plot to assassinate the crowned princes of Europe. Yet suddenly he felt as if he had stepped on a kitten. "You canna remember?"

"No." She bit her lip. It was a full lower lip, the very sort that begged for a kiss. This could prove to be dangerous indeed, Ian thought. In ways he had not yet considered.

"Darling." He took both her hands in his and drew her to her feet. The top of her head just reached his chin. "Surely you remember me. I am your one true love, your Ian."

At this the other women clustered round, jabbering and clucking like hens.

"Kiss her!" one of them urged.

"Yes, kiss her, kiss her!" The others took up the chant.

It was odd, Ian thought, looking at these hopeless, disheveled creatures. After all they'd been through, they still wanted to believe in a happy ending.

"Kiss her!" they continued to chant. A buxom woman with black hair and laughing eyes made a smooching sound with her mouth.

"Ian," Miranda repeated. Her breathing quickened, and she made a sound of distress. "Dr. Beckworth, may we please have some privacy?"

Ian was more stunned than the doctor by her request. He felt a jolt in his chest. God. She was falling for the ruse. He ought to feel pleased by his own cleverness. Instead he sensed a faint edge of panic. He might very well find himself with a fiancée before this day was out.

"Miranda, I shouldn't allow it," Beckworth said. "It would not be prop—"

"The lady made a simple request," Ian broke in.

"You may go to the empty cell across the hall." The doctor held the door for them. "I shall be outside." He aimed a meaningful stare at Miranda. "You need only call out and I'll come."

"She'll call out, right enough," said the black-haired woman. "But not for you, Beckie."

Ian glared at the doctor as they left the room. Officious little toad. *Does he think I would ravish her right here in this rank cell?*

Rather than seeming absurd, the very idea made him hard. Perhaps he was crazy, too, lusting after a woman in Bedlam, of all places. His chest felt tight when he turned to Miranda. "Does the name Stonecypher mean anything to you?"

"Stonecypher." She tasted it like an exotic fruit. "No. Should it?"

"That's your name, my love. You are Miranda Stonecypher, and I am Ian MacVane."

"My betrothed."

"Your betrothed."

She clasped her hands demurely in front of her. "Were we in love?"

The question took him by surprise. *In love.* He almost laughed aloud at the thought. Love was something that didn't happen to Ian Dale MacVane. It simply wasn't meant to be. Yet here she stood, all innocence, brimming with hope.

"Well?" she prompted. "Was it a love match?"

"Very much so." How easy it was to gaze into her

wide, trusting eyes and lie. "We were deeply in love." He traced his finger along her jawline. "I still am."

"Oh, my." Her slender throat moved sinuously as she swallowed hard. "And we were to be married?"

His thoughts came together swiftly. "Aye, we were going to Scotland so there would be no need to secure a special license." Recklessly he plunged on. "And of course, you wanted to meet my people in the Highlands."

"Why?"

"Because they've not met you, lass, and—"

"That's not what I meant." She pressed her palm to his chest. Her warmth burned into him. "Why were we going to be married?"

"I thought I explained that. We love each other. We—"

"But why marriage?" Her hand crept along his chest and slid upward to skim his collarbone. He wondered if she was at all aware that by touching him this way, she was breaking every rule of proper behavior. He wondered if she cared.

"Marriage is the institution of a corrupt society, designed to enslave women," she stated.

Ian could barely think. Was she naive or simply bold, touching him like this? He had been caressed more intimately by more brazen women, to be sure, but there was a compelling quality to the way Miranda slid her long-fingered hands over him.

"Who told you that?" he asked. "Did you learn it by reading Mary Wollstonecraft?"

"I suppose so. Dr. Beckworth urged me to remember things. It is odd. I can recite whole passages by heart, yet I can't even recall my name—" She backed away as a violent shudder racked her. "You can't know how frustrating it is."

An outraged female yell drifted in from the common room.

He saw something flicker in her eyes—fear. Settling his hands on her shoulders, he asked, "What is it?"

"This is a place of corruption. I—I wasn't prepared for that."

A chill prickled down his neck. "What do you mean?"

She folded her arms in front of her. "There is a warden called Larkin. He wanted—that is, he would have—" She looked away, pressing her lips together as if loath to speak further.

"Miranda, did he hurt you?"

She shook her head. "No, and it's silly of me to dwell on it. I convinced him that it might be dangerous to harm me." A fond smile curved her lips. "I said I was undoubtedly a great lady, with a vast fortune and a title, and that as soon as my memory was restored, I would reward those who befriended me."

Ian gave silent thanks for her quick thinking.

"But lately," she said, "he's been eyeing me. I think he's starting to suspect it's a lie."

Ian trapped her hands in his. "I want you to come away with me. Now that I've found you, you need not stay here a moment longer."

"I know you claim me, but you're a stranger. I'm sorry—"

"You'll be safe with me," he said.

"I want to believe you, but I do not know you. I cannot go with you." She shivered. "It's awful here, but it's familiar. It's all that I know."

"Believe me," he whispered, lowering his mouth toward hers, wanting just a taste of her. "Do, Miranda. Believe me."

His mouth hovered closer. She gasped and parted her lips slightly. At the last second, he changed his mind. He must not kiss her. He knew better than to kiss a woman when he wanted her this badly. He brushed his lips across her brow. "I'll keep you safe," he heard himself whisper, not knowing whether or not he was lying. "I'll keep you safe."

She glided her hands up his chest, pressing closer, skimming his shoulders.

He hissed and broke away, barking a curse. His shoulder was on fire, and for a moment he saw nothing but a red haze of pain.

"Mr. MacVane!" Miranda cried. "What happened?"

"My shoulder, lass. I was burned in the fire."

"You were in the fire?" she asked. "*My* fire?"

"Aye, lass, if you're claiming it."

"Lass," she whispered, wonder dawning on her face. "It was you, wasn't it?"

"That depends on what you're accusing me of."

"You're the man in the flames. You called me lass. You pulled me to safety. Gave me your coat."

"Aye," he said again, wishing his shoulder would stop throbbing.

"You ran off to help a small child, and that was the last I saw of you." She shuddered. "The watchman said you had both perished."

"The watchman turned out to be quite unreliable."

"You would have come back for me, but you were unable?" she asked, unwittingly making it easy for him to deceive her.

"Injured," he admitted. "Not mortally, as you can see."

"Thank God. How is the child?"

"Robbie is fine. Some bumps and bruises, a burned hand that's healing nicely."

She subjected him to a wide-eyed, wondering look that made him feel as if he had grown a foot taller. "How grateful his mother must be."

"Robbie's an orphan. He had been staying at a flash house, where they were training him as a cutpurse." Ian decided not to tell her the worst of it, the other things they were forcing Robbie to do. "He ran away from there and was living alone in an abandoned building."

"How sad. What will become of him?"

"After my assistant, McDuff, tutors him, Robbie'll be bound for public school, perhaps university." An old dream flickered in Ian's mind. A lad like Robbie should live free, racing through Highland dales and shouting with laughter, just as Ian had so many years ago.

Miranda clasped her hands to her chest. "You kept the child."

"He had nowhere to go."

She crossed to the door.

"Miranda?" he asked. "Where are you going?"

"With you."

"But you just said you wouldn't."

"I changed my mind."

"What made you change your mind?"

She gave an incredulous laugh. "I have two choices. I can stay locked in this asylum. Or I can leave with a man who not only saved me from a fire, but rescued an orphaned child and is raising him to be a gentleman."

"So you changed your mind because of my sterling character?"

"No." An unexpected glint of humor winked in her smile. "It was your devastating blue eyes."

Her wry statement caught him off guard. He stared

at her for a moment, then started to laugh. To his amazement, she joined him. "And of course," she said, "you'd never lie about something that can be so easily disproved."

Dr. Beckworth appeared at the door. "Are you quite well, Miranda?"

She bathed him in a radiant smile that made the poor man all but squirm with delight. "Oh, indeed I am, Doctor. Surely your patience and care prepared me for a full recovery of my lost memory."

It was all Ian could do to keep panic at bay. What was this? She remembered? If so, that meant she realized Ian MacVane was no part of her past.

"God be thanked." The doctor raised his eyes heavenward.

Miranda rested her fingers on Ian's sleeve and sent him an adoring look. "My dear fiancé will, of course, send a large endowment to the hospital." She glanced at the women's ward. "Enough for some sweeping improvements," she added, and the subtlest note of warning hardened her voice. "Of course, I shall check on the progress of the reforms."

With a decided spring in her step, she walked toward the main foyer. She stopped at the common room. "Things will get better here," she said to the women.

Some of them looked up, waved, and blew kisses. "We'll take care, ducks," Gwen assured her. "See if we don't."

"We still think you should kiss her," said the old lady who thought he was Bonny Prince Charlie.

I still want to, Ian realized. He followed Miranda out, joining her amid the foot traffic on the street. He stared at her, filled with bafflement and delight that quickly froze into icy suspicion.

Just how much *did* she recall?

"You say you *remember?*" he demanded.

"Lies," she said breezily, turning a giddy circle on the cobbled walk. "All lies."

"But you did it so well," he said, impressed. "I know of no one who lies quite so well, except perhaps—" He broke off, taking her elbow to steer her out of the path of a pieman's cart.

"Except whom?" She had an engaging way of tilting her head and regarding him sidewise. The look was both charmingly naive and artlessly seductive.

He thought better of elaborating. "Never mind. You were quite magnificent."

She sobered for a moment. "To survive in a place like Bedlam, one must develop certain skills."

It was not what she said, but what she did not say that told Ian she had lived a nightmare. He grimaced, imagining her bedding down in filth amid lunatics. Without volition, he slipped his arm around her shoulders. In a matter of moments they had violated a dozen rules of propriety and decorum. Either she had forgotten those rules or, like him, took pleasure in disregarding them. Or perhaps she had never known the rules in the first place.

She peered up at him with that slanted look. "So now you have rescued me. Again. If you persist in being this kind to me, our future is very bright indeed."

Though his customary long strides never faltered, Ian felt his stomach knot. He couldn't even reply. In a very short time, he would have to deliver her to an address in Great Stanhope Street. Only God knew what would happen to her then.

4

There is no greater sorrow than to recall, in misery,
the time when we were happy.

—Dante

    The authorities would try to extract information from her. Ian would not allow himself to think about the methods they might use. He worked for the English, aye, but only because they were the highest bidder for his services. He had no false ideas about their compassion for a woman they perceived as a traitor.

He brought Miranda south through London, along the crumbling river walks. When they reached the west side of London Bridge, they would take a barge and then a hansom cab to the rendezvous in Great Stanhope.

"So we will leave the City today?" she asked, standing at the edge of the river and watching the traffic of boats and barges with rapt fascination. Before he could reply with an appropriate falsehood, she said, "I know that I lived in London before the . . ." She hesitated, looking so vulnerable for a moment that he had to glance away. His heart was pure steel—he had made it so. Yet he sensed that this woman could turn steel to ash if he let her.

"Before what?" he asked.

"Just . . . before. But I don't remember it being so vital. So alive and exciting. Look at all the people. I wonder if I should know any of them." She sobered. "It is the oddest feeling, Mr. Mac . . . Ian. It's happened a few times. I feel as if I'm on the brink of something—some discovery or revelation—and then everything disappears into a fog. Dr. Beckworth said my memory would return." She raised bewildered brown eyes to him. "The question is, what made me forget this in the first place?"

Ian's heart gave a lurch. "It was the accident," he said quietly. "'Twas a miracle you survived."

"But what was I doing there?"

His gut twisted. "I don't know, love," he said. "I'm only glad I was there to get you out in time."

"I wanted to die in there," she whispered.

He hoped he had heard her wrong. "No, Miranda—"

"It's true. A calmness came over me, an acceptance. I wanted it, Ian, I did."

"You were overcome by smoke." The idea that she had craved death disturbed him deeply. *In God's name, Miranda,* he wanted to say. *What happened to you?*

But he couldn't ask that. She expected him to know.

She frowned and rubbed her temple, swaying a little.

"Are you all right?" he asked.

"A headache. They come and go." She walked a few steps along the quay, then turned and walked back. Ian watched her, trying to analyze the effect she had on him.

What was it about the lass? She was almost waif-like in the faded dress, yet the worn fabric failed to conceal the body of a temptress. And in her eyes he could see ancient, veiled secrets. A wealth of memories lived inside her. His task was to unlock them, even if he had to batter down the door.

She rubbed her temples again, wincing at the pain and closing her eyes.

"Are you certain you're all right?" he asked again.

She nodded, eyes still closed. "Can you take me to the house where I live?"

He thought swiftly of the ramshackle rooms in Blackfriars, the overturned furniture, the dried blood. "You should rest."

She opened her eyes. A shroud of shadows crept over her face. Without moving, she distanced herself from him, receding to a place he could not imagine. For a moment it was as if she lived somewhere else, in a world of her own fancy. Or was it the past?

"Miranda?" he prompted. The syllables of her name tasted sweet, spoken with his Scottish burr. He was a sick man indeed. He took a perverse pleasure in simply saying her name.

She blinked, and the distant look passed. "I try, truly I do. I try to remember." She clasped both her hands around his. Her fingers were chilly; he could feel it through his gloves. He rubbed his thumbs over them, to warm her. Or himself, he was not sure which. But in that moment he felt something—they both did; he could see it in her eyes. The startlement.

The recognition. The deep inner twist of captivation that defied all logic.

"You must tell me, Ian," she said. "You are my betrothed. Surely you know my home." She hesitated. "My family. For the love of God, what was my way of life?"

Falsehoods came to him swiftly. "Ours was a whirlwind courtship, so I confess there is much about you I do not know."

"Then tell me something you do know."

"You lived," he said, hating himself for lying but lying anyway, "to love and be loved by me."

She caught her breath, a dreamy softness suffusing her face. "Ah, Ian. That is what I want to remember most of all. Loving you, and you loving me."

He stroked her cheek, and when her eyes opened, he let a devilish smile curve his mouth. "Does this mean I must teach you all over again?"

She laughed throatily. "Perhaps. Do I have family?"

"Alas, no." He didn't look at her, didn't want to see her reaction. "You're a scholar, Miranda. A teacher. A . . . private tutor."

"Then I lived with a family. With children."

"The family recently repaired to Ireland."

"Then we must write to them."

"Aye, we must." He knew such a letter would never go farther than his waistcoat pocket. "You're tired, my darling." He did not know whether it was part of his ruse or an untapped softness in his heart that made him slip an arm around her shoulders. She nestled against his chest as if seeking shelter from a tempest. And perhaps she was, from the storm of confusion inside her.

Her hair smelled of harsh soap, yet he also detected a hint of her own unique essence, something earthy and faintly herbal, evocative as a whisper in the dark.

"Ah, Miranda, forgive me. I know so little of your former life."

"Please," she whispered. "Tell me anything."

"'Tis melancholy." The lie spun itself with quick assuredness, like a silken web produced by a spider. He borrowed from the truth but seasoned it liberally with fiction.

He explained that her mother had died in childbirth, even though Frances had found out Helena Stonecypher had run off with a lover years earlier. Miranda's father, an impoverished scholar of indifferent reputation, had raised her in haphazard fashion and had passed on more recently. Miranda had been employed as a tutor, but she had scarcely taken over the duties when the family had gone to Ireland.

"When I met you, Miranda," he finished, "you were alone, in leased rooms near Blackfriars Bridge."

She extracted herself from his arms and walked to the edge of the river. She stared at the rippling surface for so long that he wondered if her mind had wandered again.

"Did you hear me, lass?" he prodded, standing beside her.

She raised her face to him. Her cheeks were chalk pale, her eyes wide. "I was quite the pathetic soul, then," she said in a low voice.

She was as fragile as spun glass. So easy to break. He had no doubt he could crush her with words alone. Rather than softening him, the notion made him angry. She was a gift he did not want, a responsibility he could not shirk.

Determined to stir her out of her sadness, he cupped her chin in his palm and glared down at her.

"Did you expect to hear that you're some long-lost princess, and I a blue-blooded nobleman? That I'll conduct you to a vast and loving family who have been waiting for your return?"

She flinched and tried to pull away, but he held her firmly, forcing himself to regard her with fierce steadiness. She would need a stiff spine for the trials ahead. If she broke now, dissolved into tears, he would take her directly to Frances and wash his hands of the entire affair.

She swallowed, and he felt the delicate movement of her throat beneath his fingers. "Touché, Mr. MacVane," she said, surprising him with a calm regard. "Though actually I had hoped I was a lady of great learning. There are things I know, things I have read, that Dr. Beckworth considered quite extraordinary." She squared her shoulders. "But that is a common hope even for people who remember the past, is it not? To wish to be something better than we are?"

"Touché yourself," he said. He let his hand trail down to her shoulder and gave her a squeeze. "Forgive me. I'm not angry at you, but at myself. I want so much more for you."

Her smile trembled, then steadied, and she looked amazingly winsome. And also weary. "There now," he said. "You must rest, and later we'll speak of the past."

"And of the future."

"That, too," he admitted, as foul a liar as had ever crossed the border from Scotland into England. Her future was a short trip up the Thames to Biddle House, where she would endure an interview with Lady Frances.

Yet when a barge arrived and the ferryman asked where they were bound, Ian rapped out his own address. He told himself it was because information obtained under torture was notoriously unreliable. Aye, that was why he didn't want her tortured. He'd find out her secrets in his own way. In his own time.

Miranda turned in a slow circle in the foyer of Ian's opulent residence, her head angled up so she could take in the spiraling sweep of a marble staircase, the tall windows of beveled glass, the painted cherubs and clouds on the ceiling and wainscoting.

"Have I been here before?" she asked. She nearly reeled with weariness, her hair escaping from its single frayed string, yet a sense of exhilaration buoyed her up.

"Nay, lass. It's not proper for an unchaperoned lady to call on a gentleman."

The word *lady* rolled elegantly off his tongue. His Scottish burr turned mere words to poetry. She felt a ripple of delight course through her. "Have I always loved the way you talk . . . Ian?" It felt delicious and right to call him by his Christian name.

He looked at her with his gentian blue eyes, and the shiver up her back turned to a warm river of sensation. "You never told me so," he said.

"I should have."

He gave her the oddest sensation, a sort of breath-held anticipation that lodged behind her heart. Had he always had this effect on her? How in heaven's name could she have forgotten?

Miranda saw a movement from the corner of her eye. Turning, she noticed a window in the wall. A woman stood in the window, watching her. And then it hit her—this was no window, but a mirror. The first mirror she had encountered since her terrifying journey into madness had begun. Her heart pounded as she looked into the glass. A complete stranger looked back at her. Miranda lifted one hand to her cheek, skimming it along a cheekbone and across a straight dark brow. The stranger did the same.

A feeling of utter panic swept over her. What sort of oddity of nature was she, a woman so addled in the brain that she did not even know her own face? Brown eyes—what had they seen that was so horrible she had hidden from the memory? Dark curls falling across a high, clear brow—had her unremembered father ever kissed her there? An ordinary nose and a wide mouth—had she opened it to scream the night of the fire?

Who are you? She asked the image silently. What have you done with your life?

The stranger stared silently back at her. There were no answers in the unfamiliar brown eyes. Only questions. Only an endless string of questions, and the answers were locked up inside the creature in the mirror.

She looked back at Ian, feeling more lost and helpless than ever, and wanting more than ever to be swept into his world, where she knew she would be safe.

For long moments they simply stared at each other like two figures in a painting. His face was in-scrutable, while Miranda felt certain every inch of her yearning for him surely showed on her features. She wanted to tumble right into the middle of his life, and she had never been so aware of her own desire. Had she?

Then Ian looked past her and broke the spell. He said something in a rolling, guttural tongue that she recognized as Gaelic but did not understand.

"My assistant," Ian said, taking her by the shoulders and steering her around. "Angus McDuff."

She turned to see a cherubic man of middle years, dapper in black breeches and a tartan waistcoat, his gray beard forming a bristly U from ear to ear.

Angus McDuff spoke with Ian in Gaelic, then swept low in a courtly bow. "How good it is to see you safe and sound, Miss Miranda."

She inclined her head. He seemed to know her, or at least to know of her. "It is good to *be* safe," she said. "But sound?" She looked helplessly at Ian. "I cannot remember my life before the moment of the explosion."

"So he was just explaining. Some things are for the best, my dear. 'Tis a thing I have always believed."

"Thank you, Mr. McDuff."

"Call him Duffie!" piped a loud, childish voice. "He'll insist on it."

With a squeal of skin on wood, a little boy slid down the banister. He landed with a flourish, wobbled, then fell on his backside.

"And I insist," Ian said with exaggerated severity, pulling the child to his feet, "that you greet the lady properly, scamp."

Full to bursting with mischief and merriment, the boy bowed from the waist. He had a clean bandage wrapped around one hand, and she realized he was the child Ian had saved from the fire.

"Robbie MacVane, at your service, mum," he said in a clear soprano voice.

"MacVane?" Ian asked, lifting a dark eyebrow.

"Aye, if it's all the same to you," Robbie said.

Ian did not smile, but looked solemn as he nodded. "You do honor to the name, lad."

"Besides," Robbie said, "it's the only name I know how to spell."

Miranda stifled a laugh. She found the boy enchanting, from the top of his tousled head to the tips of his scuffed leather shoes. Ian hooked a thumb into the band of his breeches. Robbie did the same, perfectly copying Ian's stance. Miranda looked from the boy to the man. It was extraordinary to think that in an age when some parents abandoned their children or sold them into apprenticeships, Ian had taken in this enchanting little stranger. He was a special man indeed.

When did I fall in love with you? she wanted to ask him. *What did it feel like?*

And was it happening again?

Thinking hard, she absently brushed a deep brown lock of hair out of her face.

"Cor, mum, I know you!" Robbie was staring at her with wide, unblinking eyes.

All the hairs on the back of her neck seemed to stand on end. "Do you, Robbie?" she asked in a low, shaken voice.

Duffie took the boy by the hand. "Come along now, my wee skelper. We'll leave the master and—"

"No," Ian said hurriedly. "What do you mean, you know Miss Miranda?"

Robbie lifted his shoulders to his ears in a shrug. "Not by name, mind you. But she gave me tuppence when she passed me in the road. I knows it were her because she's got a face like the mort in that painting in St. Mary-le-Bow, the one what looks all holy even though she ain't hardly got a stitch on."

Duffie made a choking sound and put his hand up to his mouth. Robbie scurried away from him.

"Gave you tuppence?" Miranda asked. "When?"

"Just before you went in there," Robbie said, puffing up to find himself the object of such rapt attention.

"In where, lad?" Ian asked.

"Well, you know." Like a monkey, he hung in the knobby banister rails at the bottom of the staircase. "In that building what blew to smithereens."

Miranda felt nauseated. Her head started to throb. She had been there. Inside the warehouse. Sickening guilt crept up her throat, gagging her. She thought of the twist of stiff, sulfur-smelling rope she had found in her apron pocket, along with tinder and flint. She had almost caused her own death and that of this innocent child.

She remembered the victims of that night, the bleeding faces slashed by flying glass, the burned flesh, the screams and moans of the wounded. Why would she hurt them? *Why?* She swayed, and the question she dared not ask screamed through her mind. *Am I a murderer?*

"There, see?" Duffie said with comforting brusqueness. "The lady's well nigh exhausted. I'll just have the housekeeper show her to—"

"Not so fast." Ian spoke in his customary low voice, but his words rang with authority. "Robbie, was Miss Miranda alone?"

"Oh, aye, sir, and she were in a great hurry—but she took the time to toss me a copper and bid me to get myself home." His round cheeks flushed. "She didn't know about me having no home."

Ian contemplated the boy with a look that was fierce, but protective rather than frightening. "Run along, then," he said. "See if Cook's made more of those gooseberry tarts."

Robbie scampered off, and Duffie followed him out of the foyer.

Miranda faced Ian with trepidation. He knew something. But what? Was it was more than she herself knew about that night? Or less?

The icy speculation in his eyes was unmistakable. She swallowed past the dryness in her throat. "I don't suppose," she said, "you could explain why I was down at the wharves, unchaperoned."

His large and powerful hand, still sheathed in its black glove, came to rest on her arm. A shiver coursed through her.

"I'm certain you had your reasons, love," he said, leading her into an opulent parlor furnished with dark wood and deep green hangings. "Come and sit down, and we'll—"

"Excuse me, sir." A cheerful-looking man with a peg leg came into the room. On his hand he balanced a salver, and he approached them with an ease that belied his infirmity. "This just arrived for you."

Ian took the letter from the tray. "Thank you, Carmichael."

"You're welcome, sir." Carmichael sent a pleasant smile to Miranda. "And welcome to you, too, miss. We've heard so much about you—"

"Thank you, Carmichael," Ian said, louder this time. "That will be all." He helped Miranda to a settee as the servant withdrew.

"How did he lose his leg?" she asked.

"The Battle of Busaco. We were in the Thirty-second Highlanders together."

Ian MacVane, she decided, was a man who took in strays. As Miranda watched him open his letter, she wondered what sort of stray she had been when they'd first met.

"Damn it," he said.

She jumped. "Damn what?"

He crumpled the letter in his hand. "Cossacks in Hyde Park."

She felt no surprise; her knowledge of local events had remained intact. Arriving with fanfare and entourages that often occupied entire flotillas, an extraordinary group was convening in London this summer. All the crowned heads from Tsar Alexander of Russia to the prince of Saxe-Coburg had come to celebrate Bonaparte's defeat. The Cossacks, under their hetman Count Platov, were serving as life guards to the tsar.

"Have they done something wrong?" she asked.

"It seems they've challenged the Gentleman Pensioners to a horse race. A few of them had too much to drink and are terrorizing people." Ian went to the door. "I'd best go and see that order is restored."

"Why you?" She was suddenly aware that she had no notion of Ian's role in all of this.

He grinned. "It is my métier. I'll tell you more when I get back. Duffie will see to your needs."

"Ian, wait!" A flush suffused her cheeks. "Is it true— what you said earlier? About . . . going to Scotland?"

"Upon my oath," he said, then was gone.

The next morning, Ian awakened to the dreadful notion that he had pledged to take Miranda to Scotland and make her his bride.

"A simple enough idea, when you consider it," Duffie said as he laid out a clean shirt and morning coat. "Marriage happens every day."

Ian sluiced cold water over himself from the yellow-glazed Newcastle ware bowl on the washstand. "Not to me." He turned the ewer sideways and took a long drink directly from it. "Never to me, McDuff."

The diminutive man seemed to swell to twice his size. "What are you saying, then?"

Ian grabbed a towel and began scrubbing his face and hair dry. Craning his neck, he inspected his burned shoulder. He closed his eyes, felt a sickening terror pitch in his gut as he relived the moment of rescuing Robbie. Only the desperate need of a child had prodded him out of his paralyzing fear of heights, prodded him just as the bigger boys had, so many years ago, sticking pins in his bare feet to urge him to climb higher, higher through the tight, narrow passageways of the chimney pots he had been forced to clean.

"I'm waiting for an answer." Duffie snatched away the towel and gave Ian's shoulder a casual glance. "Healing nicely," he pronounced, "which is more than I can say for your paper skull if you don't answer me. What are your intentions toward the girl?"

Ian grabbed back the towel and rubbed it across his chest. Only from Angus McDuff would he tolerate this constant meddling. He heaved a sigh. "You sound like a fierce papa."

The salt-and-pepper brows beetled. "Lord knows she could use one. She's helpless as a lamb, man. Dinna eat her alive."

Ian began dressing in traveling garb of black breeches and boots, a starched and snowy shirt, waistcoat, and cravat. "I'm taking her to Scotland."

"To Scotland."

"Aye."

"To marry her."

"Nay."

For an older man, Duffie moved with surprising speed. In one swift movement he had Ian shoved back against the wall, showing no sympathy for the wounded shoulder. His face was florid, his eyes hard. "Damn you to hell, Ian MacVane. I ought to skelp your stubborn hide for you. Have you taken a knife, then, and carved out your own heart?"

Ian glared at him coldly. "Oh, aye. You know I have."

Duffie dropped his hands to his sides, but he did not retreat. "That doesna mean others are made of ice. I'll not let you ruin the girl. Not let you whisk her away, destroy her reputation, destroy any chance she has to settle down one day and find happiness."

"She's happy now," Ian said, his mouth a cruel twist, "when she knows nothing of the past."

"Fine. She knows nothing. And you care nothing for her future. It'll be no future at all if you skulk off with her, wooing her with false promises. What decent man would have her after she goes adventuring with Ian MacVane?"

"No one need know." The back of Ian's neck prickled. He didn't like feeling this way—knowing he was wrong but lacking the conscience to stop himself.

"*She* will know," Duffie said obstinately. "To her core, she is a sweet and decent soul."

"Frances thinks she is a traitor. Oh. Do pardon me. A sweet and decent traitor." Ian raked a wooden comb through his close-cropped hair. "Look, would you rather I do what I should have done in the first place?"

"And what is that?"

"Take her directly to the authorities. I could make this all very simple by marching her before them and letting them be the ones to unlock her secrets."

Duffie's cheeks paled beneath his beard. "She's a wee, fragile thing. I suspect you guessed that or you wouldna have brought her this far. There is only one solution."

Ian set down his comb. He was tired of arguing. It had taken half the night to get the hard-drinking Cossacks to return to their residence at the Pulteney Hotel. "Why do I get the feeling I'm not going to like this?"

"Because it's the kind and proper thing, which is not what you are used to doing." Duffie pointed a stubby finger and narrowed an eye as though taking aim at his employer. "You'll do exactly as you promised, my fine gentleman. You'll marry the girl. Perhaps, if you're lucky, you'll find out her secrets. And if you're luckier still, I willna skelp you."

5

We loved, sir—used to meet:
How sad and bad and mad it was—
But then, how it was sweet!
        —Robert Browning

The inmates of Bedlam were not nearly as entertaining since the endowments had started to arrive. Dr. Brian Beckworth, for one, did not regret the change. He did not miss the gawkers who paid their coppers to come and stare at the moonstruck inmates. He did not miss Warden Larkin, given the boot the same day Miranda had left.

The till at the door had dwindled, but the anonymous payments drawn on a London bank account more than made up for that. Before long, the hospital would relocate to a new building in Lambeth, and this moldering pile of rubble would be abandoned.

For years Dr. Beckworth had wanted the institution to be a place of healing. A place where people

who had lost pieces of their souls could find themselves again—or at least find solace. Now there was a
chance that it could happen.

Some of the women were hopeless, it was true. But
others simply needed care and compassion. And now
the doctor could afford to give it to them. All because
of Miranda.

Feeling a rare sense of accomplishment, Beckworth
smiled up at Gwen, who came in with his morning tea
and the London *Times*. She had started doing a few
tasks around the place and seemed to take her new
responsibilities in stride.

"Nice and strong like you favors it, sir," she said.
Today her hair was caught back neatly with a bit of ribbon, and her hands and face were scrubbed clean. She
hid less and less behind her brash, uncaring façade.

Beckworth inhaled the fragrant steam and held up
the paper, scanning the front page. Gwen turned to
leave, but her eyes widened and she bent close. "Sir,
look there! 'Tis our own Miranda, and no mistake."

With a frown, Beckworth turned the paper over
and laid it on his desk. He saw a small sketch of a
young woman with large eyes and a swirl of thick,
dark curls. The caption identified her as "Miss
Miranda Stonecypher."

For no apparent reason, an icy claw of fear
clutched at his gut. There was something sinister
about seeing her likeness, her name in bold print.

"What's it say, sir? Please." Gwen propped one hip
on his desk and bent over the sketch.

Beckworth cleared his throat. "It seems her family
is looking for her. Requests a reply to an anonymous
box at the paper. Claims she has been missing
since . . ." He scanned down the article. "Since the
day before she arrived here."

"But that can't be," Gwen stated. "Mr. MacVane already collected her."

Beckworth's mouth went dry. "He claimed he knew her, but I was never quite convinced."

"Hell and damnation," Gwen burst out. "Then MacVane played us false and stole poor Miranda away!"

From the corridor outside came a scuffle of feet and the murmur of voices, but Beckworth was more preoccupied with the extraordinary notice in the paper.

"So it would appear." He pinched the bridge of his nose. The cold clench of fear in his gut tightened. Had he let a stranger spirit the girl away?

With a less than steady hand, the doctor dipped quill in ink and scribbled an urgent message. "I shall have this delivered to the *Times,*" he said, thinking aloud for Gwen's benefit as he blotted the ink. "And another to the lodgings of Ian MacVane. I have a few questions for him."

She took the note. "I'll see that it goes out with today's post." She left through the rear door of the office.

A moment later, the other door banged open and two people pushed inside.

"How do you do?" he asked, recognizing both of his visitors. They had come before to gawk at the inmates, but he noticed they'd paid particular attention to Miranda. "I just composed a message to the *Times.* I do hope—"

"Where is she?" asked the one with the French accent.

Dr. Beckworth was taken aback by the abruptness of the voice. "She left with the Scotsman, Ian MacVane."

"When?"

"Thursday. That is why the notice in the paper surprised me. You see—"

A strong hand plunged into his hair. Dr. Beckworth found himself forced to his knees. A foot pressed into his back, shoving his chest hard against the floor. "Who took your message to the *Times*?"

By now, Beckworth understood the peril. He must not lead them to Gwen. "P-posted it myself. Just this morning."

The visitors exchanged words in French. Beckworth tried to fight, but he wasn't trained for brawling. His arms flailed, and he managed to choke out one word: "Why?"

The hand holding his hair jerked his head up and pulled back, baring his throat. An expert hand wielded the sharp, cold blade quickly, neatly. As he bled to death swiftly on the floor of his office, Dr. Brian Beckworth answered his own question. He was dying because of Miranda.

"I'm certain I've never done *this* before." Miranda gripped the forecastle rail of the sleek, swift frigate *Serendipity* and gazed out at the churning North Sea. She inhaled deeply, filling her lungs with the fresh, salty air, and threw back her head, wishing she could unbind her hair and let the wind ripple through it. She knew the winds. Somewhere in her forgotten past she had studied wind and weather, though she had no idea why.

"Done what?" Ian stood beside her. With a swath of plaid draped diagonally across his chest, he looked as regal as a Highland chieftain. She shivered with admiration at the very sight of him. How plain and mousy she felt next to her betrothed, yet at the same time, his appearance empowered her. To have the devotion of such a man was heady indeed.

"Gone on a sea voyage," she said, watching the endless rush of the waves below the bow. "I feel quite sure I've not experienced this before."

Sailors in the mizzentop raced along wooden booms, working the sails as the wind made the ship yaw back and forth. Miranda hugged herself and smiled at the sky burnished like copper by the setting sun. "It all feels brand new. And so exciting. . . . Ian—" She broke off when she saw the way he was looking at her.

As if he wanted to eat her alive.

She sometimes caught him at it, eyeing her in a manner that was both fierce and tender. Was that the way he had always loved her, with that mixture of intensity and gentleness?

"What is it?" he asked, laying one gloved finger on her wind-stung cheek.

She wondered if he had ever told her why he always wore gloves, but it felt too awkward to ask. Besides, there was something mysterious and romantic about it.

"Nothing," she said. "Just that I know you're frustrated because I can't remember anything." His touch made her tingle in secret places. Were these places he had touched . . . before?

She could not quite bring herself to ask him that, either. "I do want to, Ian. Truly I do." She felt a stirring inside her, a sharp but unfocused yearning that ached in her heart. A sense of loss and longing and emptiness came over her.

"I did recall one thing," she said.

Clear as ice shards, his gaze focused on her. His hands gripped her upper arms. "Yes?"

She so hated to disappoint him. She wanted to please him, to bring a flicker of cheer to his brooding eyes, to feel his smile like the sun on her face. "I'm afraid it's not terribly important," she confessed. "When I woke up this morning, I realized that I know Homer's *Iliad* by heart."

His grin looked strained. "Lovely."

"In Greek."

"There has never been any question of your cleverness," he said. "You trouble yourself too much, lass. The memories will come when they come."

"What if that never happens?"

"Then we'll start over," he said.

She moistened her lips, tasted the faint bitter tinge of spindrift on her mouth. The maintopmen called to one another, gathering in sail from their lofty perches, and their shouts were like a sea chantey, rhythmic and pleasant.

She studied Ian for a long time. How magnificent he was, tall and lean and rugged, his black hair and sharp eyes creating a magnetism that ran deeper than his appearance. She felt drawn to him in a hundred little ways—the brush of his gloved hand on hers, the way one corner of his mouth lifted in wry amusement, or the warmth in her chest when he gazed at her.

"Is this what love is, then?" she asked impulsively.

He frowned, clearly startled. "What?"

"The way I feel when I look up at you. Is it love?"

For a rare moment, his composure seemed to slip. He appeared raw and unguarded, unnerved and vulnerable. In the blink of an eye, his customary regard of lazy amusement returned. "This is not a conversation we've ever had before."

"It's important to me, Ian. It is." She could not take her eyes off him. "I shall describe it, then, and you can tell me if it is love or not." She kept one hand on the rail to steady herself. "You make me feel something quite jolting inside. I find myself wanting to touch you rather boldly, to hang on to you and discover your smell and your taste and— Why on earth are you laughing?"

He made no attempt to stifle himself. "That isna love you describe, delicious as it sounds, Miranda. It's lust."

Miffed, she poked her nose in the air. There was more to it than that. There had to be, for he was the only man she regarded in this way, and she had made it a point to study the sailors and officers of the *Serendipity*. She had been on the verge of baring her heart to him, and he was laughing at her.

"Not that I am averse to lust," he said quickly.

In spite of herself, she felt mirth tugging at her. "But I truly want to know," she said, sobering. "What did it feel like to love you? And will I ever feel that way again?"

He turned away, but not before she detected a glimmer of torment in his craggy face. "Not if you know what's good for you."

"What?"

Still he did not look at her. "There are things about me—" He broke off. His hands clenched around the ship's rail. "Ah, listen to me." When he turned to her again, he was smiling. "I dinna want you to have any doubts, sweet."

"Then teach me," she said, desperate to fill the emptiness inside her. "Show me how we used to love. I want to remember, Ian. Truly I do."

He said something gruff and Gaelic. "Lass, you don't know what you're asking."

She watched a gull dive for a fish in the distance, then studied the horizon, the gray edges of sea and sky, as if the answers were written there. After a while, she glanced back at him. "Help me, Ian. Help me remember."

"I don't know how," he said. "I canna simply give you your memories back, all wrapped up in a tidy parcel."

"Then tell me something, anything. A tidbit to spark my remembrance."

His blue eyes narrowed. "What sort of tidbit?"

"Conversations we've had. Experiences we've shared." She could not explain how fearsome it was, this yawning black gulf inside her. It was like missing a leg or an eye. She was not whole, and she did not know how much longer she could go on. "Please," she said. "I need to know."

He watched her for a moment, the wind mussing his glossy black hair. "I taught you to dance the waltz," he said, speaking reluctantly, as if the words were pulled from him against his will.

She cocked her head. "The waltz. It's a dance, then?"

"Aye. All the rage in London this Season. The tsar and his sister, the grand duchess of Oldenburg, have made it the sport of choice." He winked, then gripped her lightly by the waist, with one hand around hers. "The rhythm is like a heartbeat. *One,* two, three, *one,* two, three . . . Do you feel it?" He began to hum a soft melody in her ear.

"You have a beautiful voice," she said.

He kept humming and drew her along the forecastle deck, neatly avoiding coils of rope, lashed-down barrels, and the envious stares of the sailors. She followed his lead, letting his graceful maneuvering make up for her inexperience. Round and round they spun, the rich melody lilting in her ear until the rhythm finally penetrated her very bones. They moved as one, and she reveled in the way they seemed to fit together, in the light scrape of their feet on the wooden deck and the hiss of the ocean speeding past the hull.

"There is," she murmured, "something magical about dancing. Why is that?"

His hand moved in a circle on her back. "Well," he said, stretching out his Scottish burr, "dancing involves two people, holding each other, moving in a rhythm both understand, their goal to stay together, for no reason other than sheer physical pleasure." He smiled wickedly, and a shiver shot down her spine. "There is only one other circumstance in which all of that is true."

She snatched her hand out of his. Hot color surged to her cheeks. "Ian!"

He leaned against a tall spool of rope and watched her, clearly amused. "Aye, love?"

"Have we . . . did we . . . "

He threw back his head and laughed. "My dear, if you had forgotten *that*, I'd say there's not much hope for us." Seeing her unamused expression, he took both her hands in his. "Believe me, Miranda. To my eternal frustration, and through no choice of my own, we have never made love."

"We were waiting, then."

"Aye."

"For marriage."

He hesitated. "Aye."

"Mary Wollstonecraft didn't believe in marriage on principle."

"She may have a point."

Miranda found herself laughing again, feeling giddy.

"You're an incredibly desirable creature, Miss Stonecypher," Ian said.

She wondered if he had any idea how entrancing he was. "Tell me more," she said. "I feel that if I could remember even one moment, if I could just look back and *know,* then everything would come right."

"I dinna think it's that easy."

"Indulge me," she said. "Please."

"The Orangery in Hyde Park," he said.

"Should that be significant to me?"

"Oh, aye." He paused. "Your first kiss."

She felt her color deepen. "Surely a significant event if there ever was one."

"And you dinna remember it."

"No." She stared at his mouth. "I'm sorry."

"Don't be." He took her hand and led her toward the bow of the ship, where they stood in the cool evening shadows. Sails luffed in the wind, and the cry of a cormorant droned mournfully across the swells. "Actually, it's rather an advantage."

She began to tingle inside. "An advantage?"

"Oh, aye. You can have your first kiss . . . all over again."

With a discreet movement he took off his gloves, dropping them on the deck at their feet.

She felt faint, yet dizzily aware all at once. Nervously she licked her lips. "I'm afraid I don't know what to do."

"What you're doing now is just fine. For the moment."

"What am I doing?" she asked.

"Standing there. Looking bonnier than heather in bloom."

He took a step closer. His hands drifted down the

length of her arms, heating her skin. The pads of his thumbs found her racing pulse.

"Was it like this . . . before?" she asked.

"Nay, love. This is better." His hands traveled up and over her shoulders. His fingers threaded their way into her hair, sifting through the curls.

"Now what?" she whispered.

Though he did not smile, amusement glinted in his eyes. "Just keep your head tilted up. Aye, like that." He bent low, his face looming close, his breath, with the tang of his evening brandy, caressing her. He touched his lips tenderly to her eyes, first one and then the other, so that they were closed. Then he kissed her mouth, softly, tentatively.

"I can stop at any time," he whispered, "if this makes you uncomfortable."

She smiled dreamily. "Uncomfortable is not quite the word for what I feel."

He kissed her again, tugging gently on her lower lip until her mouth opened and she surged toward him, hungry, wanting. The taste and smell of him filled her—sea and leather and maleness, seasoned with the brandy they had drunk after supper. The sensation of kissing him caused passion to leap up inside her until she was straining almost painfully for him.

His hands slipped from her hair and traveled down, tracing the inward curve of her waist and the outward flare of her hip. Then he touched her breasts, hands brushing, fingers skimming the tips. Warmth seared her in places he wasn't touching, places that begged for his caress.

Then, as gradually and inevitably as the kiss began, it receded. He lifted his mouth from hers, and his hands dropped to her waist.

She kept her eyes closed, holding the moment, hovering in uncertainty and wonder and delight.

"Miranda?" he asked.

She forced her eyes open. She reached up and touched his cheek. His tanned skin was rough with evening stubble. "I feel completely starstruck, Ian. Bowled over like a ninepin. Was it like that for me before?"

"You never said." His voice sounded gruff and uneven.

"I was trying to remember what it was like to love you," she said. "But I feel as if I'm learning for the first time." That something so simple as a human touch could shake the foundations of her heart was a staggering notion. "Ah, Ian." She spoke his name on a sigh. "You are so good to be patient with me."

He took her hand, removed it from his cheek, and kissed the back of it. To her surprise, his own hand trembled. "You make it easy, Miranda." She thought she detected a note of bitterness in his voice when he added, "Too bloody easy."

Guilt was a new and decidedly unpleasant sensation for Ian MacVane. Yet as he lay awake in his narrow, damp quarters each night of the voyage, he knew guilt in all its sharp and bitter shades.

He was manipulating the feelings of a naive young woman. Whatever else Miranda's crimes might be, she was innocent when it came to matters of the heart.

But not for long, if they stayed on their present course.

I was trying to remember what it was like to love you.

Her words snapped back at him like a lash. She was driving him insane with her unwavering trust in him.

Trust. Miranda *trusted* Ian MacVane. She was by far the first woman foolish enough to do that.

She wanted memories, and he was giving them to her. False, hollow tales he dredged from his paltry stores of sentiment.

If ever a man had a past that begged to be forgotten, it was Ian MacVane.

Instead here he was building a castle of lies in order to win Miranda's faith and perhaps, if he was very lucky, find the memories she kept locked away in her mind.

He kept wondering if he should have simply handed her over to Frances. Perhaps that would have been better all the way around.

The morning they'd taken ship, Frances had shown her customary lack of surprise at his flagrant disobedience. She'd even sent him a message in cipher: *Perfect, darling. I do so love it when you do something scathingly clever and cruel. Yes, sleep with the girl. It is the best way to—dare I be so tasteless?—get her to reveal herself to you.*

At the bottom of her note, he had scribbled a reply in cipher and sent it back to her: *When I bed a woman, my dear, it's for my own reasons, not because anyone orders me to.*

Even then he had known he would find a reason. The whole matter was sordid. He had a sudden notion to turn his back on the entire affair, but he knew he would not.

Time was not critical yet. The duke of Wellington was still in Paris, ambassador to the newly restored King Louis. But once Wellington returned to England, Napoleon's allies would put their plan into motion.

Ian had pledged to foil the insane plot. Bound by his own private sense of honor, he knew he would not rest until he succeeded in stopping the conspiracy.

Even if it meant filling Miranda's head and her heart with his lies. Even if it meant a cruel betrayal of her trust. Even if it meant taking her innocence and ruining her reputation.

He pounded his fist into his hard pillow. Surely it wouldn't come to that. Surely she would regain her memory and divulge the plan before things had gone too far.

When the smoky gray mist of a Scottish dawn tinged the sky, he gave up on sleep. He had lost sleep over only one woman before Miranda, and that was his mother.

For all that Mary MacVane knew or cared.

Shoving aside thoughts of a past he could not change, Ian got up and bathed with water from a basin, then dressed in the black trousers and white shirt Duffie had set out the night before. Soon they would make landfall.

Today Ian would begin a journey from which there was no return. For him, Scotland was a place of memories and madness. Here, his world had been torn to unrecognizable bits by a stranger with greed in his eyes. His soul had been damned by the woman who had given him life.

Once he had escaped Scotland, Ian MacVane had been reborn, a creature of darkness, his past scoured clean through sheer force of will.

Perhaps that was why Miranda held such fascination for him. She had achieved what he had been trying to do all his adult life. She had obliterated the past.

Her means of doing it, however, held little appeal for him. In his soldiering days, he had seen men wake up the day after battle with no notion of the horrors they had seen, of acts that had been committed upon them, of atrocities they themselves had carried out.

At first, the postbattle blankness had seemed a blessing. But the memories always returned in one form or another, weeks or months or years later. Nightmares. Fits of rage or terror. An inability to cope with everyday life. Was that to be Miranda's fate?

He donned a waistcoat of boiled wool and reached for his gloves. Before pulling them on, he braced his hands upon a sea chest at the end of his bunk and studied them. They were large and squarish, hands suited to the son of a hardworking crofter. Except that the crofter had been murdered in cold blood, his young son sent to toil in Glasgow at tasks so grueling that they were performed only by orphans or slaves.

Ian scowled down at the stub of the last finger on his left hand. The digit had been chopped away at the first knuckle, and the only concession he had gotten after the accident was half a day's holiday and an extra slice of bread at supper.

Och, how he wanted to forget. Instead he remembered every detail with crystal clarity, as if he were viewing his past through a perfect glass that showed him not only the sights, but the smells and sounds and textures as well. The reek of soot and blood. His brother Gordon's bitter curses. Ian's own horrified screams. The dizzying view of the street far below the rooftop where he had been stranded. The sensation of abject fear that had roared through him as Gordie fell.

He made a fist, hiding his deformity. Then he forced himself to open his hand. Today, no glove. No shoving his hand into his waistcoat à la Bonaparte.

Ian MacVane would return to Scotland as he had left it: maimed and full of rage.

6

On ev'ry hand it will allowed be,
He's just—nae better than he should be.
—Robert Burns

After the landing, Ian stood on the rocky shore, oblivious to the movements around him, oblivious to the delighted shouts of young Robbie, oblivious even to Miranda, whose presence had consumed him since the moment he had laid eyes on her.

He simply stood, feeling the solid earth beneath his feet and trying to get his mind around the fact that after an exile of fifteen years, he was home. In Scotland.

How much had he changed, he wondered, from that wounded boy, skulking to freedom by hiding in a ship's hold?

He was staggered by how deeply he had missed his homeland. He drew the feeling in through his pores, and into his lungs with each breath, and the very essence of the land began to pulse through him. This was Scotland, his birthplace.

Here, he had suffered the torments of the damned—but also, in that early misty time of his youth, he had known his greatest joy. Had known the crystal sharp air of the craggy Highlands as he'd raced across the moors after a stray lamb. Had known the sweet, warm scent of a mother and the hearty affection of a father.

Ah, how long ago that had been. The boy who had gamboled through glens and boggy moors, who had fished for trout in the icy streams and chased squealing girls in the kirkyard on Sunday, was as good as dead.

Ian MacVane knew the name of his murderer. Adder, like the snake. Mr. Adder, the sly-eyed Englishman. He had swept like a storm into Crough na Muir, claiming that the crofters were trespassing on his property. And so they were, on land relinquished to him by the laird whom Adder had beggared at the gaming table.

Ian drew in another breath of Scotland. He felt as if he were falling, falling back into the hideous past, squarely into the night Adder and a troop of mercenaries had swooped down upon the croft of the MacVane. . . .

He heard a sound that didn't belong to the night. Below the living quarters, the cows blew gently in their sleep. Then the sound came again. It was a soft whistle—not an owl or a nightingale, but a human sound. The dog reacted first, leaping down from the loft, yapping wildly.

He heard a sickening thump, and the dog fell silent. By then Ian's father was up, pitchfork in hand, but it was too late. Too late. . . .

Miranda broke his fall. She did it with something as simple and as complicated as the brush of her hand on his sleeve, a tilt of her head, a querulous smile.

"You were a thousand miles away, Ian," she said. "And it was a sad place."

He fought the urge to shake her off, to lash out like a wounded wolf, to recoil from her compassion. Instead he managed a wry half smile. "Reading my moods, are you?"

"Didn't I always?"

"Of course." Christ, but this was absurd. Inventing a past for them, pretending they had a future.

No one's future was assured so long as fanatic Bonapartistes kept hatching their plots in England. Ian wondered how the British could be so blind. They and all their allies were convinced that Napoleon would rest content in his defeat in exile. But Ian understood the brilliance and determination of the emperor, the loyalty of his followers. Exile at Elba was surely but a temporary state for such a man. Bonaparte would be back. Already he was coiled like a snake, poised to strike.

Impatience stirred within Ian. He had best make quick work of the marriage—a handfasting would do—and hasten back to London.

"We've always been of one mind, lass," he said, forcing gentleness into his voice as he lied to her. "And my guess is, you're of a mind for a good bath and a meal."

"I am."

Duffie and Robbie had gone on ahead with the baggage. Ian scanned the road that wound up and around the great rising hills. He had not stood on this spot since he was a lad. Yet he knew people would still remember him in the village.

A part of him still dwelt there.

He started toward the settlement, old and tumbled and comforting as a tattered blanket.

After walking along the dusty road for a quarter mile, Miranda stopped him. "Ian."

"Aye, lass?"

"I don't remember my own past, save what you've told me. But I know nothing of your past, either."

And he would never tell her, Ian thought. The one thing he would not do with his pain was share it.

He grinned at her and winked. "I was an exemplary lad in every way. Surely there is no question of that." He took her hand and started walking again.

"Someday, Ian MacVane," Miranda said, "I am going to get the truth out of you."

Not in this life, he thought grimly. Not in this bloody life.

The pony cart that had brought their belongings from the ship had preceded them to the village. Clearly Duffie and Robbie had made a grand announcement, for townspeople were waiting expectantly just beyond the gate.

The drystone walls had crumbled low, though when the Scots had first built them to deter raiding Norsemen, the defensive structure had stood tall and sturdy. Now the barrier resembled a set of decaying teeth, weathered by the centuries and the incessant wind off the moors. Rock roses and ivy twined in and out of the stones. In the background stood the steeple of the village kirk. At the end of the lane was a stone cottage with yellow thatching on the roof and a trellis of twisted old roses framing the gate to the dooryard. Agnes's place.

Miranda stopped walking again.

"Are you all right?" Ian asked her.

"It's just that this is all so lovely. Like a painting or . . . or a dream."

To Ian, the place looked like no more than it was—

the village to which he had walked hand in hand with his father each Thursday to buy rye flour and to sell eggs. Little had changed; Crough na Muir was sturdy and drab. Yet unexpected bursts of flowers in the window boxes cheered the place, much like a smile on the face of a plain girl.

No one was smiling now. The knot of people waiting inside the town gate looked piercingly inquisitive. When last they had seen him, he'd had a rope around his neck and wrists and was being led off by English soldiers.

"As I live and breathe," said a wiry man with a gap-toothed grin. He pointed to his chest. "Callum Grundy—I was a friend of your da, and you're the very image of him." Callum scratched his head beneath a worn woolen cap. "Never thought a MacVane would tread this path again."

"'Tis grand to be back, Callum. I know you all from Agnes's letters, every one of you."

"Aye, you're the picture of your father, Lord grant him eternal peace," Flora Hunt agreed. "You have his charming, smooth way, too, laddie."

Ian tried not to see it, but the people were gaunt and unwashed, their clothes little better than rags. Under a proper laird, the crofters of the district might have flourished. But Adder had stolen good fortune from them all those years ago.

Rather than seeing to their welfare, he had merely engaged a factor to extract rents. Occasionally he sent bored English peers to the manor house, once the residence of the laird, but now a brooding hulk on the hill. According to Agnes, the visitors did nothing but drink and hunt grouse on the moors.

Just for a moment, an old dream flickered in the back of Ian's mind. Perhaps it was awakened by the nearness of Miranda. There was something about her, a special quality that awakened old, hidden desires. He did not like it, did not trust it; he feared she would cause him to care about things better ignored.

Ian sometimes dreamed that *he* was the laird, wise and benevolent, devoted to the welfare of Crough na Muir. He was a part of their lives, watching them grow up and marry, mourning with them when they buried their dead, celebrating with them over the birth of a bairn. Rather than living amid strangers, he had a place to belong. A place that belonged to him.

The yearning for it rose like an ache in his chest, and he was stunned to feel it. He had not dared to want something like this in years.

A man with gray hair and beard shuffled forward. "Is that truly Ian MacVane and his betrothed, then?" he asked in Gaelic.

A number of the villagers still had only the Gaelic, and to Ian's ears it lilted like a lullaby. For Miranda's sake he spoke in English. "Aye, this is Miss Miranda Stonecypher." He told himself he had no reason to smile, but he grinned like the village simpleton. "Soon to be my wife."

Duffie had done his work quickly and well; none of the people looked surprised by the news. Tam Alexander, who operated the ferry across Loch Fingan, nodded sagely. "They always come back to marry, eh?"

"She's a bonnie thing, isn't she?" a woman observed.

Ian scanned the crowd, spying the small figure, the wizened face. "Agnes."

She held open her arms. "Come here, laddie, and bring the lassie with you. Lord, but it's been an age." She embraced them both with her sturdy arms. "I've waited years for this day," she whispered, for their ears only. "How I've waited, Ian! Waited for you to find love, to find someone to live in your heart."

He gave her a squeeze and stepped back. In all the eventful years of his life, he had done many unspeakable things, but this was quite possibly the worst. Duffie had done his work too well, filling Agnes's head with romantic notions of a love match. Ian should set her straight. But when he saw the joy and pride in her kindly face, he could not bring himself to deny it.

Miranda kept hold of the older woman's hand. "It is fine to be here, Agnes."

"And Duffie told me much about you, *mo chridh*. If it's healing you need, you'll find it in the love Ian bears you."

They were all listening, Ian noticed. The villagers who had shaken their heads and wrung their hands over the destruction of the MacVane family now nodded to one another and murmured words of hope, of faith. Two things he had lost the day Adder had dragged him away.

Clearly Agnes still believed these were things that could be recaptured. Ian glanced at Miranda—she looked flushed and lovely amid all the attention—and he wanted to believe it, too.

"There, Agnes," he said with a cocky grin. "We're not an hour off the boat and you're getting sentimental on us."

She laughed softly. "Aye, I'll save it, then, for the wed—"

A hoarse screech rent the air. The townspeople reacted with discomfited sympathy, stepping back, exchanging glances.

"Good gracious!" Miranda looked around wildly. "Someone's been hurt."

He felt a dull horror in his gut. Someone had been

hurt, aye, but it had happened long ago. He took Miranda by the arm. "Dinna worry, love—" He broke off, feeling helpless and furious as every eye in the village watched him.

"We'd best be going, then." Tam touched Ian's shoulder. "'Tis good to see you back, lad, and on such a happy occasion."

Others murmured their farewells, but the words were drowned by the ragged roar of a tormented soul. People drifted away to go about their business, for what else could they do?

Miranda's eyes widened in outrage. "Will they all just leave, then, when someone needs help?" She pressed against Ian as if he could protect her. "We should help the poor soul," she said, still not understanding.

Ian MacVane could protect no one. He had failed his father the night Adder's men had shot him like a stray dog, and he had failed his brother the day Gordon had fallen from a rooftop. But the failure that haunted him most was embedded in the present moment, possessing him, hurling him back into the nightmare again. . . .

Weeping and shivering, he crouched beside a stone wall. The screams of women and children tore into the night sky. Flame shadows from burning crofts danced a hellish jig over the village. He saw his da pulling Gordon out of the inferno.

Across the yard, a soldier raised a musket.

He wanted to cry out, but his tongue was frozen, so it stayed as he huddled there, stayed even when the musket exploded and his father fell, and later, when the Englishmen's pawing hands and hungry mouths and brutal lust turned their attention to his mother. . . .

"What's wrong, Ian?" Miranda asked, tugging his sleeve and pulling him toward the source of the moaning. "Who is in there? Who cries out so? And why does no one care?"

Someone cares, he thought. Someone cares too much.

"I suppose you'd best meet her sooner rather than later," Ian said grimly, starting up the path to Agnes's cottage.

"Meet who?"

He paused, his hand on the door latch, his heart seeming to hammer a hole in his chest. "My mother."

The room was bright with the afternoon sun, the walls freshly whitewashed. Nothing like Bedlam, Miranda reflected, with its moldering filth strewn everywhere, its iron galleries. Still, she felt a chilling recognition when she looked into the madwoman's eyes.

They were beautiful eyes, like Ian's, blue as morning glories and deep with pain and secrets. They stared out of a face that might have been handsome once, long ago. Mary MacVane had regal cheekbones, a slender nose, a high, proud brow. Yet her mouth was an angry twist, her cheeks furrowed by lines, her steel-colored hair a mass of knots and matted tangles.

Agnes spoke to Mary in Gaelic. Mary ignored her, and Agnes withdrew. Ian stepped into the small, scrupulously clean room, bending his head slightly, for the ceiling timbers were low. He went to his mother and held out his hand. Miranda was surprised and touched by the yearning she sensed in the gesture.

"Mother," Ian said in English. "I've come back, Mother, and this is Miranda. She's to be my bride."

Mary MacVane sat like a stone. Ian touched her hand. He talked to her a while longer, speaking low in Gaelic. He reminded Miranda of a penitent praying before a statue of the Madonna, and her heart ached for him. He was a man of great charm and self-assurance, but when he faced his mother, he seemed as defenseless as a child.

It struck her then that he had deeply hidden needs. Had she known about them before? Had she dared to believe that if she loved him enough, she could drive the sadness from his soul?

When he finished speaking, the woman continued to sit and stare. He rose to his feet, then bent to kiss her on the cheek. Still she sat frozen, looking at nothing, saying nothing—until Ian turned away and reached for the door.

"I curse you, Ian MacVane," Mary said in a low snarl, her voice trembling with vitriol. "Aye, curst be your name and your union with the Sassenach woman. You might have forgotten, but I never, ever shall. It was the Sassenach who brought suffering on me and my Fergus, and poor baby Tina."

Horror and pity welled up in Miranda. She stood frozen, helpless, shocked by the words of a mother to her son.

Agnes came to the door, tears pouring down her cheeks. "Enough," she said. "You've tired yourself, Mary. You should rest." Agnes motioned for Miranda and Ian to leave. "Dinna fash yourself, dearie," she said to Mary. "And you were having such a good spell, 'tis a shame you couldna hold on and greet Ian properly. . . ."

Miranda glanced back into the madwoman's room,

and a chill slid through her. Mary had lapsed into Gaelic and was hugging herself, rocking back and forth. The woman lived in hell, and the most eerie part of all was that Miranda understood that place.

But Miranda's hell was different. She had no memories, while Mary was plagued by horrible ones. Perhaps that was why Miranda couldn't remember—perhaps there was something so terrible in the past that she had scoured her memory clean.

Shaking her head, Agnes left Mary alone and started back for the main house. Mary's quarters were separated from Agnes's cottage by a thatched arcade with ivy growing up the sides. Noting Miranda's appreciative glance over the adjacent garden, Agnes smiled. "'Tis a grand place for such as myself, eh? All Ian's doing. Starting with the first copper he ever earned, he's sent me half of everything. He's a generous lad, he is."

When they entered a small, tidy keeping room, Miranda looked at Ian and almost wished she had not. The wounds inflicted by his mother shone beneath his surface like diamonds under water, cold as ice, distant as the stars.

"She was doing so much better, lad, as I wrote to you in my letters. I was starting to hope she'd forget the past, stop letting it torment her so."

"As long as I'm alive," Ian said, "she won't get better. I'm a constant reminder. That's why I stayed away."

"There, don't be blaming yourself."

"I'm the only one left alive to blame," he said grimly.

Agnes heaved out a long-suffering breath. She went into the adjacent kitchen, leaving them alone. Duffie had gone to the village alehouse, and Robbie played in the garden, sailing an imaginary ship through rows of foxglove and lemon grass.

Miranda crossed the room and stood in front of Ian. "Why?" she asked. "Why did she curse you?"

He flinched, just for a second, as if she had probed into a wound. As of course she had.

"Because I survived, Miranda. I failed to protect her when our croft was attacked by an Englishman with hired soldiers. My father was killed that day, my baby sister abandoned in her cradle. I can still hear her infant wails in my head." He made a fist with his gloved hand. "I should have run for help."

"How old were you, Ian?"

"A lad of seven." Sweat broke out on his brow. "Jesus. I've never said these things to anyone. Ever."

Miranda was afraid to touch him. She wanted to take his hand, lift it to her lips, and soothe him. But he was dark and withdrawn; she couldn't be sure he would not lash out at her. With an effort of will, she reached past his pain, took his hand, and drew herself closer. "And your mother?" she made herself ask. "Did they harm her? Dishonor her?"

His reaction to her touch was swift and violent. He pulled her against him and glared down into her face. His strong fingers felt hard, unyielding. He was a cold stranger, and suddenly he frightened her. "Do you know what English ladies call dishonor, Miranda Stonecypher? In Scotland we call it rape."

She scowled, fearful and then furious that he had frightened her. "I know what rape is, Ian MacVane, and I'll thank you not to handle me like a sheep at shearing time." A white bolt of pain flickered in her head. She caught her breath as a voice called out in her mind. *Don't hurt her! She doesn't know anything—*

"What is it?" Ian asked.

The voice was gone as quickly as it had come, and the headache began to subside. The sense of immediacy she felt was for Ian, not herself.

She pressed her palms against his chest and was surprised to feel the racing of his heart. "You say I never knew my mother, so I cannot speak of that bond. But I know when she cursed you, it was the madness speaking, not the mother. Inside her, there is a woman who loves her son."

"What can you know of it?" he demanded.

She refused to flinch at his acid tone. "I lived with madwomen. I have eyes to see." She stepped back, dropping her hands to her sides. "I'm sorry for you, Ian. I want to help, but I don't think I can."

He was quiet for a long moment, and the rhythm of his heart gradually slowed. "You already have, Miranda," he said, an edge of surprise in his voice. "Aye, my love, you already have."

"Take me to see Scotland," Miranda said to Ian the next day.

Miranda's request startled Ian out of his brooding contemplation of the village that lay beyond the kitchen garden. In spite of himself, he let a smile curve his mouth.

"To see Scotland." He imitated her British accent. "'Tis all you Sassenach want, to come and sketch pictures of our landscape and cry, 'Oh, how quaint!'" He punctuated the statement with a limp-wristed gesture.

"I do remember my history," she said, a trace of laughter in her voice. "Scotland has not always been considered quaint."

He spread his arms. "And what of me? Am I quaint?"

Her gaze raked him boldly. "Hardly, sir. But I've come a very long way, and since you insist I'm to become your wife, I should learn the sort of place Scotland is."

Her words stung him with panic, but only for a moment. All would be well, he told himself. Surely soon she would remember. It was all a question of putting her mind at ease, making her feel safe, lulling her until the memories flowed back into her.

He took her hand. "Come along, then. I'll show you the sights."

They left through the rear door of the cottage, tiptoeing past Mary's quarters. Ian saw a jar of freshly picked wildflowers on the shelf outside his mother's room, and his heart lifted a little. Robbie, uncritical and too young to make judgments, had decided that Mary MacVane simply needed a bit of cheering up. He had vowed to gather flowers for her each day until she got better.

How simple the world appeared through the eyes of a child.

Ian and Miranda climbed a slope above Crough na Muir. "It means 'hills by the sea,'" Ian said. "They say it was first given the name by pagan priests who worshiped the trees."

"Crough na Muir," Miranda recited. "It's a lovely name."

Halfway up, he stopped and pointed across the glen. "Innes Manor," he said. To Ian, the gabled house of gray green stone, with its slender fluted chimneys and banks of tall windows, used to seem like a dwelling out of a storybook. High on the shoulder of a mountain called Ben Innes, the manor rose above the mist, a kingdom in the clouds.

"It used to be the laird's house," he said.

"Who lives there now?"

"No one. The butcher who took over the district sometimes sends guests up for grouse hunting."

"It's so lovely." Miranda smiled up at him. "I wonder what it would be like to live in such a place."

The odd thing was, he could picture her at Innes Manor, walking along the stately garden paths like a figure in a Watteau painting. "Perhaps you'll find out one day."

"We."

"What?"

"Perhaps *we* will find out one day."

The reminder jolted him. "Idle talk." He had long since ceased to question his own motives when it came to indulging Miranda's whims. It had become simply something he did, with no rhyme or reason other than his own guilt about playing her false. So he did not pause when he found himself leading her ever higher, to a place he had not visited since he was a boy.

He had not put on his gloves today, and he noticed her looking at the stump of his finger. When she saw that she'd been caught, she glanced away, blushing.

"It's all right," he said.

"I don't . . . remember that."

"An accident. Happened when I was very young." And for the first time in his life, it was all right. Almost.

He kept hold of her hand, though she needed no help. With her skirts bunched in one fist, she climbed with a sturdy gait. Her hardiness appealed to him. He had gone too long entertaining fan-fluttering London beauties whose tight corsets and meager diets made them overly delicate. Miranda, by contrast, had thrived on the sea voyage and would grow stronger

still on Agnes's robust meals and the bright, clear air
of the Highlands.

The meadows lay in green velvet folds between the
vales. Wildflowers rioted underfoot and clung stubbornly to the steep, rock-strewn slopes. He brought
Miranda to Ben Ocelfa, the highest peak of the range.
They found a level spot of ground so smooth that it
resembled a table covered by a green baize cloth.

He loosened his collar and lifted his face to the
endless summer sky. "I used to think this was the top
of the world."

She turned in a slow circle, arms outspread. "It is
the top of the world. Surely it is." When she turned
back to him, her eyes shone. For a moment, he forgot
the mysteries and memories that hid inside her, forgot
that his sole purpose was to unlock them. She was simply a woman whose face lit up when she looked at him.

"It's beautiful, Ian," she said. "Thank you."

"It's the bonniest place I know," he said, half to
himself. And so it was, the blue sky melting into the
soft green of the distant hills, the black striated veins
of rock peeking through flower-studded meadows.
Below and to the east lay the immeasurable sea, midnight blue and shifting at the base of a sheared-off
cliff. To the south, the town huddled in a meander of
the river. Round the bend, the stream poured itself
into Loch Fingan.

Before he could stop them, memories rushed like
the tide into the sucking sea-caves on the coast. Once
again he was looking through that unblinking glass,
seeing and hearing a past he tried each day to forget.

Someone shouted at him to run. Gordon seized his
hand and the two brothers raced blindly toward the
mountain. The screams of their mother pierced the
air, halted them as surely as an iron manacle. Black

smoke plumed skyward from the burning thatch, stinging Ian's eyes and nose with a sharp reek.

"What shall we do with the pair of them, Mr. Adder?" a soldier asked, dragging the boys before a man with thick lips and hard eyes. How tall and gaunt Adder looked, high on his horse. He wore coarse clothes and had a thick ginger beard. His manner was so cold, he didn't even flinch at the sound of a woman begging for her baby's life.

"Send them to my factor in Glasgow." Adder raised his voice above the hoarse shrieks of Mary MacVane. His speech was coarse and ugly. "They'll make a fine pair of climbing boys."

Miranda touched Ian, and he came back into the sunlit day, with the peaceful hills all around him. "There you were again, drifting off," she scolded gently. "What is it that troubles you on such a fine summer day? Look at this scenery. Am I allowed to say it's quaint?"

Ian laughed briefly, quietly. "If you must."

"But actually, it's not. It's majestic. Magnificent. How blessed you are to have known such a place."

The irony of the words seared him, but she was an enchanting distraction. He *wanted* her to distract him, if only for a moment. Surrounded by the splendor of the Highlands, she looked lovelier than ever, her cheeks blooming, her hair gleaming in the sunlight, her expression open, almost enraptured.

"Can we stay long?" she asked. "Must we hurry back to London?"

"We must," he said, though he, too, felt reluctant. How remote and absurd it seemed from here, the idea that Bonaparte's spies were planning to assassinate all the leaders of Europe. "After we're" —he hesitated— "after the handfast, we'll be off."

"Handfast," she said. "I do know of this custom, so I must have read of it somewhere." She regarded him soberly. "And did I agree to it?"

"Sweetheart, you couldna wait." He grinned affably.

"But why a handfast, and not a proper marriage?"

He thought fast. "You're a follower of Wollstonecraft, remember? The crusader for free love."

"So we're to be handfasted. A trial marriage. If I conceive in the first year, the bond endures. If not . . . "

"You're free."

"Free." Her voice caught on the word. "As I am now? Knowing nothing and no one except you?"

He turned away, brooding down at the vale of the river. He had deemed the handfast more humane, in the end, than actual marriage. A true marriage would be a sentence of shame for her, for it would require an act of Parliament to dissolve. The handfast held out the possibility of escape.

He had no doubt she would want to escape him one day.

"I mean you no dishonor, lass," he said, turning back, sliding his arm around her waist. "'Tis just that we had agreed. We wanted to be together right away. Agnes has been urging me to come back for years. So it seemed reasonable to marry in the Scottish fashion."

He expected an outburst of resentment. Instead she favored him with a smile so brilliant that it made him blink. "You are the dearest man, Ian MacVane."

He nearly choked on an outraged laugh. "I? Dear? Call me pleasant if you must. I would even sit still for charming. But dear? Madam, please!"

She laughed. "I am in earnest. There is something irresistibly dear about a man who is so eager to wed that he would sail the seas and bend the very law of the land in order to be with her."

Ian found himself in the awkward position of having to both hide a smile and stifle a curse. Duffie again. The statement reeked of Angus McDuff. He had been putting inconvenient notions into her head for days.

"That is exactly the case," he forced himself to admit. "I cannot wait to marry you." The hot discomfort in his body added conviction to his statement. He was startled to realize it was not wholly a lie.

How could this be happening to him? In general he disliked the English, despite the fact that he had found notoriety and fortune in their society. He particularly disliked the women and should hold *this* particular woman in high disdain. Yet he didn't. She might be party to an assassination plot, but at the moment she looked the very flower of virtue.

She stood with her hands at her sides, the breeze plucking curls from beneath the kerchief she wore over her head. "May I speak frankly with you, Ian?"

"Aye, of course." *Tell me everything, Miranda. Everything you know, and then I can set you free.*

Her slim fingers toyed with the folds of her dress. "I can believe that all is just as you've told me—the way we met, my circumstances, my past. You've described it so vividly that sometimes I think I *do* remember."

His heart seemed to lift in his chest. What a wonder, to think that he could pretend that the past was golden, that he had loved and had been worthy of her love. "Go on."

"There is one matter that still confuses me. I want to remember loving you, but I do not." She lifted a hand to her mouth, and he was horrified to see that she was on the verge of tears. "What sort of creature am I? Why can't I remember that?"

Ian took her in his arms. "I can't explain it to you, Miranda, for I don't understand it myself." He smoothed a hand down her back, pressing her against him. He forced out the lie. "My own memories are vivid enough for both of us. We have set each other on fire, Miranda, *mo chridh*. I used to . . ." He bent his head and nipped at her ear, then whispered a wicked suggestion to her.

She caught her breath with a high-pitched gasp. "You didn't!"

"Aye, Miranda. I did. *We* did."

Her cheeks flamed, and her velvety brown eyes shone, but not with tears, not now. "And did I—did I let you?"

"You not only let me, but you liked it. And—" This time he bent to her other ear, curling his tongue inside it and whispering a description of a trick he had learned at a brothel in Naples, long ago.

She jumped back with a little scream. "You are too shocking to live, Ian MacVane." Before he could reply, she hurled herself back into his arms. "And when can we do it again?"

"Would this very moment suit you?" He wondered if he was going too far into this make-believe world. But he could not stop himself.

"Yes. Oh, yes."

He tumbled back on the soft summer grass, taking her weight on top of him and, just for a moment, feeling a pure unearned joy. He slid his hands beneath her loose white blouse, filling his palms with smooth warm flesh, filling his mind with naught but pure lust.

"Wench," he said, half dazed by the heat racing through him. "You have no shame."

"Did I ever?"

"None at all." Under her chemise, his thumbs brushed the tips of her breasts.

Her eyes drifted halfway shut. "I'm glad I was a sensible sort." She shifted, and he could tell by the expression on her face that she felt his hardness.

He smiled wickedly. "You're a tempting woman, Miranda Stonecypher. You should be properly shocked."

"I don't believe I'm properly anything." She shifted again and laughed softly at his pained expression. "Mr. MacVane, I think a hasty marriage is a very good idea indeed."

She leaned down and pressed her mouth to his, and her lips parted. There was no reason he could not take her right here, right now. His every instinct urged him to do so.

"Ah, Ian, Ian, did you tell me the truth before, when you swore we had never made love?" she begged to know, her mouth dragging down his throat, her hands clinging to his straining shoulders. "Did we ever join our bodies?"

Summoning all his restraint, he forced himself to put her aside. The heat in his loins was driving him mad, but he managed a crooked smile. "Miranda, my sweet, what I said before is true. If I had joined my body with yours, I promise you wouldna forget it."

7

*Needles and pins, needles and pins,
When a man marries his trouble begins.*
      —Anonymous, Nursery Rhyme

Miranda had done the impossible, Ian realized. She had made him see Scotland in a new way. The land was no longer the dark, forbidding place of nightmares he had envisioned for so many years, but a country of such wild beauty it took his breath away.

He had managed to forget that—until Miranda had reminded him.

Early the next morning he struck out for the manor house, taking the worn cow path along the ridge of Ben Innes. A dark sense of satisfaction streamed through him. Callum had heard that Adder had been obliged to sell the place; presumably the Sassenach had fallen on hard times.

Though the house and gardens had been neglected, an air of majesty still hung about the place. Wildflowers and roses gone awry flourished

around the gateways and along the paths to the terrace.

Ian turned and looked out over the valley and
beyond the cliffs to the sea. A frigate, looking as small
as a toy and flying the Union Jack, pushed into the
harbor.

What a thing it must have been, to be the laird. To
stand in this spot and to know he was master of all he
surveyed.

The old dream tugged at him like the persistent
ache of an unhealed battle wound. How could he dare
to hope to live here one day, in the place that was as
much a part of him as his eyes or his hands?

To remind himself of the futility of dreaming, he
looked down, studied his maimed hand as it gripped
the stone wall at the edge of the terrace garden. He
still felt his finger, a phantom digit, as if it were still
there. Unlike Miranda, he had no trouble remembering, in vivid detail, every moment of his past.

"Hold it steady, there's a lad." *The voice belonged
to Smudge, the sweep's idiot nephew. The size of a
small bullock, he was like a giant child, with the
strength of two men. When the sweep told him to separate the pieces of a broken chimney pot that had
been soldered by burnt creosote to the brick, he set
himself diligently to the task, with Ian in assistance.*

*They positioned themselves beside the pot on the
roof, with Ian holding back a sheet of beaten metal
while Smudge raised a shovel high. The reek of old
soot and creosote seared his nostrils.*

*"Wait, Smudge," Ian said. "You'll have my arm
off with that shovel if—"*

*He leaped back, but not in time. The blade of the
shovel came down and caught his hand. The pain
shot like a hot lance up his arm. He sank onto the flat*

rooftop and stared at the blood pulsing out, spreading in a wide red pool onto the black tar. His severed finger lay on the flat rooftop. The world spun in crazy circles.

"Sorry about your finger, ducks," said Smudge.

The raucous caw of a crow startled Ian.

"Jesus." He had broken out in a sweat. Dizzy, he looked away from his hand on the wall and made himself take deep, cleansing breaths of the morning air as he ran back down the mountain to the village.

Childish shouts rose up, and children ran by in a herd, chasing a hoop. Robbie was among them, and Ian paused to watch.

Aye, it had been a good plan to bring the laddie here. No more flash houses for that one, no nightmare of service as a climbing boy. Robbie would stay here, growing braw and red-cheeked in the Highland air.

"You blethering little Sassenach snot!" The taunt pierced Ian's thoughts.

The Scobie twins advanced on Robbie, who turned to run for his life, stumbled, and fell into a puddle. The twins, hale as their wheelwright papa, leaped upon him, fists flying. Robbie howled with outrage.

Ian started toward them to break up the fight, but he stopped in his tracks when he saw his mother rush out of the garden gate in front of Agnes's house. She was like an avenging angel, her robes flying and her hair loose. Heedless of the mud, she plucked the Scobie twins off Robbie and gathered the lad in her arms. The village children backed off, some of them making a hex sign with their fingers in superstition.

Ian stood amazed. He approached cautiously,

praying she wouldn't hurt the lad. By the time he reached them, Mary was hugging Robbie close, and he was sobbing into her ample breast.

"He's only a wee laddie," she said to the twins. "Just a wee lad. He canna fight the likes of you."

She glanced up, spying Ian. He stared at his mother and she stared back, her face mottled but curiously regal as she rested her chin on the top of Robbie's head. For a moment, the fog of madness and the estrangement of years fell away.

Ian's stomach clenched. He waited for her to rage at him, to curse him, to accuse him of failing her, but she simply said, "He's just a wee lad. He canna fight the lot of them."

Calm as anyone's favorite grandmother, she straightened up and took Robbie into the house with her.

Ian stood there, incredulous. Then he felt it—a smile began in his heart and unfurled on his lips. "All this before breakfast," he muttered. Then his grin disappeared as he remembered that today was only the beginning.

Today was his wedding day.

Since arriving in Scotland, Miranda had developed an excellent understanding of male pride. Ian was supremely confident of his gifts as a great lover. She tried very hard to grow annoyed at him.

Instead she found herself intrigued. More than that. Warm and slightly breathless each time he came near. Shamelessly eager to touch him, to be touched by him.

While the villagers constructed a bonfire of celebration to be lit that evening, she watched the activity. Before the night was out, she would be married to Ian MacVane.

"You're staring." Coming up behind her, Ian whispered the words into her ear, raising shivers along her spine. "You're staring and you're frowning. 'Tis a bad portent."

Even the mere whisper of his breath affected her. All of her flesh began to tingle. He ignited an undeniable power inside her, a force strong enough to burn past her will, past good sense, past all her reservations. She wanted him, and her body told her so frankly, without shame.

"I'm thinking," she explained.

"Is it something you've remembered?" His voice was taut with strain.

She shook her head. "I'm wondering about what will take place here tonight. Becoming a married lady is a pivotal event. Surely it warrants a moment of silence." She turned to face him and nearly swayed back into the pile of firewood.

"Oh, Lord." Her gaze raked him from the top of his glengarry to the tips of his leather shoes.

He planted himself squarely before her. "What's wrong, lass? I thought you'd be pleased to find me dressed early for the wedding. Duffie would have it no other way."

"Wrong?" The word came out in a breathless rush. "What is *wrong*, Ian MacVane, is that you have done the unforgivable."

His shadowy eyes narrowed. "And what is that?"

"There are many things I cannot remember, but I do know there is one cardinal rule in weddings. The groom must never outshine the bride."

He cocked his head to one side. "Outshine? Love, I have no idea what you—"

"Do not deny it." She planted her hands on her hips. "You should have warned me that you look that way in a kilt."

He spread his arms, all innocence. "What way?"

"Like . . . Rob Roy. Like a hero out of a fireside tale." She glared at the badger sporran covering his groin. The lifeless eyes of the badger mocked her. "Did no one ever teach you that it's vulgar to flaunt one's physique?"

He let loose with a howl of unrepentant laughter. "It wasna part of my boyhood training, I assure you."

He had washed his hair, and beneath the woolen cap it flashed blue black in the sunlight. The snowy shirt billowed out at the sleeves, broadening his shoulders. The shirt and leather waistcoat were parted at the throat to display an enticing expanse of sun-browned chest and throat. The kilt was woven of a plaid she recognized as the MacVane tartan, bright red shot through with black and sea green. The hem brushed his long, powerful legs, the movement drawing the eye, teasing the passions.

But Ian's appeal was made of more than the dashing Highland costume. His customary look of weary disdain was gone, replaced by a barely veiled hunger when he studied her lips, her throat, her bosom. Without speaking, without touching her, he was letting her know he wanted her, and Miranda found it appallingly thrilling.

"Even so," she said at last, "you have dragged my vanity in the dirt." She clasped her hands in front of her, pressing them against the heat in her belly. "I should thank you, I suppose. For you've reminded me that I do possess a sense of vanity. I wasn't sure until now."

He took her hands and pried them apart, cradling them in his. He exhaled a long, slow breath. "Let me see if I have the right of this. You're fashed with me because I dressed my best for our wedding."

"You make me sound petty and silly," she said. "It's just one more way you outshine me, Ian. You've had me at a disadvantage from the start. You, not me, have been the keeper of my past. All I know, I know from your lips."

He gripped her hands in his. "Lass, I'm sorry."

She saw guilt in his eyes. "I'm not certain what you're apologizing for, Ian."

He looked past her, to the village green where the men were building the bonfire. "For . . . knowing things that you don't, lass. For not being able to help you remember."

The sweetness of his words humbled her. "I *am* petty, aren't I? The way I look shouldn't matter to me, but it does, and there you are. It matters."

His eyes shone, and his lips pressed together as if he were keeping in more laughter. God help him, if he laughed at her again, she would march to London and never look back.

But he didn't laugh. He touched her hands with that rare tenderness he sometimes showed when he wasn't keeping himself under rigid control. Gently his knuckles grazed her fingertips.

"Tell me, how was I to know?" he asked quietly.

She cocked her head. "To know what?"

"That I—with my blouse flapping and my great, hairy legs exposed for all the world to see—could possibly outshine you? God's light, lass, you look as fresh and lovely as moon on the moors, a far comelier sight than myself in a moldering old costume first made for my great-grandsire."

She searched his face for a trace of insincerity and found none. "Was your great-grandsire a gentleman, then?"

"He was a MacVane. He lost most of what he had in the clan wars, and then the English took the rest." He cleared his throat as if to banish the bitterness from his tone. "Almost all. He did leave me a fine kilt and sporran. Though I doubt he meant for it to annoy my future wife."

She smiled before she remembered she was angry with him. Then she realized her anger had fled, insubstantial as morning mist on the loch. "I don't feel you're mocking me. It's just that when I saw you dressed this way, it occurred to me that you could have any woman you choose. A great beauty. A famous lady. A noblewoman or a notorious wit."

"How do you know you aren't all of those, Miranda? Perhaps you are, and I've simply neglected to tell you."

Despite his teasing tone, the words hit her hard. Who was she? Did she even deserve this man?

Before she could make herself ask him, he called over his shoulder, "Agnes, can you help?"

The older woman bustled out and snatched Miranda from Ian's grip. "Agnes," he said, "Miranda needs your help in getting ready for the—"

Waving her hand, Agnes shooed him silent. "Weesht now, I have eyes to see, Ian MacVane!" She stopped in the dooryard amid the chickens poking at seeds on the ground and raked him from head to foot with her gaze. "Vain male baggage," she muttered, then steered Miranda inside.

*   *   *

Ian MacVane had played many roles in his life, but bridegroom was a new one for him. And one, he decided, for which he was grossly ill suited. Moments before he was to appear on the steps of the kirk, he hesitated in the keeping room of Agnes's house.

He was about to promise Miranda Stonecypher a year of his life. And if, God forbid, she were to conceive a child, the year could stretch out to forever.

How did a man pretend all his dreams were coming true when his life was a waking nightmare?

How did he pretend to be in love with a woman when all he wanted from her were her secrets?

And how, by all that was holy, could he make love to Miranda, steal her innocence and her honor, and expect to live with himself after?

The questions consumed him, even when a rider rushed in with a hastily scrawled message in semaphore cipher. "Abel Jack from Kirkcaldy said you'd give me a half crown for this," the rider stated.

Ian paid him without comment and dismissed him with a nod of his head. He unfolded the message and held it in the light from the small window. The letter was dated the day before, so he knew right away the semaphore towers, signaling news from one end of England to the other, were in place and functioning.

There was something quite amazing about the new system of communication. Men stood vigil atop lofty towers, squinting at other distant towers, waiting for a signal. In a matter of moments the signaling was done, the man put aside his lever-driven flags, and then stood to await yet another message.

Fog and darkness often interrupted transmissions, but when the system worked, its speed boggled the mind. Here in Scotland, he held in his hands a thought that had been formed in London only a day before.

It was a very angry thought. Tersely stated, as were all semaphore messages.

Return to me immediately.

He wadded up the paper and tossed it onto the crumbling peat logs in the grate. So Frances was not happy with his change of plans, the meddlesome harpy. She had told him to put himself on intimate terms with Miranda. To make love to her, to learn her secrets.

Fanny didn't understand his need to protect Miranda when she was in this lost, memoryless state. To salvage her honor by marrying her. Hell, he didn't even understand it himself. But Fanny should know better than to interfere. He had always done his job, and done it well.

"Cor, sir, you look right silly in them skirts!"

Ian turned away from the hearth to see Robbie watching him with a mixture of disgust and merriment. The lad was flourishing like springtime itself, and Ian was surprised to feel a rush of pride. Robbie's cheeks were bright red and growing rounder on Agnes's good brown bread and apricots from the orchard, trout from the streams and lakes. His London pallor was gone, thanks to the fine, robust quality of the Highland air. He wore the puffy bruise beneath his right eye like a medal of honor.

"Sir," Ian said with mock severity, "I'll have you know these skirts you find so silly have been the garb of kings since time out of mind."

Robbie dubiously studied Ian's bald knees. "Why?"

"I suppose," Ian said, recalling Miranda's perusal earlier, "'tis because Scottish women like the view, and they make the clothes."

Robbie cocked his head skeptically. He walked in a

slow circle around Ian, his young face solemn and thoughtful. "I suppose it could be useful if you have to piss in a hurry."

Ian laughed and went to the door. "How is your bruise, lad?"

Robbie touched the bony rim under his eye. "Doesn't hurt at all. Mistress Mary chased off the Scobies quick as you please."

"I saw." Ian's throat ached.

"She was asking about you, Mistress Mary was."

His heart thudded slowly, audibly, against the wall of his chest. "Asking—"

"About your London house and where you nicked all that money you're always sending her. I told her she should ask you." Robbie grinned. "I wager she will."

"Dinna wager too much." He draped an arm around the boy. "Come, we've a wedding to attend."

Just as they were about to leave the cottage, a faint rustle came from the rooms in the back. His mother. Did she have any notion of what was happening today? Did she know her only surviving son was about to take a wife? And if she did, would her hatred for him extend to Miranda?

Age-old pain twisted through him. No matter how much time had passed, he could never think of his mother without feeling the sad yearning.

His face felt carven in stone as he took the boy's hand and stepped out into the path toward the kirk. It took all of his control to hide his sorrow. And in the end he failed, for Robbie stopped and glanced back at the house. "'Twill be all right, sir. You'll see."

Before Ian could stop him, Robbie broke away and ran off. At the same moment, Duffie and some of the local men swept Ian into their wake. Buoyed by copious pints of heather ale, they conveyed him to the kirk. Ribald comments salted the air, and Ian slipped uneasily into the role of bridegroom.

Attended by Agnes and the women of the town, Miranda waited on the steps.

Ian stopped in his tracks. He had sworn earlier that her beauty needed no artifices or enhancements, and that was true. Yet under Agnes's care, Miranda's loveliness had taken on an almost painful intensity.

She wore a crown of flowers, laurel and daisy and heather interwoven with her sleek, nut brown hair. She was draped in a gown of sheer, pale green. With her enormous eyes and soft mouth, she resembled a pagan wood nymph, savage and fey, impossible to hold yet equally impossible to relinquish.

A light breeze swept down from the heights, tearing a storm of petals from the berry bushes that surrounded the kirkyard. Miranda lifted her face to the swirling petals. God's light, she took his breath away. He felt a warmth somewhere in the region of his heart, and the sensation was so unfamiliar that he had nearly forgotten its name. Happiness.

This was not supposed to happen to him. He was not supposed to become smitten with Miranda Stonecypher. He was not supposed to look at her and see someone who could, if he let her, bring him joy and peace and all the things that most men were allowed to have.

"A blessing upon you!" shouted Hamish Dunn. He was the town blacksmith, but when disputes arose he served as magistrate, and at least twice a year he acted as kirk deacon. For as long as anyone could remember, Hamish had officiated at the births, deaths, and marriages of Crough na Muir.

Ian reached the stone steps under the curving lintel

of the village church. Stray petals settled on his shoulders and chest. He glanced down at Miranda and felt a jolt of panic. Only moments from now, she would be his wife.

"My friends," Hamish said in his broad, deep burr, "we are gathered to hear the vows of fidelity of Ian MacVane and Miss Miranda Stonecypher. Do you both agree to abide by the custom of handfasting?"

"I do," Miranda said softly.

Ian suspected that she had romanticized the notion of handfast. He did nothing to correct her, for it suited his purposes to let her think it fanciful and poetic. In sooth, it was sometimes a cold-blooded means to test a woman's fertility.

"Aye," said Ian. He knew exactly what he was agreeing to. The clasping of hands, the speaking of vows, bound them in marriage for just one day over a year. Once their time was up, they could part or live together as they chose.

"And is there any among us who can name a reason this man and this woman should not be joined?" Hamish went on. "For if there be one—"

"*Wait.*"

Every person present turned toward the kirk gate. Hushed whispers flurried like petals through the air.

With a dawning sense of dread, Ian pivoted on his heel. He heard the sharp intake of Miranda's breath. His hand went to the handle of his dirk, but what he saw was no enemy who could be vanquished by a blade.

His mother. She wore her matted hair unbound, a shapeless dress dragging its hem in the grass and flowers of the kirkyard. The air of wildness and unpredictability hovered around her like a musky perfume. Her gaze was steely and magnetic, holding everyone silent as she made her way to the steps.

Ian braced himself for the storm of her rage. Once again, she would tell him how worthless he was. How he had failed to save her and his family. How he should have died with the rest of them.

But the fury never came, and when his initial shock had passed, he realized why. Robbie. The boy held her hand, escorting her proudly, with a broad grin on his face, as if she were his own dear mother.

The meddling little blighter. Ian had told him to stay away from Mary, that she could lash out and hurt him. But she hadn't. She'd let him bring her flowers every day. When she stopped in front of the kirk and let go of Robbie's hand, Ian saw the mother-love in her pale, lined face.

Then she looked up at Ian and Miranda, and her expression did not change. Did not shift to bitterness and animal fury.

"He brought me," Mary said. "The little lad. He made me see things that were hiding inside my grief. Old, old things. Because, you ken, he's just a wee lad. Nae bigger than you were yourself, my Ian, when the bad men came to our croft." Her hand, rough and papery dry, came up to caress Ian's cheek. "Bless you, lad," she said. "Bless you and the lassie, too. Bless you."

He lost control then and there. Ian MacVane, who had bullied and cheated his way to wealth and power, who had fought on the battlefields of Spain and sailed the high seas, who was known to all London as a man lacking sentiment or soul, gave way to searing tears of gratitude. Silently they crept down his face, and his mother wiped them away with her trembling hand.

The moment, punctuated only by Miranda's faint sobs, passed quickly. Mary MacVane handed Miranda a scrap of linen. "A handkerchief," she explained.

"My own dear mother made it for me. Part of my dowry, it was, but that's all that's left. The rest is ashes. Ashes." She seemed to drift off then, to become vague and distant. She wobbled, as if the effort of walking to the kirk had sapped her strength.

Agnes gave a loud, sentimental snort and took Mary by the arm. "Come along, then, dear one. 'Tis a wearying thing, rejoining the world, but I always knew you would one day. You'll want a bit of a rest."

Mary allowed Agnes and Robbie to lead her to a stone garden seat beneath a linden tree. And Ian, his soul on fire, pondered the terrible irony of it all. His mother had given him the gift of hope just at the moment he was about to commit his greatest deception.

He clasped Miranda by the hand and pledged to make her his wife.

8

There may, perhaps, in such a scene,
Some recollection be
Of days that have as happy been,
And you'll remember me.
—Alfred Bunn,
The Bohemian Girl, III

When the brief ceremony was over, the villagers clanged tankards and goblets together, raising toasts to the newlyweds. The men brought forth a set of pipes and a skin drum, and Hamish sawed out tune after tune on his fiddle. People danced reels and jigs or sometimes simply stood by and stamped the rhythm with their feet or clapped their hands.

Miranda, fresh and breathless from a wild reel, went in search of Ian. She found him standing off by himself, bathed in the wavering golden light of the bonfire.

"There you are, Mr. MacVane. 'Tis Mrs. MacVane here." She felt merry and giddy, filled with anticipation.

"I feel as if I've never truly lived until now. Because of you."

A pained expression darkened his face. "Dinna say that, lass. Dinna make me responsible for your happiness."

"But you are," she said, unwilling to let his moodiness dim her cheer. He had been pensive ever since his mother had given her blessing at the wedding. "You've made me very happy, Ian. You've given me a life again. A goal. I am going to devote myself to you."

"Ah, Miranda." His smile was warm and weary all at once. "You're a stubborn woman, you are."

"And have I always been?"

"Since the first moment I met you." He lifted his horn cup and drank deeply. The piper skirled a loud salute. Gaelic yells filled the air.

Miranda peered at the shining faces in the crowd. Ian's people. Hers now. What a remarkable concept. The aching void inside her was filling slowly. She needed to belong. Perhaps here, amid these people who had welcomed her, was where her healing would begin. "What are they saying?" she asked Ian.

"You dinna want to know," he said, his voice low with restrained laughter.

"I do," she protested, watching Tam Alexander lift his cup and pantomime a rocking motion with his hips while his friends howled with laughter. "It has to do with me, doesn't it? With us?" At the very thought, all the heat in her body pooled in secret places, places that longed for his touch. "You can tell me, Ian."

His strong arm snaked around her and drew her close. She felt the heat of him through his shirt and through the stout woolen tartan of his kilt. "Tell you?" He lifted an inquisitive eyebrow, then bent and nipped at the lobe of her ear. "And spoil the surprise?"

The promise in his voice and in his touch took her breath away. She wanted this man with a deep, piercing longing. It hardly mattered that she could not remember him, for the feelings that drummed in her chest were as old as time itself. She could almost believe she had known him in another lifetime, for one life span was hardly enough to love him the way she wanted.

To the delight of the laughing crowd, she wound her arms around his neck. "I love you, Ian MacVane," she said. "I'm certain I do. Surely I always have."

He muttered something in Gaelic, then kissed her long and hungrily. The hooting and stamping of the crowd rose to a crescendo.

"To bed," shouted Tam Alexander. "To bed! Take her to bed, lest you spark another bonfire where you stand!"

"To bed! To bed!" people called, roaring with laughter.

Ian lifted his mouth from hers. "To bed?"

"They all appear to be demanding it."

"And what do you demand, Miranda?"

He seemed to want to hear her say it, though she was certain her desire was written clearly on her face. "Take me to bed, Ian MacVane. Now."

The villagers formed two lines leading to the cottage. They would have the cozy dwelling all to themselves; a night of privacy would be Agnes's gift to them. She and Robbie would stay with Mary in the adjacent quarters.

As Ian took Miranda's hand and led her up the path toward the rough plank door, the crowd and the noise seemed to fade away, and there was Ian, only Ian, towering over her, his every touch a tender promise.

Miranda knew she had read love poems in the past. She had viewed paintings and heard music that was supposed to express the depths of sensual desire. But none of them even came close to what she felt in that moment, just before he opened the door.

They stood at the threshold, she feeling overheated and sweetly needy, he cloaked in shadow and looking unbearably handsome. She heard someone yell at Ian to pick her up, to carry her over the threshold. He reached for her, swept her up into his arms in a towering, romantic gesture that left her dazed.

A chorus of *oooh*s and wistful sighs rose up from the villagers.

A distant pounding drummed on the road, unexpected. Uninvited. Unwelcome. Torches bobbed above the heads of a half-dozen riders. Past the crumbling wall, the riders poured in, boiling along the main road on galloping horses.

Forcing a curse past his gritted teeth, Ian set Miranda down on the path.

"What is happening?" she asked, trying not to raise her voice in frustration. She was not about to let her wedding night be spoiled. "Ian?"

"Damned if I know."

The bonfire bathed the lead rider in gold. The bright hues of the flames matched his blond, Brutus cut hair. He wore Hessians and tight riding breeches, a perfectly fitted waistcoat and frock coat. The men who rode behind him were as immaculately clad and humorless as soldiers on review.

Ian spat a curse. "Robbie, where are you, lad?"

The boy scurried from the direction of the banqueting

tables. "Take Mistress Mary away," Ian said. "Can you do that?"

Robbie's eyes rounded like saucers. "Are the soldiers here to hurt us, Ian?"

"Nay, lad, not this time, and they couldn't if they tried. But my mother won't understand. I dinna want to see her upset."

Robbie nodded and hurried off. A moment later, Miranda saw him leading Mary MacVane off to her quarters.

Ian strode down the path and planted himself in the middle of the roadway. The men brought their horses up short, five of them falling back while the lead rider pushed forward and dismounted.

Feeling as if she had come awake halfway through a dream, Miranda walked toward the newcomers. The golden man fascinated her so.

Ian grabbed her arm. "Have a care," he said through his teeth. "You don't know what they're about."

Her head pounded with a peculiar throbbing that was familiar by now. The pain always preceded an episode of remembrance. "He won't hurt me," she said.

Some of the villagers began to grumble. "There's naught but trouble for you here," Hamish yelled.

"State your business and be gone," said Tam Alexander.

"Miranda!" In two strides the golden man reached her. He took her in his arms and hauled her against him. He smelled, not unpleasantly, of sweat and horse. "Ah, Miranda, I've found you at last!"

She heard a hiss of fury from Ian and quickly pushed away from the man. "Sir, if you please!"

The Englishman was tall and broad, his arms and chest and shoulders hard with muscles. To her astonishment, tears gathered in his eyes.

He was a stranger. Yet he knew her name. She felt a chill, a sense of unreality, as if this were a dream about someone else.

With a small cry, she glanced back at Ian. She wanted to take shelter in his arms, but he wasn't offering his embrace. He was glaring at the newcomer.

"Who the devil are you?" he demanded.

"Miranda?" the man asked, ignoring the question. He was handsome in a balanced, classical way, his face composed of bold planes and angles all perfectly arranged, his hair long and wavy in the fashion of the day. He dabbed at his eyes with a clean handkerchief. "Miranda," he went on, "I've been frantic with worry. I've searched for you—quite literally—over the length and breadth of England." He smiled with genuine pleasure, his eyes still bright and moist. "You're looking well, sweet Miranda. Simply lovely."

Ian swore and shouldered forward through the encroaching villagers. "If you've business with the lady, it can wait."

Miranda swallowed but could barely speak past the lump of fear and confusion in her throat. "Ian, no. I must speak to him." The pounding in her head increased. "Sir," she said, her voice low and trembling. "Sir, forgive me, but I don't know who you are."

One of his companions sidled over on his mount. The horse's breathing sounded loud in the tense, waiting silence. "Remember, my lord, what the black-haired wench from the hospital said. Memory lapses and all."

Wench from the hospital. Gwen? Had they spoken to Gwen?

"She doesna want you here. Get out," Ian ordered.

His shadow loomed like a protective cloak over Miranda.

Determinedly, the fair-haired man disregarded him. "It can't be." He looked at Miranda with an intensity and absorption that made her cheeks go hot. "Darling, you must remember me. I am Lucas Chesney."

"Lucas." She tested the word. It meant nothing to her.

He grasped her by the shoulders, his grip firm. "Lucas Chesney, Viscount Lisle. The man you love, Miranda. *Your betrothed.*"

With a growl of rage, Ian stepped in. "Get your bloody paws off the lady."

The man's grip loosened. She stumbled back.

"Lucas Chesney," Ian muttered as if the name meant something to him. "You'd do well to take yourself off, for you've come at a very bad time."

The villagers tried to crowd in closer, but Chesney's men held them at bay with muskets angled low across their bodies.

Something hot and blinding flashed in Miranda's brain. She was reminded of the ordeal in the warehouse, when the explosions erupted all around her while she stood still, certain she was about to perish. The shock held her immobile, speechless. Lucas Chesney. Her betrothed.

But how in heaven could that be?

Ian advanced on the stranger. "The lady says she doesna know you. I'd say you came a long way for naught."

Chesney's nostrils thinned. Miranda could see his gaze flick over Ian; The men with him exchanged nervous glances.

"I came," Chesney said, "to reclaim my betrothed."

Ian's chin jutted upward. "Who sent you? How did you know to come here?"

"I am the Viscount Lisle. Not unknown in certain circles."

"I've no use for a fancy title. Nor, I would think, does a Bedlamite named Gwen. How is it that you know her?"

"Gwen informed me—" The viscount blinked, but his voice never faltered. "By God, I shall not do this! I shall not answer to some Jacobite in kilts."

Ian's fist twisted into the stock of Chesney's shirt. "I have a very bad reaction to Sassenachs who come to Scotland looking for trouble."

Two of the soldiers grabbed for Ian. Miranda swayed on her feet. She looked from Lucas's handsome, golden face to Ian, who stared down his opponent with a brooding intensity that suddenly terrified her.

And then the anger started, surprising her with its force. "Damn you both," she said. Again her voice trembled, but this time it was with rage. "Damn you both to hell." She slammed her fist down on the top of the dooryard gate. "I have lost my memory, not my wits. And I demand an answer. This instant. Which one of you is lying?"

"You had best hope," Ian said, shoving Lucas back against his men, "that it isn't me, love, since you just married me." He rested his palm at the small of her back.

For a fraction of a second, she responded to his touch, her body coming to life for him and him alone, all her wanting centered on him. But she forced herself to step away from him, to confront the shock on Lucas's face.

"Miranda!" Lucas said. "Oh, my poor Miranda. I've come too late."

She felt as if a cold steel rod supported her rigid back. "Yes and no, Mr. Chesney."

"What does that mean?"

"I'll tell you what it means," Ian roared. "Get your fancy arse back to England."

She could not bring herself to look at Ian, for if she did, her courage would falter. She understood what she had to do, and she could not allow herself to waver.

"It means, my lord, that yes, you are too late to stop me from marrying Ian MacVane, if that is your purpose in coming here."

Lucas plowed a broad hand through his hair. "Ah, God, Miranda—"

"But it also means," she went on, hearing the steely coldness in her voice, "that you are *not* too late to put an end to this farce."

"Darling, I don't know what you mean," Lucas said.

"Mind how you address my wife, Sassenach," Ian said.

"You may not call me darling," she said to Lucas. At last she dared to look at Ian. He stood there, painted by flame and shadow, tall and forbidding, yet somehow aloof. "And *you* may not call me wife."

His eyes narrowed dangerously, but she forced herself to continue. "Since the—since my accident, I have allowed myself to be buffeted about by men. By the constable who sold me to the warden of Bedlam. By the doctor there. By you, Ian." Fighting a terrible feeling of loss and confusion, she turned back to Lucas. "And now by you."

"I'm here to help you," Lucas said. "To protect you from this scoundrel."

"So was the constable. The warden. The doctor. And Ian MacVane." Seared by betrayal, Miranda took a step back, wanting to be away from them all, wanting to hide in the dark like a wounded animal. "I no longer know whom to trust, so I'll trust no one. No one except myself."

"Ah, Miranda." Lucas's face appeared pale in the firelight. "I was hoping for a moment of privacy so I could tell you—"

"You'd do better to hope for the moon to fall out of the sky," Ian snapped.

"Weesht!" Miranda said, borrowing Agnes's phrase. She turned back to Lucas. "Tell me what?"

"About your father. He—he's gone, Miranda. Presumed dead."

There was a strange quality to the emptiness that yawned inside her. Since she could not picture the man who had been her father, it was like looking down into a black well. "Ian told me."

"Did he tell you Gideon Stonecypher was murdered?" Lucas demanded.

The black well turned to blinding, raging whiteness. Her father, her own flesh and blood, was dead. Murdered. Yet she could not react properly, could not grieve properly, because her past had been stolen from her. Somehow her life had been bound up with these men, but she could not sort out the ways. "Then I must find out what happened to him," she said.

Duffie came forward, his face lined with worry. "Lassie, please, dinna do anything rash—"

"I shan't, Mr. McDuff. I promise you that. All I ask is that I be allowed to return to London. Let me find out on my own who I am, what happened to me and to my father." She glanced from Ian to Lucas. "Let me find out who lied, and who told the truth. It's what I should have done from the beginning."

A sense of revulsion ran like icewater through her blood. She walked past Ian, then paused and turned back to him. "If everything has been the way you say, then I shall come back to you, if you'll have me." She felt as if she were awakening from a golden dream to cold reality.

"You canna trust him," Ian stated.

"I can't trust anyone but myself."

He gripped her shoulders, bent low, and whispered in her ear, "You said you loved me, lass."

Confusion spiraled through her. *Did he tell you Gideon Stonecypher was murdered?*

"That is what I said," she whispered brokenly.

"Then stay, lass. Stay, and we'll go to London together later."

He would never know the strength it cost her to wrench herself from his grip, to step back. "I have to go now. I have to find out the truth."

She started down the road, brushing past the astonished Englishmen.

"Goddamn it!" Ian roared. "God—"

A dull thud sounded. She whirled around in time to see him staggering back, clutching his jaw, sinking to the ground. The crowd clustered around him while Lucas Chesney flexed his hand.

Miranda felt as if a block of ice encased her. She looked neither right nor left as she walked toward the harbor. She did not want to see the disappointment in the faces of these people. She did not want to think about the sense of belonging she had felt with them. The joy she'd felt in Ian's arms. The happiness she might have found here.

"You should feel relieved," Angus McDuff told his master the next day. "It was fate itself intervening.

Keeping you from doing a grave injury to the lassie's honor."

Ian glowered at him. His head throbbed from the ale he had consumed the previous night. Pints and pints of it. But no matter how much he drank, he could not banish Miranda Stonecypher from his mind. Miranda Stonecypher MacVane, he reminded himself.

He should rejoice at her departure. Now he could put Frances in charge of finding out what Miranda knew. He had done his best and made a disaster of it.

Ah, Frances. Did she know that Lucas Chesney, on whom her sights had been set for years, fancied himself in love with Miranda? Of course she did, Ian thought in disgust, and she probably had from the start. Fanny knew everything. No wonder she didn't care if Miranda lived or died.

"Fate itself," Duffie repeated sagely.

"And wasn't it you, my good McDuff," Ian asked, "who threatened to skelp me if I didn't marry her?"

"Aye." Duffie leaned forward over the washbasin to examine his beard in the looking glass. He plucked a hair, wincing a little. "That was because you were going to bed her to learn her secrets. Bad business, that."

"Bedding?"

Duffie laughed and turned away from the looking glass. "Nay, but doing so under false pretenses is bad business indeed. It were better that you married her first."

"Now I've wed a woman who will not have me."

Amusement twinkled in Duffie's eyes. "So you did, laddie."

"I fail to see what's so funny about that."

"You're accustomed to getting your due, Ian. You

always were, ever since you ran away from Glasgow and fought your way through the ranks of the army. And you know what I find so sad? Once you survived the ordeal of your youth, all you touched, all you did, was golden, yet it's brought you no happiness."

Ian stalked up and down the length of the room. The motion made his head hurt, his bruised jaw throb. "I have everything a man could want. Wealth. Privilege. The attention of beautiful women, the admiration of powerful men."

"And you're miserable. Or at least, you *were* miserable. But I saw that change last night, my friend."

"What the hell does that mean?"

"Miranda was going to make you happy for the first time in your life, and the very idea terrified you."

"Blather, old fool." Ian's ears felt hot.

"Your mother gave you her blessing, she smiled on you," Duffie reminded him. "We all saw it. She hadn't smiled on you since you were a lad. Don't you see? The healing was about to start."

"You're romanticizing, man."

"You were pleased to be marrying Miranda."

"She's got the body of a goddess, and I was about to avail myself of it when we were so rudely interrupted."

"It's more than that. You wanted the lass, wanted her in a manner I've never seen you desire something before. Now she's gone away, and you have to get her back."

"You're awfully cheerful about it all."

"That's because you're going to have to struggle to win her. It's going to be the fight of a lifetime. And the rewards, if you succeed, will be so great you canna even imagine them."

Ian washed himself in the basin, scrubbing away

the vestiges of last night's escape into drunken oblivion. He looked in the mirror to see Duffie sitting on the bed, grinning like an idiot. "I worry about you, Duffie. Truly I do."

"You'd best hurry. The ship's leaving with the tide."

"I am aware of that."

"I dinna think you'd just let her go!"

"I'm not letting her go. She's *mine.*" Ian surprised himself with his own vehemence. And with his speed as he readied himself, stopping only once to puke into the chamber pot, causing new howls of mirth to erupt from Duffie. Within minutes, Ian was dressed and mounted on Bruce Hume's old hunter, galloping for the coast.

Barely visible through the thick morning fog, the ship lay at anchor in the little harbor. Her sails luffed indolently in the breeze as she awaited the tide.

He had no idea what he would say to Miranda. Perhaps the square-jawed viscount had already convinced her that Ian MacVane was a liar and a cheat.

But perhaps not.

Ian knew he had not imagined Miranda's attraction to him. He had not imagined the earnestness in her voice when she had said that she loved him. He remembered the words exactly: *I love you, Ian MacVane. I'm certain I do. Surely I always have.*

She loved him.

Fool woman. Didn't she know better than to love someone like Ian MacVane?

Of course she didn't. He had lied to her, had manipulated her emotions, had used his low tricks of seduction to cloud her judgment, all so that she would trust him.

He should turn his back, let Lucas Chesney teach her the truth about her past. He should, but he knew already he would not. Miranda had come to mean more to him than a puzzle to be solved.

Did Chesney understand that? Was he aware that people were after Miranda, people who would not balk at hurting her to get what they wanted?

An ugly thought stabbed at Ian. What if the yellow-haired viscount was not what he seemed?

Spitting curses between his clenched teeth, Ian launched a dory from the shore and began rowing toward the ship.

Miranda stood at the rail and stared down at the cold waters of the North Sea lapping against the hull. Deep fog hid the shoreline from view so that she felt suspended in an eerie world of ghosts.

She had spent a sleepless night in a cramped cabin, wondering how in the world to ferret out her own past. She had no idea who was lying and who was telling the truth. Her mind was filled with memories, but only recent ones.

It was as if she had been born the day Ian MacVane had walked into Bedlam and swept her into his arms, into his world. From that moment onward, her life had been bound up with his. Her hungry mind had devoured the things he had told her, even as her heart and her body had turned to him for comfort, for reassurance.

I love you, Ian MacVane. I'm certain I do. The words she had spoken only the night before came back to humiliate and haunt her. Had she made the declaration based on lies he'd woven?

She clung to the things she knew were real—the joy she felt in his embrace. The tears on his face when his mother had forgiven him. The pride in his voice when he had taken her to the crest of Crough na Muir and shown her his homeland. The open acceptance of the townspeople, who had embraced her without question.

And she was leaving all that behind. For what?

Because a handsome stranger had filled her with the need to find out what had happened to her father. She ached with uncertainty. Regardless of what lay hidden in the past, she had wanted Ian with a fierce, driven passion that was as real as the wooden planks beneath her feet.

"We'll weigh anchor within the hour." Lucas's cultured tenor voice called through the fog.

Miranda turned, pressing her back against the rail. She knew nothing about this man, yet she was certain he was not the sort who would waltz with her on the deck of a ship. "Good morning, my lord," she said.

Lucas Chesney sent her a brilliant smile. "Ah, Miranda. You mustn't be so formal with me. I swear I am who I claim to be. The man you had promised to marry."

She shivered. He did not frighten her; what frightened her was the sense of not knowing. "That is what Ian MacVane said."

His mouth hardened. "I know. The lying dog."

"How do I know that you're not the liar, my lord?" she demanded. "What I don't understand is why either of you would lie in order to have me for a wife."

He reached out and gently grazed her chin with his knuckles. "You're a beautiful woman, Miranda. You're clever and sweet-natured."

She drew back from his touch. Caresses and love words only confused her. "Perhaps I have a hidden fortune neither of you has bothered to tell me about."

"That," Lucas said, a hooded darkness coming over his sun-bronzed features, "is definitely not the case."

She tilted back her head and let the breeze lift the hair at the nape of her neck. "Tell me your version of the truth. Tell me what my past was like. Tell me why I have no memory of you or anyone else in my life. Tell me why I nearly died in a warehouse explosion. And tell me why Ian, and not you, was there to save me."

"I knew nothing of the accident until your friend at Bedlam explained it to me." He took both her hands in his. "Come. Sit here, and I'll try to explain."

She went with him stiffly and seated herself on a banquette formed by a plank set across two upended buckets. She braced herself. Perhaps Lucas would tell her what she feared to remember—that she was an evil person, bent on mischief or murder in the warehouse.

"We met," Lucas began, seating himself beside her, "at a scientific exhibit at the London Institution. You were assisting your father with a demonstration of aeronautics. He had designed a balloon."

She closed her eyes. She knew a great deal about ballooning, but that was no revelation. She knew at least three languages, and how to play the pianoforte, and she could recite Homer and Virgil from memory. She had no idea how she had come by any of her skills. "My father," she said quietly. "Tell me about him."

"Gideon Stonecypher was a gifted man, gifted at dreaming and talking. I never approved of the way he raised you, dragging you from salon to salon, barely able to keep you in frocks."

Miranda forced herself to ask, "Why do you say he was murdered?"

"Your lodgings had been ransacked. I found Midge there—"

"Midge?"

"A servant. You don't remember her, either?"

She shuddered. "No."

He pinched the bridge of his nose, and she thought she recognized true horror in his face, in the white lines about his mouth. "Are you certain you want to hear this?"

"I must."

"Midge had been injured and was dying by the time I found her. She was able to speak, but barely. She said you and your father had been taken, perhaps killed." Miranda watched him grow pale. Lucas Chesney was either a very gifted actor or he was telling the truth.

"But you didn't find . . . his body," she said faintly. "So that could mean he is alive." A sense of urgency built inside her. "Perhaps he's in trouble." She pressed her fingers to her temples. "Oh, why, why can't I remember him?"

He took her hands away from her face and rubbed the insides of her wrists. The touch was meant to be soothing, but instead his caress only agitated her. "Go on with what you were telling me," she said.

"I went straight to the authorities. It was a notice in the *Times* that finally led me to Bethlehem Hospital."

"You put a notice in the *Times*?"

"No. An anonymous person ran a drawing—a rather good likeness."

"So someone else is looking for me."

"Someone who means you harm." He stared down at his hands, and his discomfiture softened her toward him.

"It could be my father."

"I doubt it." He drew a deep breath. "Another murder had occurred at Bedlam. A Dr. Beckworth had been killed in his chambers, and the entire place was draped in mourning black."

Miranda gripped the edge of the bench until her hands ached. "Dear God. Not Dr. Beckworth."

"You knew him?"

"Yes. He was a decent man. At least I think he was." She regarded him pointedly.

"They say he had been making bold reforms at the hospital. But the inmates I saw were being treated like animals. Only one woman—her name was Gwen—was lucid enough to speak to me. She told me a dark Scotsman had come and taken you away."

A dark Scotsman. It was the perfect description of Ian MacVane. She remembered him in his Highland regalia, looking like a bridegroom out of every young girl's dreams. She had gazed at him with her heart in her eyes and declared that she loved him.

The memory stung. She jumped up from the bench and paced the deck. She could not let herself love anyone—not Ian MacVane, not the handsome Viscount Lisle—until she discovered the truth.

"Miranda, please listen." Lucas got up and followed her. "There's so much to discuss—" The rest of his words were drowned out by a shrill whistle. Sailors swarmed over the decks and up into the rigging as the ship prepared to weigh anchor and set sail.

Miranda's heart ached. She was leaving Ian behind. Leaving behind the green mountains and fields of heather and people who made her feel as if she belonged with them.

A moment later, a trumpet sounded. Lucas mounted a short ladder to the sterncastle deck. "What is it, Edgerton?"

"A dory there, my lord." He pointed.

Miranda followed, holding her skirts in one hand and squinting through the shrouds of morning fog that seethed across the shifting water. A lone man rowed toward the ship. Her heart jolted as she went to the rail and clutched at the smooth wood. *Ian.*

Cloaked in pale shrouds of fog, he had come for her. Part of her acknowledged that she had hoped and prayed for him to do so. To assert his claim on her. To prove to her that he had not been lying.

Yet she knew that his coming here, now, could mean only trouble. She glanced up at Lucas Chesney and froze.

He stood behind three soldiers as they aimed their muskets at the approaching man.

"Just a warning shot, mind you," Lucas said.

Something was wrong with her voice. Her throat was full and constricted by panic. "No!" she forced out, but it was little more than a whisper. "Ian, look out!"

The three muskets discharged, shattering the foggy stillness of the morning. Miranda saw a blinding flash of light, heard a voice screaming in her head: *It's the only way to stop them, Papa. I must destroy the warehouse. . . .*

Then a waking nightmare scoured the memory from her mind as the sulfurous smoke cleared. She saw one oar hanging limply from its oarlock. Ian MacVane lay slumped over in the dory.

Suddenly her voice returned with a vengeance. She screamed loud and long, screamed until her throat felt near to bursting.

"You shot him! You shot my Ian!"

9

Here malice, rapine, accident conspire
And now a rabble rages, now a fire;
Their ambush here relentless ruffians lay,
And here the fell attorney prowls for prey.
                            —Samuel Johnson,
                                    London

"Will there be anything more, ma'am?" asked a portly, smiling maid.

Miranda looked up at the woman, blinking slowly. "Pardon me? . . . Oh. No. Thank you." She viewed the world through a gray mist like the one that had enshrouded Ian MacVane the moment he was shot.

She'd been in London for three days, but it might have been three years for all that she noted the passing of the hours. The enormity of her loss was almost too much to grasp. She had been wedded and widowed the same day. Fate—in the form of an Englishman's musket—had robbed her of the chance to be a wife.

It was like some tragic theatrical play, almost ridiculous in the sweep of its drama. But in the center of all her grief and confusion, like a poison pellet, lay one terrible question. Who was Ian MacVane?

Lucas had promised to find out. Twisted into knots of guilt, he exuded a sympathy that seemed genuine. Still, he failed to penetrate her icy cocoon of shock and grief. She had sworn to learn the truth about her past, but since arriving in London, she had done nothing.

She was terrified of finding out she had been wrong about Ian.

Since she had no other place to go, Lucas Chesney had brought her to his family's town residence, a rambling house set too close to the river, where the furnishings were just a little shabby, the soup just a little watery, the company just a little dotty.

"Dotty Aunt Dorcas," Lucas called his kinswoman, and so she was, spending most of the day sleeping. During her waking hours she was a benign presence, so advanced in years that she had no notion who Miranda was, nor any urge to find out.

"She's the perfect chaperone," Lucas had explained, his gaze warm with affection as he'd bent to kiss his sleeping aunt on the forehead below the lacy fringe of her old-fashioned mobcap. "With her present, there will be no breach of propriety, but just the same, there will be nothing for us to explain."

Lucas had such a smooth way about him. He made everything so *easy.* So comfortable. Ian had been just the opposite. Challenging her. Making her think difficult thoughts. Rousing emotions so powerful, they left her dazed. She wondered if, in the past, she had been capable of such extremes of passion.

It was so much simpler to be pulled along in the wake of Lucas's buoyant charm.

Miranda made no move when she heard the door open and close as the maid let herself out. "Good day, my lord," the servant murmured, and then there was a clump of leather boots as Lucas Chesney entered.

Aunt Dorcas, dozing on a tufted chaise by the hearth, blinked vaguely. "Mind the step, Alfonso," she muttered, addressing her dead husband as she often did. "We'll have no accidents today."

"Of course, dear heart." Lucas bowed and kissed her hand. "I am yours to command."

Miranda kept her gaze trained out the window. It was a brilliant summer day. Brisk traffic passed by in the roadway, and flowers rioted along the verges. Yet all she saw was the fog, the endless gray fog that seemed to swallow up the world.

"I'd hoped," Lucas said tenderly, "to find you less melancholy today." A chair creaked as he seated himself across from her.

She forced herself to look at him, to look at his perfect, bronzed face. "You'll pardon me," she said, "if I fail to exude gaiety after watching a man shot to death in cold blood."

Lucas hissed as if her words were a poisoned dart. "Ian MacVane was a dangerous man." He spoke gently, but with conviction. "I've spent the past three days trying to find out who he was, why he would kidnap an innocent young woman and force her to marry him."

"There was no force involved, my lord." Briefly she shut her eyes. She remembered her excitement the night of the wedding, the sturdy feel of Ian's arms around her, and the dark, sweet promises in his eyes as he gazed down at her. She had refuted those promises with her doubts and her insistence on tracing down her past. And Ian had paid the price.

Lucas captured her hands in his. He had beautiful hands, long fingered and elegant, the nails neatly pared. So unlike Ian with his blunt workman's hands and the missing finger he loathed to show the world.

"Miranda, please listen to me. I've been all over London inquiring about this man. The clubs are full of gossip. MacVane had an unscrupulous nature. He was a liar. He manipulated you for his own purpose—"

"And what might that purpose be?" she asked dully. "What possible interest could he have had in me?"

"Of that, I'm not certain," Lucas admitted. "But it's bound to be an evil one."

She surged to her feet and stalked across the room, her movement causing an antique tapestry to waft against a wall, raising a small cloud of dust. "I won't listen to this."

Lucas brought her to a halt next to a pianoforte. "You will. You must face facts, Miranda."

"My lord, I would love to face facts. It's just that I don't know what the truth is."

He leaned closer, commanding but not threatening. "Then work with what you do know. Miranda Stonecypher, if I had been your bridegroom that night, all the powers of heaven and hell could not have torn you away from me. Yet MacVane simply stepped aside and let you leave with me."

"He came after me and paid with his life," she spat.

"Do you think a man who truly loved you, truly wanted you, would have let you out of his sight? He let you go because he knew you'd find out he'd played you false. What other lies did he tell? What other promises did he break?"

She twisted away from him and went to the window, clinging to a musty drape and staring out, seeing nothing but a blur of summer color, softened by the fog that hung between her and the world.

"Miranda, listen. Ian MacVane is a Scottish mercenary. He came to the attention of the British authorities after joining a regiment in 1805 under the duke of York."

"I remember that," Aunt Dorcas said to no one in particular. "Couldn't get decent wine for a king's ransom. Family fortune went to hell in a handbasket that year, didn't it, Alfonso?"

There was a clink of glass as Lucas poured himself a drink at the sideboard. "MacVane had a reputation for being hot tempered and disobedient, and a habit of volunteering for hazardous—sometimes hopeless—duties. When they needed a man who did not care whether he lived or died, they chose MacVane."

She closed her eyes, remembering Ian. The report had the ring of truth. There was a darkness about him she'd noticed from the start, a recklessness. The night of the explosion, he had plunged into a burning building to save her, then Robbie, with no thought to himself. "What else did you learn?" she asked softly.

"He saw battle action in the Peninsular Wars. In 1810 he was drafted to perform specialized acts of espionage and sabotage for England. His training made him into a master of disguise, the perfect counterfeit Highland laird, a popular guest at any gathering of the *ton*." Lucas gulped down his brandy. "At White's club, he was a familiar face. He was extravagant—both at winning and at losing. I'm told that women found him fascinating."

"There's a surprise," Miranda murmured with a humorless smile.

Lucas's glass thumped on a leather-topped desk. "He was never to be trusted."

"The British government trusted him," she shot back.

"They used him as a bloody mercenary because that's all a man like Ian MacVane was good for. Everyone I spoke with underscored that again and again. No one has any idea what he was doing in London this Season, but he was surely up to no good. What with all the visiting foreign royalty, plots hatch like fleas. He's bound to have been a part of them."

"Did no one ever teach you to speak kindly of the dead?"

With a shaking hand, Lucas set down his glass. "It was a horrible accident. And after the"—he mopped his forehead with a handkerchief—"after the mishap, I sent out a tender to find him."

"And you failed to locate him." The moments after the shooting were all a blur. She recalled shouts, running feet, the whine of rope through a pulley, the splash of the tender hitting the water. The hopeless yell of the search party.

She squeezed her eyes shut. "And so that, as they say, is that. A man who claimed to love me is dead because of a horrible accident."

"Love you." An angry flush darkened Lucas's neck and cheeks. "He didn't know you. He had some foul purpose in mind."

"And what of you, my lord? What is your purpose?"

"Can you not remember, Miranda? Can you not remember me at all?"

She looked at him and concentrated. Gray eyes, sensual lips. An air of weary concern. But . . . nothing. He was as strange to her as Ian had been when he'd fetched her from Bedlam. "No," she said quietly.

"We used to meet in secret."

"Why in secret?"

"No good comes of keeping secrets," Aunt Dorcas said in a singsong voice.

He hung his head. "That is the worst of it. That is why I can barely live with myself for the shame of it." He plowed his splayed fingers through his golden mane. "All my life, I was taught that I must make a good marriage. No, a grand marriage. To a woman with a vast dowry, a celebrated bloodline."

"A duke's daughter or better," Aunt Dorcas interjected.

He lifted his head and gave Miranda a smile that was tinged with melancholy and regret. "I almost believed I could be content with that sort of existence. And then I met you. After you, I could not bring myself to make a cold business arrangement with some chosen woman, to breed with her and bring up more children who would be as wretched as I was."

In spite of herself, she grew interested in this man. The fog around her seemed to part a little. He was giving her a glimpse into his soul, and she didn't despise what she saw.

"I love you, Miranda. I have from the first moment I saw you. But I failed you. I was afraid of what my family would say, afraid they'd treat you cruelly because you weren't wealthy or noble."

Lucas's clear-eyed gaze radiated sincerity. "It would be so much simpler if I didn't care what they thought. But the truth is, I love my family, and they're on the verge of ruin. If I marry well, I could save them all. Give my sisters a proper entrée into society. Give my younger brother a fine education. Make certain my parents will always be free from want."

"I should like to meet them," she said. Compassion

broke through the numbness that had enveloped her. She could not remember having a family, but she understood the affection and despair in his voice. "Have you ever considered other choices? Why not earn your keep as so many men do?"

He smiled wearily. "In trade, you mean."

"Yes."

"Seeing me go into trade is the only thing my family would deem worse than—" He broke off.

But he had not caught himself in time. "Worse than marrying a nobody like Miranda Stonecypher," she finished for him.

"I'm so sorry. I'd dig ditches if I thought it was a way to have you. In fact, we talked about the possibilities. I was going to help you patent your design for the aerial balloon." His smile glowed with pride. "You're the most clever woman in England. You used to blush when I said that."

"A balloon." She tried hard to remember. Riding the winds beneath a billow of silk that looked as big as the globe. Had she ever done it?

"All your designs were attributed to your father, of course. He even signed his name to the plans."

The mention of her father closed like a fist around her heart. "The plans, then. Where are they now? Perhaps seeing them will help me remember."

"They were stolen the night of—the night I lost you."

She felt exhausted, betrayed, confused. Her head ached. Each time she tried to see into the past, she met a black wall.

"We don't need the plans now, darling," Lucas said. "I've found a way to save the Chesney family fortune. Honorably. Just think, Miranda, we can be together—"

"You assume that's what I want," she said.

He didn't seem to hear her, but plunged on. "I've met a gentleman called Silas Addingham. Actually, he is not a gentleman, but that's why this will work. He has some very lofty social ambitions and more money than Golden Ball. I, on the other hand, have more social connections than the Hanover family tree. I provide Silas with an entrée into the best circles—"

"And he pays you for the privilege."

"Exactly. What do you think?"

"I think it proves there is nothing that cannot be bought and sold like a commodity. What shall we package and sell next? Virtue? Honor? Temperance?"

A rueful smile curved his mouth. "It's a sight better than digging ditches."

She stared down at their joined hands. Before she could stop herself, she asked, "Just how close were we, Lucas?"

His cheeks flamed with color. "My dear, you're a proper lady and should not discuss such things."

She had asked the same of Ian—and had gotten a far different response. In her heart, she suspected that she had never been a proper lady. "If you knew me well," she said to Lucas, "you'd know I embrace the philosophies of the radicals. The ones who are so shocking to the *haut ton.*"

"No, my love. You've never been anything but demure and compliant."

That elicited a humorless laugh from her. "I fear the rebellious aspect of my character has come through intact, Lucas."

He closed his eyes. "How good it is to hear you speak my name. You've done it twice, you know." He opened his eyes again and grasped her by the shoulders. His face loomed close, and she smelled his spicy scent of ambergris and brandy. "Damn it, Miranda, you were mine. Mine, before you even knew the name Ian MacVane!"

A sense of helplessness swirled through her, dizzying her. "I can't remember. Lucas, what if I never remember? I'm not the same person as I was before. Will I ever come to love you as you claim I used to?"

"You must." He feathered enticing kisses along her brow. "Ah, we were close, Miranda. So close. If I must, I'll prove it." He traced the curve of her throat, and then his fingers moved downward, alluring and dangerous, flirting with the low neckline of her gown.

She could not decide how his touch made her feel. Aunt Dorcas inhaled with a snore, exhaled with a whistle. The protective haze that had enveloped Miranda thickened.

"Shall I describe your birthmark?" he whispered.

"What?"

"Your birthmark. You claimed no one but I ever saw it." His hand trailed lower, gently cupping her breast. "It's just here. A small mark the color of a rose. Shaped like a map of the Isle of Man."

The fog cleared from her mind. His words clanged like an alarm in her head, making her temples ache. She jerked away, seared by the intrusion of his caress. He was right. *He was right.*

"I must go," she said, hastening toward the door. "I cannot take your word for everything. I have to find out for myself."

"Miranda, wait! Where are you going?"

"Back to the lodgings where you say I used to live. Back to the warehouse. I have to unravel this mess— *on my own.*"

"But what about us? Our plans? Our marriage?"

She turned to face him. Even now, thoughts of

another man consumed her. She could not relinquish her memories of the husband she had lost, the answers he had taken with him to the grave. "*Your* plans, Lucas, not mine. I have to find out what I want. At the moment, it most definitely is not marriage."

His fist hit the window frame with a thud. Aunt Dorcas flinched in her sleep. "Damn it, Miranda, I want you—"

"I believe," said a silken voice from the doorway, "that the lady does not want you, my lord."

Miranda turned to see a most remarkable woman. Petite and blond, she wore a frothy bonnet and a pink gown with a scalloped hem. In her dainty, gloved hand she carried a matching parasol at half-mast. Her cupid's-bow lips were set in a pout, and her china blue eyes were wide and guileless.

"Isn't that right, my dear?" she asked, walking into the room with mincing steps. "Ah, how unforgivably *méchante* of me. *Tiens,* you must think me as gauche as a scholar's daughter. You, most surely, are Miranda Stonecypher."

Intrigued, though not at all oblivious to the insult, Miranda took the tiny gloved hand in hers. "And you?"

Laughter trilled from the woman. "I am Lady Frances Higgenbottom."

"Dear Fanny," Lucas said, venom dripping from his voice. "What a surprise."

She giggled. "Oh, you don't know the half of it, Lisle." She turned back toward the door. "Here she is, *mon cher connard.* Safe and sound, just as you'd hoped."

From the drafty corridor outside the room came the sound of a closing door and a heavy tread. Aunt Dorcas blinked herself awake. "It's about time, dear Alfonso," she called, fixing a vague smile on her face.

Miranda felt a sudden twinge of awareness, subtle yet electric, skittering through her like a flicker of close lightning. She caught hold of the back of a chair to steady herself and stared at the doorway.

Dark and brooding as a thundercloud, Ian MacVane walked into the room. He had his arm in a sling, a fierce smile on his face, and his hand on the hilt of a razor-thin rapier. "My little wife," he said in his rich brogue. "I've found you again."

His dress sword slapping at his thigh and his kilt snapping in a brisk breeze around his knees, Ian paced up and down in front of Carlton House. The imposing edifice, residence of the prince regent, was lit by dozens of torches. The air hummed with the sounds of music, laughter, clinking glasses, and the cacophony of a dozen foreign tongues.

"So get your Scottish hide in there, laddie, and see if the rumors are true," Duffie urged him. The older man lounged against a marble post and drank from a silver flask. "See if your fine Lady Fanny has brought a butterfly out of the chrysalis. I thought it was right nice of her to take young Miranda under her wing."

"Fanny never does anything just to be nice," Ian grumbled.

A week had passed since he had found Miranda again—found her in the faintly shabby drawing room of the Viscount Lisle. Even now, the memory hung about his mind like an uninvited guest. Miranda, looking thinner, wearier, even than she had in Bedlam. Lucas at her side, glaring in resentment at a smirking Lady Frances.

Fanny had made no secret of wanting Lisle. What a

hideous jest it had been for her to discover that his reason for spurning her was Miranda—the very woman suspected of treason. Fanny had managed to keep her mouth shut when Ian had explained how he'd survived.

It was the puking that saved him. Still greensick from his alcoholic frenzy, he had leaned over the side of the dory. The musket ball had merely grazed his upper arm. They had come looking for him, of course, but he was too much the Highlander to be found by a party of Sassenachs in the fog.

"She's done no harm, man," Duffie was saying, still speaking of Fanny.

"Not yet, she hasn't." But Ian had to acknowledge that in the week since he had returned to London to find Miranda, Fanny had been thoroughly solicitous. She had taken Miranda to Biddle House to be her personal guest. She'd introduced her to the grand duchess of Oldenburg. As the sister of Tsar Alexander of Russia, Catherine Pavlovna was the ranking noblewoman in London, second only to Princess Caroline and her rebellious daughter Charlotte.

Anyone basking in the favor of Her Grace was accepted at every party, every soiree, every tête-à-tête. The new friendship between the grand duchess and Miranda was an example of Fanny's cleverness. No one would dare question Miranda's place in society now.

"I hear Prince Frederick of Prussia is thoroughly smitten with her," Duffie said.

"With whom?"

"As if you didn't know. With Miranda. I hear he had a gondola full of daylilies delivered to her this morning. Of course, he's not the only one. They're all after her. All smitten," Duffie repeated, making a fist and striking himself on the brow. "Right between the eyes."

Ian's patience snapped. "And I'm supposed to care?"

Duffie laughed. "You're not supposed to. But you do. You're consumed with the lassie."

"I'm married to her."

"You call that sorry folk custom a marriage? Ha! You're no more married to her than you are to Fanny." Duffie winked. "Of course, you can take solace in the fact that she's barred the pretty viscount from her presence as well."

"Miranda's a distraction," Ian said between his teeth, half to himself. "I've got a job to do, and she distracts me."

"My heart bleeds for you."

Irritated, Ian scanned the bank of brightly lit windows along the loggia of the building. "That's not the only thing that might bleed before the night is out." Scowling, he recognized a round dozen dignitaries as they waltzed past the windows. He spied Field Marshal von Blucher, hero of the Battle of Leipzig, resplendent with his silver hair and grand thirst for wine.

The duke of Wellington, just back from France, was quieter but no less impressive as he accepted curtsies from grateful ladies. Tsar Alexander of Russia, imperial in tight green livery with gold epaulets, conversed with William of Orange, the Austrian chancellor Prince Metternich, and the Prussian chancellor Prince Hardenberg. A moment later, the tsar's lively sister, broad faced and laughing, waltzed past on the arm of King Frederick William of Prussia. The prince regent himself paraded through the crowd with the duke of Gloucester and the lord chancellor trailing in his wake. A host of lesser nobility orbited their more celebrated peers.

It was an assassin's dream. Unsuspecting and silly

with drink, the crowned heads of Europe had amassed themselves in one well-lit room. Ian almost wished he had thrown in his lot with Bonaparte. Lord knew it was easy enough.

A movement in the corner of the loggia beneath an ivy trellis caught his eye. Instantly he came alert, sensing danger. Duffie had seen the movement, too, and they slipped through the shadows until they were close enough to hear the whispered conversation.

" . . . should fatten your purse considerably, and none will be the wiser." The speaker was a tall, imposing man, merely a silhouette. Yet something about him—his posture or perhaps a tic in his manner—grated on Ian, flooded his mouth with the rusty taste of suspicion. Odd, for he was certain he did not recognize the stranger.

"Just don't commit an unforgivable faux pas tonight, Mr. Addingham. Do not make me regret our little arrangement." With a twist of cynical distaste, Ian did recognize the second speaker. Lucas Chesney of the square jaw and knight-in-shining-armor demeanor.

Duffie jabbed Ian in the ribs. "Guess the viscount found a way out of beggary," he whispered. "Interesting."

"Aye."

" . . . don't let them know you're in trade. Confine yourself to mild gossip and fox hunting, and you'll be fine," Chesney was saying to Addingham. Coins clinked; then the two slipped back inside.

"I agree," Ian said. "It's interesting. But probably not all that unusual. Addingham wouldn't be the first Englishman to buy his way into society."

"Blasted waste of money," Duffie said. "To think a man would actually pay to be part of that." He jerked a thumb toward the broad windows where the elite of society postured and preened.

"It's all a game," Ian said. "Just a game. Tomorrow, see what you can find out about Mr. Addingham. Who is he? Where did he get his money? And just what is it that he's buying from Lucas Chesney?"

"Verra good," Duffie said, taking another swig from his flask.

"If you'll excuse me . . ." Ian strolled slowly across the long porch, trying to decide on the most advantageous moment to make his entrance.

Then he spotted her—Miranda, in a peach-colored gown, her sable curls bobbing, her sparkling gaze lifted to Lucas Chesney.

"That's it," Ian said through gritted teeth. "I've had enough." Duffie called something after him, but he didn't hear. He took the steps two at a time, strode brusquely past a bank of servants and retainers, and plowed a path onto the dance floor.

Feminine gasps and a flutter of fans greeted him. Hungry eyes devoured his kilt. It was remarkable what effect a bit of Highland regalia had on these English game hens. Ian sometimes found it amusing to dally with the ladies, to shove them into barely concealed corners and turn them into whores with his rough caresses; but not tonight.

Tonight he wanted Miranda. Only Miranda.

His sense of danger, a sixth sense that never quite rested, remained alert to the dynamics of the room. Even as he jostled his way through the dancing couples, trying not to disturb the bandage on his wounded arm, he was aware of the Cossacks who stood vigil on the fringes of the dance floor. Of all of them, the tsar was the only one with the sense to take a bodyguard wherever he went.

Lucas and Miranda were caught up in a waltz. Ian had taught her well, he thought cynically, there on the deck of the ship. She danced like a flower in a gentle breeze, bending and swaying and swirling while her delicate skirts belled out, brushing the polished boots of her escort.

Christ, he wanted her. He was going crazy with it. This woman would be the death of him yet.

Ian tapped Lucas on the shoulder, none too gently. "It's time I danced with my wife," he stated.

Lucas froze. He held Miranda against him. The sight enraged Ian, though he was careful not to let it show.

"Hello, Ian," Miranda said, her voice sounding slightly breathless.

Was she glad to see him? Ian wondered. Did her blood heat as his did? "You'll excuse us," he said coldly to Lucas.

"Over my dead body," Lucas said just as coldly.

"If you insist, I'd be pleased to oblige."

Lucas stepped away from Miranda. "Is that a challenge, sir?"

Ian laughed. "That depends."

"On what?" Lucas demanded.

"On whether or not you're willing to die for her tonight."

Miranda planted herself between them. "What in heaven's name are the two of you blathering about?"

With long white feathers nodding over the brim of a ridiculous hat, Frances sailed into their midst. "Ah, my dear, it's so exciting! They've just challenged each other to a duel!"

10

The heart is very treacherous, and if we do not guard its first emotions, we shall not afterward be able to prevent its sighing for impossibilities.

—Dr. Fordyce's
Sermons for Young Women

"*I hope you're jesting,*" Miranda said. She willed herself not to look at Ian, not to weaken. When he had walked into Lucas's house a week ago, she had wanted to fling her arms around him, to cover his face with kisses and thank God he had not been killed by the musketeers.

Instead she'd reminded herself of all the unanswered questions Lucas had raised, and she had managed to greet Ian coolly. That alone seemed to win the esteem of Lady Frances, who had taken Miranda under her wing.

Like so many of the people Miranda had met in the past week, Frances was an enigma. Her dress and manner were those of the most artful and superficial of *merveilleuses,* yet Miranda suspected that it was all an act designed to conceal a shrewd and very active mind.

Now her gaze clung to her hostess as she asked again, "They are having us on about fighting a duel, aren't they?"

"Certainly not."

"Isn't dueling illegal?" Miranda scanned the gathering crowd for the prince regent. Resplendent in a military-style frock coat and red-heeled buckle shoes, His portly Highness had stopped along with the other guests and was looking on with avid interest.

"I'm afraid that doesn't matter," Lucas snapped, his voice harsh, as it had been that night in Scotland when he had torn her from the arms of the man she had just married.

Miranda confronted them both, Lucas's chiseled, angry face and Ian's roughly handsome one. "Correct me if I'm wrong," she said, hiding abject terror behind sarcasm, "but isn't a duel a fight with pistols until one of you dies?"

"That rather sums it up," Ian said, his lips thinning in an almost smile.

"It's the most idiotic thing I've ever heard of."

"Isn't it, though?" Ian turned to Lucas. "Shall we go?"

"Now?" Lucas asked.

"Are you turning yellow on me, Your Lordship?"

"It's pitch dark outside!"

"That should make it more interesting. Besides, isn't shooting blind your specialty?" Ian glanced meaningfully at his wounded arm.

She grabbed Frances's hand. "Can't you do something?"

Frances smiled. "Ah, yes. Seconds. They shall need seconds, and someone to officiate."

Miranda felt ill. "That is not what I meant." She spied Wellington, who stood tall and straight, his perfect military bearing inspiring faith. "My lord, if you please." She dipped a curtsy. "You've watched men shed their blood for the sake of England. Surely you'll not allow it to be spilled in the name of foolish male pride."

He studied her a moment, looking down over his long, aquiline nose. "A matter of honor is a sacred thing, and—" Wellington broke off and bent low, suddenly studying Miranda so intently that a chill blew through her. "Miss, have we met before?"

Her knees wobbled. She had to struggle to remain standing.

"Tell!" commanded Prinny. "She is our famous mystery lady. Lost her memory in a terrible accident." He rubbed his palms together. "It's too delicious."

"Can't remember a thing, can you?" asked Silas Addingham. Of all the people she had met in this whirlwind, he was the most enigmatic. Unfailingly correct, he seemed to live in horror of committing a faux pas. Lucas had begged her to be gracious to his benefactor. She simply did not care for him, the way his gaze followed her when he thought she didn't notice.

Disgusted, she moved away from them. These people were more concerned about their own amusement than the fact that two men were about to kill each other.

Buoyed on a wave of excitement, the company moved en masse into the gardens to observe the duel. Large torches, their flaming heads reflecting in a man-made pond, bathed the area in bright light.

Everything happened so swiftly that Miranda hardly had time to take it all in. Pistols appeared,

lying on their sides in a polished walnut case. Duffie
stepped forward as Ian's second. Seemingly beloved
of all the nobility present, Lucas had at least six vol-
unteers to choose from.

She appealed to General von Blucher next. "You
must stop this. It's insane."

"All violence is insane," von Blucher declared in
his rich, rumbling, accented English. The scent of
wine hung thick in the air around him. "That is why
men love it so."

Lady Frances took Miranda's arm and drew her
out of the way. "Save your breath. They won't listen."

"Don't you even care?" Miranda demanded,
wrenching away.

"Hysterics won't solve a thing."

"Nor will standing here like a pair of birdwits!"

The tsar's lifeguards held the crowd at bay, lining
the edges of the lawn. As she watched Ian and Lucas
pace off the distance between them, Miranda felt a
wash of fear so powerful that her chest ached. Strong
featured and looking as if he were the subject of a
classical painting, Lucas embodied honor and ancient
tradition. Dark and fascinating, as rugged as the
Highlands of his birth, Ian was the sort of man one
heard warnings about in Sunday sermons.

Lover or liar? Which man was which? Lucas made
her feel safe, cherished, protected. Ian made her feel
wild, womanly, free. The only fact she knew for certain was that she did not want either of them to die.

" . . . eight . . . nine . . . ten!" the field marshal
barked. "Fire!"

At the same moment, Lucas and Ian turned to face
each other. Miranda lurched forward unthinkingly,
but Frances grabbed her hand and pulled her back.
With a flash of burning powder, Lucas discharged his

pistol. The sharp report pierced Miranda like a blow to the head. She let out an involuntary sob and pressed the heels of her hands to her eyes. Gasps rose from the crowd.

"God," Miranda whispered. "Oh, God." She forced her eyes open.

"Ian's still standing," Frances said. "He wasn't hit. But . . ." She blinked her wide, pretty eyes at the clearing smoke around Lucas. To Miranda's amazement, tears began to stream down Lady Frances's cheeks. "But he hasn't fired yet, and now he has a clear shot. Ah, Lucas, my dearest," she said in the faintest of whispers. "You poor fool."

Miranda clasped her hand, suddenly understanding. Lady Frances was in love with Lucas Chesney. When had that happened? she wondered. "Perhaps Ian will miss."

"Ian MacVane *never* misses," Frances hissed.

"Stop!" Miranda shouted as Ian extended his good arm. "For the love of God, stop! If this is about me, then I should be the one to resolve it."

Lucas stood unmoving, staring blankly at his opponent. His broad chest rose and fell with weary resignation. He lifted his chin and gazed calmly across the green, his sense of fatalism both tragic and infuriating.

With a broad, insolent grin, but without lowering the pistol, Ian turned to Miranda. "Very well, lass," he said, "resolve it."

"Resolve *what*?" Like a festooned river barge, the grand duchess of Oldenburg crossed the garden. She spoke in French, for her English was poor. Her bodyguards swarmed in a panic around her.

Speaking in Russian, the tsar said something urgent and irritated to his sister.

"Why haven't you fired, MacVane?" demanded the prince of Wales, slurring his words. "I say, isn't it unsportsmanlike to be so long taking aim? And what in blue heaven *is* this quarrel about?"

Ian bowed from the waist. "It's quite simple, Your Highness. Miss Stonecypher married me, yet Lord Lisle claims a prior betrothal to him." He waited for the excited chatter to die down, then turned to Miranda.

He was no longer smiling, but fierce and deadly serious. "Whom are you going to believe—your wedded husband and his clan, who accepted you as one of their own, or this liar who cannot produce a shred of evidence that he ever knew you?"

Then, lowering his hand and letting the pistol dangle from his fingers, he glared across the broad yard at Lucas. "What I ask is simple enough, my lord. You need only point out *one* person who can corroborate your story. Or tell me *one* irrefutable fact that proves your prior claim on her."

Duffie huffed out his cheeks and said something in Scottish, but Ian kept his gaze on Lucas.

Miranda held her breath. Now was the perfect time for Lucas to mention her birthmark. She braced herself for the shame of having her private affairs revealed to all.

Lucas hesitated, but only for a moment. "I have no evidence," he said in a taut, strained voice, "save my own word of honor."

Miranda let out the breath she had been holding. She realized that part of her wished one man would prove himself a scoundrel without question and make the truth apparent.

"Then why," Ian asked pointedly, "would a woman care for a man who, until tonight, has refused to declare himself publicly?"

More chatter erupted from the crowd.

"Sir," Lucas called in a voice like striking lightning, "take your shot!"

Ian laughed and handed his pistol to Duffie. The older man took it with a gusty sigh of relief. "That would be unsporting at this point, wouldn't you say? I'm not going to shoot you, Lisle." He made a grand show of holding out his sling and placing his arm back in it. "I'm sure to regret it one day, but no, I'm not going to shoot you."

The incident established, once and for all, Miranda's reputation as an Original. That, Lady Frances explained, was a splendid coup. When one was an Original, no one dared question her background or bloodlines. They simply accepted and adored her because she was especially entertaining or fascinating or amusing or attractive.

"In your case," Lady Frances said, tightening her mouth into a wry pout, "all four."

They were seated in one of the many parlors at Biddle House, and Frances was teaching Miranda the rules of piquet and of society, flitting back and forth from the game to life as if they were one and the same.

"Never show by your face what you hold in your hand," she advised. "Or, for that matter, in your heart."

"Why not?"

"Because it causes nothing but embarrassment."

"So you were embarrassed last night, when you wept for fear of losing Lucas?" Miranda lifted one eyebrow.

"I did no such thing," Frances shot back. Her yellow curls bobbed as if in stubborn agreement.

"As you wish." Miranda sighed, bored with the game. She seemed to have an abnormal understanding of numbers and ratios. Using the pattern of the four suits with thirteen cards in each, she was able to calculate the odds with lightning swiftness. Such knowledge seemed to take the sport out of the game.

She wondered if, in her former life, she had been a cardsharp. For a moment, the thought tantalized her. Perhaps she was even a cheater; that was easy enough to do, at least with Frances. Maybe the incident at the wharves was the revenge of someone she had cheated.

Her restive gaze shifted to the window. The bough of a huge chestnut tree bobbed above the avenue, where coaches and pedestrians passed in a steady stream. The emptiness inside her yawned into a great, aching void. How lonely it was to have no past, no memories to cling to. The occasional, frightening glimpses of violence and terror that plagued her were hardly a comfort.

"When will you decide?" Lady Frances asked in a crisp, no-nonsense voice.

"Decide what?"

"Which man you want."

Miranda stared at her. For a moment, she had the distinct feeling that Frances knew which man she had loved before she'd lost her memory. But that was silly. If Frances knew, she would have been the first to speak up. She was a gossip extraordinaire.

The door opened with a discreet swish. A butler stepped inside. "Delivery for Miss Miranda Stonecypher."

A parade of footmen came in, each bearing an

armload of fresh flowers. As Miranda's jaw dropped in astonishment, the next wave arrived, these carrying salvers of delicate chocolates and petits fours, comfits and dainty sweetmeats.

The last servant presented, with a bow and a flourish, a young woman with a sweet smile and a crisp blue serge dress. "I am Yvette Deschamps," she said with a small curtsy. "I am to be your lady's maid."

"But I don't need a—"

"Monsieur was most insistent." Yvette held out a note on heavy stock. Miranda opened it and glanced at the bold handwriting: *All my love, Lucas.*

Guiltily she crushed the note in her palm, but not before Frances had seen the writing. "You needn't try to spare me," Frances said in a brittle voice. "Lovesick fool." She moved gracefully to the window. "Bloody lovesick fool. He can't afford such grand gestures."

The same thought had crossed Miranda's mind. If what Lucas had said was true, that his family teetered on the brink of ruin, why would he be so extravagant?

Was he being helped by his secret benefactor? The thought of Silas Addingham niggled at her. She could not put her finger on the cause for her distaste. Lucas swore the man was an angel in disguise.

"I can't accept such a gift," she said to the maid. "It is nothing to do with you; it is simply inappropriate."

Yvette's lower lip trembled. "If mademoiselle sends me away, I shall be disgraced."

Miranda tamped back a feeling of exasperation. Had she always been dim? she wondered. She felt like a fool, relying on Lucas or Ian or Frances rather than controlling her own life. If only she had her memories back—

"Please, mademoiselle, give me a chance. I am well trained."

Miranda regarded her soberly. "I have absolutely no doubt of that, Yvette."

The maid folded her hands carefully in front of her. "If you will not keep me on, I'll have nowhere to go."

"Just for a time, then," Miranda said wearily, exchanging a glance with Frances. "Just until Lucas finds you another situation."

"Bless you, mademoiselle," Yvette said, her eyes filled with gratitude. "You will not be sorry."

For the rest of the day, Miranda avoided the flower-filled parlor, retreating to her suite of rooms on the pretext of getting Yvette settled in.

"Tell me," she said as Yvette brought her carpetbag into the small chamber adjacent to the dressing room. "Have you known Lord Lisle for a long time? Are you a family retainer?"

Yvette shook her head and opened the bag. "Yes and no, mademoiselle. I have known Lord Lisle for several years. But I am no longer a family retainer."

Miranda expected humble belongings to come from the carpetbag. The quality of Yvette's petticoats and night rails, their fine embroidery, surprised her, but she said nothing.

"I was let go of necessity." Yvette gave a dainty sigh. "But His Lordship was good to me. He found me a position with Monsieur Addingham."

Addingham again. He was pleasant. Carefully groomed. And full of pretenses. "A merchant trying to claw his way into society," Frances had pronounced, dismissing him with a careless shrug.

"But Lord Lisle sent you," she said to Yvette.

"Yes. He and Monsieur Addingham came to an

arrangement." Yvette smiled. She was vivacious, with small deft hands and an air of competence. *"Tiens. You have been invited for an outing in Hyde Park. We must get you ready."*

While Yvette bustled her into the dressing room, Miranda frowned. "How did you know about the invitation from the grand duchess?"

"Her card on the hall table."

Miranda nodded. There was no reason that Yvette should not have read a card left out in the open. She did not think she had ever had a lady's maid before. Perhaps it was a maid's place to keep track of one's social engagements.

The grand duchess of Oldenburg had summoned her on a ride through Hyde Park in an open landau. It was strange and not entirely pleasant to be surrounded by heavily armed bodyguards. Count Matvei Platov ordered his men to range in a tight and menacing circle around the slowly traveling rig.

The duchess seemed accustomed to such treatment and chattered blithely in French about her romantic liaisons, her infuriatingly proper brother, Alexander, her whirlwind travels, her dearly departed young husband. By the time they returned to Biddle House, Miranda was quite certain that she had no ambitions to join the ranks of the nobility.

A butler greeted her at the entrance. "This was delivered while you were gone."

Unhappily, Miranda took a small silver box from the tray he held and wandered up to her room. Yvette appeared immediately, standing at attention.

"Does mademoiselle need anything?"

"No," Miranda said distractedly. "No, thank you, Yvette."

The maid curtsied and went through the dressing

room to her own small chamber. Miranda sat on the edge of the bed and opened the box, certain she would find a bauble that Lucas could not possibly afford.

Instead she discovered a single sprig of heather. She was not prepared for the stumble her heart gave when she lifted the blossom to her face, inhaled the light, spicy scent. In that instant she was transported back to the Highlands, to the green-carpeted hills and the village where everyone knew her name, everyone smiled at her and welcomed her as a friend. Where Ian, clad in native tartan, his dark eyes full of promises, had made her his wife.

False promises.

At the bottom of the box lay a tiny, folded card.

Her fingers were clumsy as she opened it. Ian had not written her a note. The message was a printed notice, an announcement that Bedlam Hospital had been endowed with even greater funds, enough to move the institution to a modern site in Lambeth. The endowment was made in memory of Dr. Brian Beckworth.

She knew then that she *did* have memories. She remembered, with crystal-sharp clarity, every single moment she had spent with Ian MacVane. Now those moments came hurling back at her, hitting her with painful force. She saw Ian smiling down at Robbie, giving the orphan a name, a family. Saw him kneeling before his mother, offering her his heart. Saw him standing atop a mountain, filled with the splendor of the Highlands . . . and sharing it with her.

Breathless with the intensity of her longing, she doubled over on the bed, curling her knees to her chest and staring out the window at the darkening sky. She feared darkness. She feared sleep. Lately her dreams had been filled with mystery and violence. She sensed she was on the verge of remembering her past.

And that was what she feared the most.

"*All* of them?" Ian asked Frances with a cynical edge in his voice. "Prinny is insisting that *all* of them pose for the portrait?"

Though she looked impeccable as always, strain pulled taut lines about Frances's lovely eyes. Ian was furious at the way she had swept Miranda into her care, and he felt grimly satisfied that the effort of sheltering Lucas Chesney's one true love was proving to be a trial to Frances.

"Prinny," she said, rolling the name in imitation of Ian's brogue, "is convinced that such an illustrious collection of dignitaries has never been brought together before. He has decided that the events and people of this singular celebration must be recorded for posterity. He's commissioned Thomas Lawrence to paint a portrait. Promised a knighthood for Lawrence to boot. People are all agog."

Ian swore and went to the edge of the garden maze. He and Frances had met in St. James Park to discuss what, if any, progress had been made in uncovering the plot against the Allies. It was becoming increasingly clear that Miranda was still their best hope. But until she remembered the past, they knew nothing.

"I'm agog, too," he said. "Prinny must be working secretly for Bonaparte. Damn the man! He keeps bringing these people together as if they were clay pigeons at target practice. Does he have no notion at all that it might not be healthy for all the world leaders to gather in one place at one time?"

Frances twirled her parasol and sent him an artful smile. "So that is my news. And you haven't once asked me about Miranda."

Ian made certain that his cynical expression did not change. He had plenty of practice hiding his emotions. He had discovered, at an early age, how to conceal his true thoughts from the men who had tormented him. They had forced him to work as a climbing boy, to watch his brother fall to his death from a sooty rooftop. Yes, it was safer to hide his feelings. It was safest of all to have no feelings whatsoever.

He said to Frances, "I assume if you had any news on that front, you would have reported it. So our mystery woman is still a mystery."

"Quite so. I haven't had any better luck than you did. But you've gone too far with this one. *Marriage,* for heaven's sake." She shuddered. "That's so . . . so *permanent.*"

"Not in Scotland," he reminded her.

"God, you're cold, MacVane. I could almost feel sorry for the girl." She pulled distractedly on a golden ringlet. "Perhaps I should torture her."

Ian refused to rise to the bait. "Go ahead. You might get her to tell us more than we've extracted by being kind."

"Or I might drive her over the brink into madness, and then she'll be no help at all."

"I'll leave the choice to you, Fanny. You're so seldom wrong in these things. Just—" He broke off, angry at himself for letting his voice roughen. "Just make certain you watch over the girl. She has no defenses. Look what happened at Bedlam. Beckworth obviously couldn't tell his assailants what they wanted to know."

"I thought the maid was a clever touch," she said as if thinking aloud.

Ian thought of the pretty Frenchwoman Lucas had sent to serve Miranda. "Lisle should know that spending money he doesna have is unlikely to impress Miranda."

"Darling," said Frances, "*all* the best people spend money they *doona* have." She laughed. "At least the maid's good with a needle. All Macbeth does is steal food from the pantry. Mangy beast. Where did you get him, anyway?"

"Won him in a game of faro. He's a fine beastie, isn't he, though?" Ian grinned, picturing the ungainly Scottish deerhound bounding about Frances's house and gardens. He had sent the dog to Miranda for protection. And for each of them, it had been love at first sight. Dog and woman had formed a bond, becoming virtually inseparable.

The summer wind swept through the garden, which had been planted with special care in honor of all the dignitaries. A flurry of petals showered over them. "Now," he said, jerking his thoughts firmly away from Miranda for the moment. "Just when and where is the sitting for this historic portrait?"

"I wouldn't miss it for the world," Miranda said to the grand duchess and Frances. In truth, she had no desire at all to witness the posing and posturing of a group of noblemen and war heroes. She had been in their midst, had taken meals with them and danced and conversed with them, and she'd had her fill.

But one did not cross the duchess of Oldenburg. Miranda pasted on a bright smile as footmen helped them from the coach and they entered the grand salon of St. James Palace together.

Thomas Lawrence, the long-suffering artist, was shrieking about light sources and composition and clashing uniforms and gowns. Prinny was flitting from group to group like an enormous butterfly seeking nectar.

Prince Frederick of Prussia spied Miranda and started shouldering a path toward her. "Pardon me," she murmured to Frances.

She took a sharp turn and found herself in a dim alcove window, conveniently equipped with a heavy drape. She stepped back into the alcove and hoped Frederick had not seen.

The curtain parted slightly, revealing the figure of a large man. She thought she recognized him as part of the entourage of the archduke of Austria, but she wasn't certain. "There you are," he said, acting as though he knew her. *"Aimez-vous la violette?"*

"Il reviendra au printemps," she replied automatically.

The man slipped away. Miranda stared after him, appalled and confused. Her past was returning to her, creeping back in dangerous bits and pieces, like a rogue tide swamping a village.

"Wait," she called, hurrying after the man. "Please, I must speak to you."

He gave one swift glance over his shoulder and ducked out a side door. By the time Miranda followed, she found herself in an empty garden. Empty.

She pressed her hands to her stomach, feeling sick. The exchange had occurred in a matter of seconds. There was no thought involved, no will, no choice.

The words seemed innocuous enough: *Do you like violets?* he'd asked. *They will come back in the spring,* she'd replied.

Yet deep in her guilt-racked soul she understood that the violet was the symbol for Bonaparte. Napoleon Bonaparte, who had cut a bloody swath through Europe, who had caused the death and starvation of millions. He was supposed to be harmless now, living in exile on the isle of Elba.

But Miranda, the old Miranda, the Miranda she did not dare to trust, seemed to know something. She seemed to believe that Bonaparte would return with the spring.

How could she know that, unless she was privy to a terrible plot? She committed to memory the face of the man who had approached her. Dark hair. Bland, pale face. The tiniest of ridged scars on his chin. Black clothing, lacking adornment. He could be one of hundreds of retainers in the service of some monarch or prince.

She started walking through the garden, searching for him, searching for answers. What had he hoped to accomplish by approaching her? She suspected—she feared—he was checking to see if her loyalty was still intact. If she remembered.

Her reply to him had been instant and automatic, a reflex. He had seemed quite satisfied.

He made her skin crawl.

The air was sweet with the fragrance of blooming larkspur and roses. A fountain murmured, trickling into a large basin. Bubbles rose lazily to the surface.

She stared down into the water, stared at the stranger who had her face, and wondered what that face concealed.

"Running away, love?"

With a gasp, she turned. Ian MacVane came striding across the lawn toward her. "I thought," he said, "you were learning to enjoy the company of great men."

She pressed her back against the rim of the basin. "Whatever gave you that idea?" Her gaze clung to him. He looked devilishly appealing, his dark hair shining in the sun, his understated breeches and boots and waistcoat singling him out amid the garish blooms in the garden.

"You've become a favorite. I never realized you had social ambitions, but apparently *La Grande* Catherine has turned your head."

"I think you never knew me at all," she said.

She should have known he would see through such a bald challenge. He merely smiled. "Ah, Miranda." To her dismay, he stepped very close and touched her lower lip with his finger. "Not nearly as well as I'd like."

After the encounter with the mysterious man, she was in no mood to spar with Ian MacVane.

"Something happened just now," she said. "I think it might be important."

"Aye? Go on." He leaned against the basin next to her.

"I was approached by a man who recognized me—from before."

She understood Ian well enough now to realize that though he showed no outward reaction, his every sense had come alert. His gaze became just a little keener, his posture a little stiffer. "Is that so?"

"Yes. It was only a brief encounter. We exchanged no words of note." She thought it safer to lie. "But he seemed to know me."

"Who was he? Describe him."

"Just a man. An ordinary man with a small scar on

his chin. I thought he might be attached to the arch-duke, but I could be wrong. He left quickly, and I don't know where he went."

"Did he call you by name? What did he seem to want?"

"He didn't say my name." Ah, why couldn't she remember? Her head ached with the need to know. She turned and gazed at the surface of the water where small bubbles clung to the leaves of the lily pads.

All of a sudden, a jagged white light streaked across her vision. It felt like thousands of hammers on the inside of her head, trying to pound their way out. The pressure built until she was certain she would explode.

Her throat clogged. She could not force words out, or her breath in. Ian took her arm to steady her, but she barely felt his touch. She was seeing something. She was looking into the water and seeing something.

"They threw his body into the river," she said when at last she found her voice. "They tried to kill my father. They threw him into the Thames."

She remembered it in sharp snatches that stung like darts. Her father's broken form. Blood smearing the cobbles of the walkway. A brick with the mortar crumbling, carelessly tied around Papa's limp ankle.

Her mouth opened in horror. But when she tried to scream, there was only silence.

Ian was there, solid as an anchor, his hands holding her shoulders. "Tell me, Miranda," he said. "Tell me what you remember."

"Nighttime," she said. "Raining. A little wind, because the curtains were blowing. They . . . they came to the flat."

"Who?"

"I don't know." Menacing shadows darkened her

soul. The pounding in her head grew louder, fiercer. "They were black shapes. Three of them. Gruff voices. *I don't know.*"

She took a long, ragged breath as shards of memory dug into her. "They beat my father, beat him until he was silent, and dragged us both away." She rubbed her wrists over and over again, feeling the burn of the rope that had bound her. "They said if I made a sound, they'd kill us both. The place where they took us was like a prison cell. Dark and dank. The hours seemed like days. My father would talk to me."

She heard it all again, his voice breaking through the hammering in her head. *Mindy, my dear, you must forget what you overheard. All that you know. All our plans. All our projects. You know nothing. Nothing. Forget it all. It's the only way to stay safe . . . .*

"He called me by a pet name—Mindy. He told me to forget . . . everything. Even when he"—her voice broke—"even when they were beating him, he would say to me, 'You're not seeing this. You don't see me. This is not happening.'" She lifted her heated face to the wind and said, "It worked for a while. But now it's coming back in broken pieces, and I don't know why."

Ian's hands massaged her shoulders. "Ah, love. You have to let yourself remember. What else? The beatings—they got worse?"

"Yes. They thought they killed him." Hope flickered inside her. "But as they dragged me away from the river, I noticed something they'd overlooked."

She saw it all again. A pale hand emerging from the churning water. Fingers clutching at a piling under a dock. "Ian," she said, "I think my father is alive!"

11

*Such things we know are neither rich nor rare
But wonder how the Devil they got there.*
        —George Gordon, Lord Byron

Ian kept his face carefully blank, though a murderous rage was burning a hole in his heart. Someone had forced her to watch her father beaten nearly to death. Just as Ian had watched his own father and brother die. No wonder she had fled from the memories.

He felt her trembling beneath his hands and knew the force of the images coming back to her now could easily shatter her. Very gently he gathered her to his chest and held tight, tucking her head against him and stroking her hair.

Meanwhile his mind raced. She was remembering the past in bit and pieces. She was remembering. But the memories were not what he had expected.

"Can you tell me more?" he asked, bracing himself. Any moment now, she might remember that she had never known a man called Ian MacVane, had never loved him or shared her dreams with him or promised to marry him. Any moment now she might realize he was a liar.

It shouldn't bother him. He had lied to kings and ambassadors and battle commanders, to ladies who had given more of themselves to him than Miranda ever had.

Yet the thought that she might soon realize the extent of his deception jabbed unpleasantly at his conscience. He pictured her wounded expression and decided that hurting Miranda was his own private version of hell.

"They took me . . . I'm not sure where," she said, her voice muffled against his chest. "It was a small room with a single candle burning. One window, and outside I could see ships' masts, so I knew we were not far from the river. I was seated in a chair, and then . . . then the questions began."

"Questions."

"About our work. Manned balloon flight. Missiles. Navigation and the wind. We did . . . our most advanced work in those fields."

"I don't understand," Ian said. "Why would they have abandoned your father and questioned you?"

She drew back from him and stepped away, looking small and infinitely fragile. Yet he knew better. He knew she had endured agonies beyond bearing, had been subjected to horrors so stark that her mind had recoiled, wrapped itself in a cocoon of forgetting.

"That," she said, "is my fault. Entirely my fault." Her eyes glistened with unshed tears. "I thought admitting the truth would protect my father. I thought they would set him free and concentrate on extracting the information from me."

"Why you and not your father?"

A bitter smile twisted her mouth. "Because he didn't know anything. The information they wanted was here." She pointed to her temple. "It was always that way. Scholars, like the rest of society, could not accept erudition from a woman. So my father always pretended my inventions were his, and that I was merely his assistant." A single tear escaped and rolled down her cheek. "My father could not save himself by surrendering information under torture because he had nothing to confess."

Ian felt shocked. This was important information to be so lightly admitted.

She raised her tear-drenched gaze to him. "Why didn't you tell me, Ian? Why didn't you tell me about our projects?"

Hating himself, he said, "It was a secret you kept even from me." He took out a handkerchief and daubed at her cheek. "Ah, Miranda. You canna blame yourself, lass."

"I should have known they'd kill him once they realized he knew nothing."

"They," he repeated. "Do you know the names of these men? Can you remember what they looked like?"

She frowned and closed her eyes for a few moments. Ian held his breath. Even in a state of despair she was lovely—and he kept expecting her to open her eyes and look upon him with hatred.

Instead she shook her head and let out a long, weary sigh. "Everything is all jumbled up inside my head."

"Can you remember how you managed to escape them, or why you ended up in that warehouse?"

She shuddered. "I have no idea. I just recall a feeling of utter compulsion. I *had* to go there. But the reason . . . ?"

"The place housed explosives. We've known that from the start." Ian watched her closely, but her grave face gave him no indication that she was hiding something.

"So I must have been trying to destroy the explosives—or something else, something concealed in the warehouse." She shook her head, looking pale and drawn as she tucked her hand into the crook of Ian's arm. "We had best go inside. The grand duchess was most insistent that I attend the sitting for the portrait."

Ian felt a wave of guilt. He was supposed to be scanning the premises, for the cream of European royalty had all arrived. Another perfect opportunity for an assassin.

Yet not to save all the crowned heads of Europe would he abandon Miranda. Duffie and Frances were inside, Ian reasoned. Between the two of them they would spot anything suspicious.

He understood now why Miranda was so sought after. Her genius was the sort that darker minds would try to exploit. It was up to him to discover just what she knew and who was after her. A sense of startlement gripped him. In the manly world of scientific invention, Miranda shone like a star—but hid her light behind her father.

"So now, at least, I know what I must do," she said, her hand firm and warm on his arm.

"What is that?"

"I must find my father, of course."

Ian took her hand in his. "Has it occurred to you that your plan could be dangerous?"

"Of course. The men who kidnapped us are murderers. But tell me, Ian. Do I really have a choice in this?"

He smiled, and surprised himself because it was a genuine smile, warm and heartfelt. "Ah, lass. And do I?"

"You know," Frances said that evening, "if he chooses to claim his conjugal rights, no one can legally stop him."

Miranda looked up from her copious notes and stared across the drawing room at her. "Ian, you mean?"

"Of course." A tinge of bitterness crept into her voice as she added, "Not every woman can flit back and forth between two extraordinary men."

Miranda's grip on her stylus tightened. "I do not flit. I'm doing everything I can think of to avoid flitting with anyone, Frances."

Macbeth, the deerhound sent by Ian, wandered over and placed his huge, hairy muzzle in Miranda's lap. She patted his broad head and looked lovingly into his large, liquid brown eyes.

A gift from Ian. He and Lucas were playing a game with her as the unwilling prize. Each time one man sent an offering, the other tried to surpass it with one of his own. The sweets and flowers from Lucas had been disconcerting enough. The services of Yvette suggested an intimacy that Lucas believed was warranted.

Yet Ian's gifts were gifts of the heart. The endowment. A sprig of heather. And now this creature. Macbeth was a handsome, gentle beast the size of a small pony. He had endured much cooing and fussing from the grand duchess, but his loyalty lay with Miranda.

"He's a gray, smelly thing, isn't he?" Frances said, wrinkling her nose at Macbeth.

"I suppose so, but he has other virtues." Miranda scratched his ear, and the dog stretched his neck in ecstasy. "I think what I like best about him is that I don't have to question his loyalty."

Frances sniffed. "I hope you're not implying that you question *mine.*"

Miranda smiled. "It's only male animals that plague me." She had explained to Frances all that she had remembered at the fountain that afternoon. Her Ladyship had pledged to help her find her father, and even now they were trying to decide where to begin.

Miranda rubbed her eyes, then scanned the pages on the desk in front of her.

"Did you find anything useful?" Frances asked.

"No." Miranda scowled at the notes. "This was a wasted exercise."

It had been her own idea—to write down every detail she remembered in the hope that she might scribble some telling fact that would lead her to her father. Instead, after two hours of laborious writing, all she had were masses of disjointed phrases and images that got her no further than her talk with Ian had.

Ian. She still had no idea how he fit into her unremembered past. She would never admit it, but most of the writings on the desk before her concerned him. It was as if her life had begun the day he had rescued her from Bedlam, and every moment was almost mystically bound up with him.

Now she had a more urgent purpose. To locate her father. To find out if he had indeed survived. Though he had not been as gifted a scholar as his colleagues thought, Gideon Stonecypher was a still brilliant man. His area of expertise lay in ciphering; he had always been fascinated by remote communication.

Miranda dipped her stylus in ink and wrote, "Semaphores."

Something in her expression must have changed, for Frances stood and crossed the room. "What is it?"

"Much of my father's work involved semaphores."

Frances's reaction was curious. She flushed a deep, becoming shade of red, as if something had embarrassed her. "Really? How very interesting."

"I never found it particularly so," Miranda said. "But Papa did, so I left him to it. We even had use of a semaphore tower in—" She scratched her pen and looked down at what she had written. The letter *H* and the letter *W*. Unconnected.

"Where?" Frances asked urgently.

Her stomach knotted with disappointment. "I'm sorry. I can't. I started to write something—Lord knows what—and then everything just turned gray and foggy." She kneaded her temples. "This is so damned nettlesome!"

"Perhaps you're trying too hard, dear," Frances murmured sympathetically. "Why don't you go to bed, rest awhile?"

"All right. Come, Macbeth. To bed with us." Miranda rose from the desk, leaving the notes scattered there. She bade good night to Frances and made her way slowly through the long, gilded halls of Biddle House.

Having deep emotions, she realized, was exhausting business. Although she couldn't be certain, she suspected that before the fire, she had been uninvolved in matters that set entire nations to war. But now the conflict had become personal. They had taken her father. Perhaps killed him.

How dare they? she thought. How dare they?

She stopped walking and clutched the marble rail

of the winding staircase. Rage came over her in a blinding flash. Macbeth stopped on the landing and sat back on his haunches. The images that seared into Miranda's mind at that moment made no sense. She saw Lucas's glittering smile, then the flamelike intensity of Ian MacVane's blue eyes.

How dared they?

Frances was right. She *was* exhausted, and Lucas and Ian only muddled her thinking. In different ways, she was attracted to both of them. She was dazzled by Lucas's social and physical perfection, his charming manners and easy wit. At the same time, she felt drawn to Ian's darkness, to the complex depths of him. In Scotland, she had been so certain of her love for him. Now she knew, with a painful surge of her heart, that one day she might have to choose between the two of them and that the choice might end up hurting her.

Lucas kept telling her of their past, of the secret affection they shared, of their hopes and dreams. Ian no longer spoke of the past; he seemed to think she should accept him on faith alone.

She could not. She must proclaim her independence. She must discover the truth for herself rather than leave it up to any man.

She started walking again, very slowly, up the grand, curving staircase. Recessed alcoves at regular intervals supported busts of important historical figures. Their blank-eyed stares and smooth marble faces haunted her. She recognized each one—Isaac Newton, Alexander Pope, Linnaeus.

And the headache started again.

Someday you'll be famous for this, Papa. You know that, don't you?

And it'll all be a lie, Mindy love. All a lie. The hon-

*ors should rightfully go to you. But I wonder, sweet, if
you've thought beyond the obvious.*

I don't know what you mean, Papa.

*Couldn't someone with an evil purpose exploit
your gift? Use it to cause harm rather than good?*

*Oh, honestly, Papa. Who in their right mind would
ever do such a thing as that?*

Miranda shuddered, trying to look back at the memory without recoiling. She wasn't sure precisely what
they had been speaking of. She did not know when or
where she'd had the conversation with her father, but
it seemed his dire prediction had come true.

At the top of the stairs, long, golden triangles of
light wavered on the marble floor, cast there by a single lamp set at the newel post at the top of the winding stairs. She put her hand on the knob.

Macbeth whined softly.

"In a moment, boy," she said, knowing he was
eager to get to the bowl of kitchen scraps she had set
out. She opened the door and stepped inside.

Cool air from a high, open window rushed over
her. She felt a faint stab of surprise, for Yvette always
kept a lamp or candle burning each night until
Miranda came to bed. The wind must have blown out
the flame. Only the uncertain, wavering gray light of
the moon spilled through the glass door leading out
to the balcony.

Macbeth whined again; then a growl rumbled in
his throat.

"Yvette?" Miranda called. "Are you there?" Putting
out a hand, she made her way into the room and toward
the door that led to the maid's quarters. "Yvette?" she
called again.

A faint thump sounded somewhere near the
window.

Macbeth's low growl crescendoed to a ragged snarl.

Miranda turned toward the window.

A hulking shadow streaked toward her. She had no time to scream, no time to think. The hulk slammed her back against a wall. Something closed around her throat, biting into her neck, choking off her breath.

No no no no . . . She could offer only silent protests. She kicked out, but her skirts hampered her.

One hundred pounds of furious, smelly deerhound leaped at the assailant. Miranda felt the pressure on her neck loosen, then drop. In the pitch darkness she saw nothing, but she could hear the dog growling and cloth ripping.

A moment later, she heard the sound of the shattering window. She staggered up and made her way to the balcony door. Broken glass crunched under her shoes. A shard sliced into her finger when she freed the latch on the window and gingerly swung it open.

Macbeth pushed past her and put his front paws on the balcony ledge.

"Stay," Miranda said in a rasping, breathless voice. The trembling started in her heart and then radiated outward along her limbs until she was shaking uncontrollably.

Thick shadows hung in the gardens below. Somewhere in the gloom was the man who had just tried to kill her.

12

*Almost all our misfortunes in life
come from the wrong notions we have
about the things that happen to us.*
                              —Stendhal

Ian dreamed of flying again.

In his dream he was a boy fleeing along the dales of
Crough na Muir while darkness, like a cloud shadow,
raced to overcome him. Determined to escape, he
pushed his feet off the ground and soared.

The village receded below, and the great, vast sea
spread out endlessly before him. He flew toward the
sun, to a place of light, closer and closer until he
could feel its golden warmth. His cares melted
away—the English mercenaries could not reach him
here. He could no longer hear their lewd laughter or
see their idiot grins or their cruel hands with the bay-
oneted muskets and torches.

But he stayed too long in the intensity of the sun,
and the warmth became an unbearable heat that

roared through him like an inferno. Then he was falling, burning and falling, toward the white-veined surface of the sea, where the water was as cold and hard as marble.

He opened his mouth to scream, but no sound came out; his throat was frozen, his hands clutching at emptiness—

"You should lay off the whiskey." Duffie's voice sounded through the terror. "It makes you sleep badly."

Reeling in his emotions, Ian shuddered, then rubbed his eyes and sat up in bed. He glowered at the brightness of the early sun streaming through the window, long yellow bars of light aimed at his face.

"Why do I always dream of flying?" he muttered, shoving himself out of bed.

While Ian bent over the washbasin and started to shave, Duffie busied himself with coffee and brioches at the sideboard and spoke over his shoulder. "Because you fear heights."

"I'd be lost without your wisdom." He angled his razor across his jaw.

"*She* doesna fear heights. She knows all about flying. Just the other day she explained how to use coal gas to fill an aerial balloon. It could work, you know."

Ian didn't have to ask who *she* was. "Flying balloons," he muttered in disgust, shaking soap from the razor blade. "It's not natural." Scowling, he applied the blade to his chin.

"Miranda says that with coal gas, decent winds, and judicious ballasting, a balloon could cross the Channel in less than two hours." Duffie took a sip of coffee and dabbed a napkin at his neat beard. "By the by, she wants to see you this morning."

The razor blade nicked into his chin. Ian drew

back, and the blade cut his finger. Cursing, he snatched up a towel. "Why didn't you say so?"

"I just did." Duffie placidly regarded the blood dripping from Ian's finger and chin. "Lovely, my lad. Just lovely."

Within moments Ian was dressed, his appearance somewhat diminished by the presence of bits of cloth pressed to his chin and finger. With the exception of his tartan waistcoat, he wore his usual black.

"Excellent choice, laddie." Duffie eyed the cut of Ian's frock coat. "That's the one that makes the ladies go 'ooh!'"

"I don't give a damn about making the ladies go 'ooh!'"

"Yes, you do."

"No, I don't."

"Yes, you—"

Ian glared him into silence. They traveled unfashionably on horseback, because Ian was in a hurry. He told himself he felt a sense of urgency because Miranda had remembered more. But in his heart he knew it was because she affected him as no other person ever had. She brought a rare sense of peace to his soul. She made him dare to believe that there could be something more to life than struggle.

"It makes a man stupid, Duffie, and no mistake."

"What makes a man stupid?"

"This marriage thing."

Duffie chuckled. "Love, you mean."

Ian gave a derisive snort. "Old fool. I'm just not used to being responsible for another person."

"You care about her."

"I care about doing my job." From time to time, he admitted to himself, he and Miranda came perilously close to the intimacy he both craved and feared, but one or the other—usually Ian—always drew back, recoiling from something new and uniquely threatening. "She's beginning to remember. I believe Miranda was not in league with the traitors, but was their victim."

Duffie nodded. "I knew it all along."

"Thank you for speaking up sooner."

"You wouldna hae believed me sooner. Now. What has she told you about her abductors?"

"She can't remember who they are, what they look like, what they wanted, or where they took her."

"A marvelous start," Duffie said wryly.

Ian felt as if he were up against a stone wall. But patience and kindness had drawn the first memories from her. Perhaps during the night she had recalled something. Perhaps that was why she had summoned him.

Dread thudded in his gut. Perhaps today was the day Miranda remembered she had never known a man named Ian MacVane.

A footman led them into a drawing room grandly decked in radiant gold and white. Fanny had never been one to employ subtlety. Miranda waited alone, sitting stiff backed upon a gold brocade chaise. The strong sunlight of the summer morning streamed over her, giving her a winsome glow that took his breath away. Her hair was an abundant cloud of curls; her grave face resembled that of an angel.

She looked dainty and refined, wearing a high-waisted, pale green dress and little green slippers. Macbeth, whose mission in life seemed to be to sleep with his muzzle between his front paws, dozed at her feet.

"Good morning." Ian greeted her with a bow.

"Sit down," she said, not even cracking a smile.

"What is it?" His soul recoiled from the look of accusation in her eyes.

"Last night, a man tried to kill me," she said, her voice weary and low with an unhealthy rasp. "Was it you, MacVane?"

Panic and fury flamed through him. "Tried to—" He plunged himself down beside her and grabbed her shoulders. She flinched, but he made no apology for his roughness. "Damn it, woman, why didn't you send for me?"

"I did."

"Last night, I mean. Right after you—right after it happened."

"I did," she said again, pulling out of his grasp. "I was told you were out."

Ian clenched his jaw. Out. The tavern. The whiskey. He had not been there when Miranda had needed him. Just as he had not been there for his mother so long ago. But this time he had no excuse. He was no sniveling boy, but a man—one who should know better than to lower his guard.

"Lucas came. He stayed nearby the entire night."

If Ian had not been so busy hating himself at the moment, he would have turned his venom on Lucas. "His Lordship does have some practical value, then. Miranda, what happened?"

"Someone entered my room through the balcony window. He tried to strangle me." She bent and curled her fingers into the deerhound's shaggy hair. "Macbeth chased him off. He managed to bite him a time or two, I think." She leaned forward, peering at Ian's face. "How did you get that cut on your chin?"

He flushed scarlet. "Shaving. Goddamn it, I cut myself shaving." He made himself pause, draw a deep breath. Loud and furious protests would only make him look more guilty.

Miranda gave a small shudder. "Lady Frances informed Her Grace of Oldenburg this morning."

Ian felt nauseated. "The grand duchess?"

"She's a friend, Ian."

He wondered. Catherine Pavlovna adored games of intrigue. Could she be playing cat and mouse with Miranda? The Russians had suffered at Bonaparte's hands. If they believed Miranda to be in league with Napoleon, they would not balk at killing her.

"She's sending Cossack guards to patrol the house and grounds night and day," Miranda added.

Cossack guards. A band of foreign horsemen armed with curved blades and nasty tempers. Ian thrust himself to his feet and started to pace. "Surely you can't believe it was I."

She sent him a long, weary look. "I can't trust anyone. But I still think of Scotland, Ian. Do you?"

Her question knifed into him. *Every day,* his heart answered. *Every waking moment.* Appalled at his own sentimentality, he sped up his pacing.

"It must be someone who wants me to die before I regain my memory," she said simply. "And it's rather odd, MacVane, that the first person I told my memories to was you."

"Jesus." He stopped pacing and glared at her. "You're not still saying—"

"She doesn't have to say." Lucas strode into the room. In his morning suit of gray serge, he looked as immaculate as an altar boy. "The evidence speaks for itself."

"What evidence?" Ian demanded, feeling his hackles rise.

Lucas reached inside his waistcoat and drew out a white silk cravat. "*This* is what she was strangled with. Miranda found it on the floor after the attacker escaped."

The blood rushed out of Ian's face and seemed to pool in his gut. He snatched the fabric from Lucas and held it up. He didn't have to look at the white-on-white monogram, but he did anyway. "IDM." The letters stood for Ian Dale MacVane.

He crumpled the cravat in his gloved hand and whirled to face Miranda. For a moment, he was too furious to speak. Too confused. He was used to being in control, to being the calculating one. The perfect spy. The master of disguise.

In the Peninsular Wars, he had led lightning raids, headed off ambushes, saved his regiment—all because he'd stayed one jump ahead of the enemy. Knowing the workings of an evil and violent mind was his specialty.

Obviously he was losing his touch.

The idea that someone had helped himself to one of his cravats, then had breached the citadel of Frances's residence and almost choked the life out of Miranda, was too much to bear. So was hearing Miranda accuse him.

"Surely you know this idea is ridiculous." He was surprised—and not displeased—to hear a cold, calm edge in his voice.

"I know nothing of the sort." Her hand went to her throat.

That was when he saw the bruises. The reality of what had happened barreled into him, searing his soul with rage. Someone had tried to kill her. Had almost succeeded.

Without taking his eyes off Miranda, off the pur-

pling bruises on her swan white throat, he called,
"Duffie!"

McDuff came in. "Aye?"

"Fetch my things. I am coming to stay at Biddle
House."

"Verra good, sir!"

"You'll do nothing of the sort," Lucas said. His
voice rang with steely contempt and the high-cultured
accents of Eton and Oxford. "I'm staying, so we have
no need of you. Someone must protect Miranda.
Someone she trusts."

"The dog I gave her is more trustworthy than
that sly French maid of yours." Ian still held
Miranda in his gaze and wondered how he could
have ever let her out of it. "Don't start fussing and
fuming at me, Lisle. I've more of a right to protect
her than you."

"Only because you forced her to marry you under
false pretenses."

Miranda blinked once, slowly. Her face showed no
expression, yet Ian sensed a storm brewing inside her.
She was being pushed to the breaking point. Perhaps
even now, memories were flooding into her. He
couldn't worry about that at the moment. He turned
his attention to Lisle.

"There was no force involved." He put his face
close to Lucas's and poked a finger at his chest.

Lucas shoved him back. "English law doesn't recognize a handfast marriage."

"Dinna push me, Lisle. You're the one who doesn't
belong here."

"You are no husband," Lucas said. "Unless you've
forced your way into her bed as well—"

Ian's fist flew, connecting with Lucas's jaw. A sickening thud sounded.

To his credit, Lucas merely staggered a little. "Scottish scapegrace."

"I should have finished you when I had the chance, on the dueling green—"

"Stop it!" Like a dreamer awakening, Miranda shot to her feet. "I won't let either of you stay if this is the way you're going to behave. I'd rather throw in my lot with the Cossacks."

Ian turned to her, though his senses were on alert for a sneak attack by Lucas. "Someone doesna want you to remember the past," he said. "It's up to me to find out who."

She glared at him. "Nothing of the sort is up to you. Loss of memory is not the same as loss of wits, Ian. *I* shall decide how to cope with this." She looked from Ian to Lucas and back again. "Perhaps one of the men in my life is a murderer."

"Then you had better be certain you know which is which," Ian said with a dangerous smile.

She tossed her head, looking magnificent. She grew stronger every day, and while some women would have been reduced to hysterics by the events of the previous night, Miranda seemed determined to confront them. The vulnerable waif he'd found huddled in Bedlam had grown into a formidable woman. She had faced danger and was refusing to let it destroy her. "You may both stay so long as you vow to live in peace," she stated.

"Preposterous." Rubbing his jaw, Lucas stalked to the mantel and turned. "It would be moral and social suicide."

"And you're such an authority," Ian said.

"As it happens, I am."

"And well paid for your expertise."

Lucas flushed as if a fire had started inside him.

"Don't worry," Ian drawled. "I won't let out your little secret. For now."

Lucas thrust his open hand through his hair, mussing its golden perfection. "Miranda, elevating you in society was all we used to dream about. We knew it was the only way we could be together openly, without subterfuge."

"I don't remember that," she said, yet her voice had softened.

Ian felt an ominous thrum of sentiment. Jealousy. The steel-edged teeth of it sank into him. He braced himself against it. She was an Englishwoman, a Sassenach. She was supposed to mean nothing to him. Nothing at all.

"It's true," Lucas said. "If only polite society would accept you, we could go openly to my family, be together with their blessing."

Family. Another poisoned stab at Ian. Though apparently in dire straits financially, Lucas had a warm and loving clan who looked to him, counted on him, loved him. Ian's mother had finally offered forgiveness, but even that would not replace all the stolen years, all the times he used to lie awake at night and hear her accusations in his head.

"You forget one small detail," Ian said, his fist closing again. "Miranda is married to me."

"Illegal Scottish handfast nonsense. It would never hold up in court."

"Enough." Miranda cut the air with her hand. "In the first place, Lucas, I cannot believe I ever put stock in the opinions of polite society. What they declare to be right or wrong is the most offensive and presumptuous tripe I ever heard. Their customs and mannerisms baffle me. Whoever heard of going about leaving cards on silver trays rather than paying a visit? Or dragging out a fashion plate in order to make certain you've dressed properly? I refuse to bow to artificial and irrelevant social rules. I feel quite certain I never have, and I never shall."

Ian felt a smile form inside him, but he refused to let it out. He clung to his fury. Prior to his meeting Miranda, her safety had meant nothing to him. There was a time when he had known her only as a name-less, faceless traitor. He had been prepared to murder her, if need be, on behalf of British intelligence.

He had chosen instead to safeguard her. Or per-haps it was not a choice at all, but a way to affirm that he was still human, that a part of him was still decent enough to balk at harming a woman.

He had taught himself not to care about anyone, but Miranda threatened to bring about a sea change inside him, touching emotions he had never felt. She reminded him that he was a man capable of feeling love and affection and jealousy and contentment. And desire. Good God, until Miranda, he had not even come close to knowing the meaning of desire.

Now someone else was after her—someone who wanted her to die before she regained her memory. Before Ian could tap into his newfound well of emo-tions.

He would not fail her. If he had to lay down his very life to keep her safe, he would gladly do so.

"Well?" she demanded, setting her hands on her hips. "Do both of you agree to abide by my rules?"

"Fine," Lucas muttered, "but I think you're over-looking the obvious." He indicated the crumpled white cravat.

"Just make certain he stays out of my sight," Ian said, jerking his head toward Lucas.

For the first time that morning, Miranda smiled.

Coldly. Sarcastically. Frances had taught her well. "You are both such a comfort to me."

The next day found Frances and her three guests mounted and headed for Hyde Park. It was yet another glorious summer day, pleasantly warm, the colors rich and lush in the sunlight. Miranda felt far more nervous than she should have, riding a dainty, even-tempered pony. Frances sat sidesaddle with a haughty assurance Miranda did not even try to emulate.

"I don't think I did much riding in the past," she confessed to Frances.

Lady Frances's nostrils flared. She looked pointedly at Miranda's death grip on the reins. "So I gathered." Yet when Lucas arrived on a chestnut hack, looking as glorious as the morning itself, Frances's control slipped and she allowed a smile. "Good morning, my lord."

He lifted his hat to her. "Good. MacVane's not here yet," he said.

Miranda watched the two of them thoughtfully. He claimed he was the man she loved. That may or may not be true, but what she could see for certain was that Frances adored him. The fact was clear to everyone except Lucas.

One of the few things Miranda knew without question was that the people in her life were all liars. For civilized people, they lied constantly.

"Mr. MacVane," she said when Ian rode up, "I was just thinking about you."

His sleek gelding put Lucas's hack to shame. He led the way from the yard to the main entrance, where two footmen swung wide the wrought-iron gate. At Hyde Park, the Ladies' Mile was jammed with curricles, chaises, landaus, and ladies draped fashionably over sidesaddled ponies. Traffic was equally heavy on Rotten Row, sandy and more popular with the men.

This park, at this particular hour, Miranda now knew, was *the* place to be seen in London. Within a few minutes, she had recognized important ambassadors and princes and war heroes. Catherine of Oldenburg bellowed a loud "Halloo!" when she spied them. As generous as she was outrageous, she loved being surrounded by her new friends. "My guards, they do well, yes?" she called.

"Very well indeed," Miranda said.

"When they're not reeling drunk on vodka or bathing in the fountains," Frances murmured in an undertone.

Miranda pasted on a smile.

Satisfied, Catherine ordered her driver to take her back to the Pulteney Hotel for breakfast. Miranda watched the ornate buggy go. Like a gathering storm, a headache started behind her eyes. By now the sensation was familiar, and she did not fight it. She simply surrendered to the blinding agony, inviting in the shards of memory.

Where the hell have you been, anyway? You reek of horse dung. Rough speech. A stranger's voice.

Then you needn't bother to ask where I've been. It's where they all go. Like pigeons in a shooting gallery.

No! It's too risky. We must stay the course, wait for the hour of glory. And you know when that is. You know precisely when that is.

When? Miranda wanted to scream. But already the voices were sinking back into cobwebby black shadows, and she could not retrieve them. It was an exchange she remembered hearing, but she did not know the speakers. "Even if something were to happen," she said, speaking aloud to herself, "why would it be today?"

Ian winked at her. "Because you're here."

"Hah," Lucas said disagreeably. "Because *you're* here."

Miranda sighed in exasperation. They had argued late into the night, each pointing the finger of accusation at the other. This morning, Lucas sported a faint bruise on his jaw.

She reflected on how it felt to have men come to blows over her. Unpleasant in the extreme, she decided.

"We'll get nowhere if you bicker," she said.

Frances led the way along Rotten Row, nodding regally at the people she passed. Miranda surprised herself by knowing quite a few of them. Lady Cowper and Lady Melbourne. Count Platov and the duke of Gloucester. The notorious Lady Holland, braving censure by sending plum preserves to Napoleon on Elba. Mr. Silas Addingham on a wildly expensive Irish Thoroughbred. The duke of Wellington. The crown prince of Prussia.

What a singular time to be in London, she thought. Every important person in the world was here. Possibly here in this park.

Wellington drew rein on his horse to exchange a few words with Lady Frances. Miranda's mentor, it seemed, had something to say to everyone. "Dear me, your grace," Frances said with flutter of eyelashes, "what is this I hear about your wife having her servants wear French colors?"

"To honor the return of the Bourbon king,"

Wellington explained with an indulgent smile. "Surely you see no wrong in—"

"They clash!" Frances said, touching her palms to her cheeks in mortification. "Red and blue simply shout vulgarity. . . ."

Miranda shook her head. Over coffee this morning, Frances had argued with Ian about interest rates at the Amsterdam banks. Yet in public she took pains to harbor no thought deeper than the color of a ribbon.

Ian's mount was restless, so he let it sidle back and forth on the green beside the track. Lucas had his hands full trying to keep his hack from grazing. Miranda waited beneath the bough of a chestnut tree. The broad, five-fingered leaves nodded in a gentle breeze. It was so pleasant here, verdant and fragrant and alive with the voices of people visiting, greeting each other. Sometimes the sound of a lark would penetrate the socializing, but not often.

Then she heard something odd. Felt it, rather. It was like the buzzing of bees, somewhere in the back of her head.

A cracking sound split the air. A large chunk of the tree trunk exploded outward, splinters of fresh, moist wood arrowing into Wellington, striking his cockade, knocking his hat to the ground.

Miranda felt a stinging sensation on her face. Her pony reared. She lost her grip on the reins and clung to the edge of the saddle, but to no avail. She heard her gown tear, felt a thud all the way to her bones as she landed on the dusty track.

A pair of strong arms went around her, holding her close. Ian, she thought. Thank God he was here.

But when she looked up at him, she found herself gazing into Lucas's eyes.

"MacVane bolted like a craven at the first sign of

trouble," he said, explaining before she could even form a question. "Are you all right?"

Like pigeons in a shooting gallery. The stranger's voice still haunted her.

She listened to the thump of hooves as Wellington calmed his horse. He and Lady Frances examined the wound gouged out of the tree. Count Platov gave a whistle, and the Cossacks formed a human shield around the tsar and his entourage.

"A shooting in Hyde Park," Lucas said through gritted teeth. "What the devil is next?"

"A cannonade at Almacks?" She attempted to lighten the moment with a thin smile. *A warehouse explosion?*

Why had she been there? *Why?* The question raged at her, but she clung to Lucas, wanting nothing more than to close her eyes and shut out the world.

He seemed only too happy to oblige her, drawing her partway into his lap and cradling her against his chest. "There, love," he said, his voice a comforting hum in her ear. "I'm here. I've always been here. Someday you'll remember that, I swear it."

His hand was infinitely gentle as he took a handkerchief and dabbed at her cheek. "Just a surface wound," he said. "A tiny scrape. It won't scar, darling. But look up at me, there's another cut just here."

She turned her face up to him. He bent his head very close, his thumb massaging her temple. Perhaps it was the shock of the sneak attack, perhaps the heat of the rising sun or the fact that she had not eaten, but she felt weak, willing to surrender, at least for a moment, to his tender ministrations.

Vaguely she heard Lady Frances's huff of indignation, but she didn't care, not now. . . . Something was coming at her, slipping over her like a shadow. A memory. She tried to grasp at it. Strong masculine arms. Holding her. *Doing what?* Hurting or helping? The low thrum of a voice. *Saying what?* An endearment or a threat?

"Lucas," she whispered, trying to tell him to help her to remember. But the shadow kept sliding over her, darker and darker. She forced her eyes open, and there was Ian astride his horse with the rising sun lighting him from behind. She remembered how he had looked the night of the fire, broad shouldered, striding toward her, heedless of the flames that roared like dragons' tongues at him. He looked at her, just for a moment, then dug his heels into his horse's flanks and rode away.

13

*A wise woman never yields by appointment. It should
always be an unforeseen happiness.*

—Stendhal

Miranda couldn't sleep that night because
she was thinking about her father. He might be alive.
Somewhere. He had to be. Her conviction that he had
survived was simply too strong. But where in heaven's
name had he gone? And who had tried to kill her?

She sprang from the bed, went to the door, and
opened it quietly. Since the attack with the cravat—
Ian's cravat, she forced herself to admit—the suites of
rooms on either side of her had been occupied.

The one on the right housed Lucas; the one on the
left, Ian.

She supposed she should be flattered that two
handsome men, both well respected in London,
should set themselves up as her protectors.

Instead she felt torn and deeply suspicious. One
moment she was certain Lucas was telling the truth

about their past, their secret trysts, the tender flower-
ing of their love. But then she looked at Ian and
remembered the way he made her feel when he
touched her, and she was certain *he* was the only man
she could have loved.

She still felt a deep inner twist of longing when Ian
entered a room. Still remembered the whisper of his
hand over her cheek just before he kissed her.

She stepped out into the dark corridor. A slice of
light from her bedside lamp illuminated the marble
pillars and gilded walls. She stood there a moment,
the need to talk to someone burning inside her.

She could wake Frances, but all she was likely to
get was a grumble and a decidedly horrific glimpse of
Lady Frances with her hair rolled in rags, her face
slathered with a mask of clay, and her eyes covered
with the black silk band she wore to block out the
morning sun.

Miranda thought of Lucas's tenderness after the
shooting and knew he would listen with sympathy.

But she did not need sympathy now. She needed
answers.

Before her courage failed her, she went to the door
on her left and tapped lightly at the wood paneling.

It opened immediately, as if he had been waiting
for her. For a moment she stood and studied Ian. He
looked charmingly dissolute in a rumpled shirt with
his cravat untied and trailing down his chest, his feet
bare and his waistcoat and frock coat long discarded.
He was not wearing his gloves.

She found his appearance shocking and provoca-
tive and appealing. Well, why not? she asked herself. She had seen less toothsome sights than a dark
Scotsman in a state of half undress. He was fascinating, an expert at deviltry, an object of desire,

and—when he didn't think anyone was looking—a man capable of compassion.

He held a tumbler of brandy, which sloshed as he stepped back and gestured to her. "Come in, then."

"You act as though you expected me." But she stepped obediently into the room and stood before the hearth. A few coals lay scattered there, emitting faint light and warmth. A single taper burned on the mantel, dripping carelessly into its holder.

"I knew you were up."

She frowned. "The floor doesn't squeak. I checked."

He took a sip of brandy. "But the bed does. And I didn't hear it. So I could only conclude that you weren't in it."

The idea that he could hear the sounds of her in bed caused a strange flutter in her stomach. "And where did you conclude I was?"

His expression went hard, belying his casual pose at the sideboard. "Ah, then you want me to say it. You want me to say I feared you were in the arms of Lord Lisle."

Color flooded her face. She made no protest when he poured a glass of brandy and pushed it into her hand. She recalled the moment that morning when Ian had seen her in Lucas's arms, and guilt shot through her.

"I have no cause to apologize," she said stubbornly, as much for her own benefit as for his. "Until I know what happened in the past, I don't belong to either of you. But—" She broke off, biting her lip to stop herself.

"But what?"

He had the most uncanny way of coaxing words from her, of knowing when something was bothering her. "This morning, after the shooting, he stayed with me, and you bolted."

His silky laughter drifted through the dark to her. "I never claimed to be a knight in shining armor," he said.

"But with so many people around, I thought—" Again she bit her lip.

He chuckled again. "You thought I'd feel compelled to prance to and fro, shouting for everyone to take cover. That would've made a nice show."

"Still, to turn tail like that—"

"Unforgivable," he agreed cheerfully, with a tiny slur in his Scottish brogue. "Call me fickle, but at the moment, it seemed judicious to find the source of the shot to see if I could apprehend the shooter."

She took a healthy gulp of brandy, welcoming its burn in the pit of her stomach. There was always an explanation. She should give up even trying to catch him out. "Oh. I hadn't thought of that."

"Neither, it seemed, did anyone else, which is why I went."

"And did you find anything?"

"No." He grew agitated, tossing back his drink and slamming the glass on a table. "It came from a rifle-barreled musket of the sort that was issued to thousands of British infantry. By the time I reached the cover of bushes, there was no one in sight. Just a mild haze of powder burn."

"Do you think it was fired by someone who was after me?" She shuddered, thinking of the shadows that followed her, the sense of invasion she awoke with after a bad dream.

"I can't be certain. Wellington has his share of enemies." His mouth tightened in a wry grin. "All heroes do. And heroines."

She thought it an odd thing to say. She took another

sip of brandy, shook off the speculation, looked into his eyes, and wondered. Lover or liar? Lover or liar?

He stepped close to her, very close, so that she could feel the warmth emanating from him, see the curls of midnight hair that tumbled down his brow. "Why did you come here, Miranda?" he asked provocatively. "Why did you come to me tonight?"

"I can't stop thinking about my father. I keep getting the feeling that I should do something. Go somewhere. But I have no idea where to begin."

His knuckles grazed her cheek, just below the place where a wood splinter had scratched her. "Perhaps you're trying too hard. Getting in your own way. I've tried to find a pattern to your returning memories. They seem to come through a side door in your mind, Miranda. When you're not trying to summon them. Does that make sense?"

She nodded, faintly astounded that he had been so observant where she was concerned. Was it because he could hardly bear to wait for her to remember that he was her one true love? Or was it because he was worried that she might look at him and realize she had never known him?

That was ridiculous, she told herself. Ian knew her better than she knew herself.

"Lass," he said with a gentle burr, "forgive me for asking, but if your father survived, why do you suppose he hasn't contacted you?"

"Perhaps he has tried, but how would he know where to find me? Perhaps he is a prisoner again, or—" A chill slid through her, and she clenched her hands around her glass. "Or perhaps he is staying away from me in order to protect me." She shut her eyes, trying to picture this man she wanted so desperately to find.

Papa. She had always called him Papa. In her mind's eye, she saw the ragged ends of an old-fashioned tailcoat, regarding him from the perspective of a child.

Can't we stay with Lady Montfort, Papa? She was ever so nice to me.

I'm afraid we've worn out our welcome, poppet—

The explanation was interrupted by the memory of shattering glass. *And don't you dare come back, Gideon Stonecypher!*

Miranda flinched and opened her eyes. She could not say why, but it was a comfort to see Ian there, waiting.

"I think," she said with a trace of amusement, "that my father is a bit of a rake."

"Can you remember any of his lady friends?" Ian asked. "Maybe he went to stay with one of them."

"Lady Montfort," she said. "Does that mean anything to you?"

"A tidy fortune and a terrible temper. And she passed away a few years ago."

"I think she knew him." Miranda thought of the shabby tails of the outmoded coat. "It must have been when I was very small."

"Anyone else? Any clue at all?"

Miranda shook her head despondently. "No doubt there were others. Ah, God." She sank to the chaise in front of the hearth. "Why, *why* can't I simply remember? What is wrong with me? What happened that was so horrible I cannot remember it?"

He sank down beside her. She gulped back the last of her brandy. He set aside her glass, took her face between his hands, and regarded her steadily. "There is nothing wrong with you, Miranda. I dinna want you to blame yourself, ever."

She wanted to say more, to tell him how fearful

she was of what her memories concealed, but she looked at him in the candlelight and could not make her voice work. There was a dark invitation in his eyes, in the full curve of his lip. She bent forward slightly, at first more inquisitive than anything else, curious to see if kissing him now would be as devastating as it had been the last time.

It was worse. Far worse, and at the same time more incredible than anything she could possibly imagine. She seemed to fall into the kiss, her lips coming down to cover his and drink from them. He made a low, rumbling sound in his throat, something like a warning, but she would not be put off. The taste of cherry brandy, warmed by his mouth and tongue, had a sweetly narcotic effect on her.

She draped her arms around his neck, hungry, needy, knowing she had exhausted all her efforts to resist this moment. Despite his claim on her, Ian had kept his distance, and now she felt his struggle, too, as he pulled back to gaze at her.

"Is this the beginning of what I think it is?" he asked in a hushed, rasping voice.

"Yes," she heard herself whisper.

"Then," he said, "you have about five seconds to tell me to stop."

"What happens after five seconds?" she asked.

"After that, a whole army of wailing Cossacks couldna make me stop."

"So I'm five seconds away from being ravished?" Her fingers curled into his hair, into the texture of black silk. It felt sleek beneath her hand, and she was struck by the intimacy of it.

"Three, now."

"Two," she said, amazed by her own boldness. "One."

"You didna tell me to stop, lass."

"I know. I want you to go on." She lifted her face and kissed him. Again. Then again. "And on . . . and on."

"I suppose," he said in a slightly strangled voice, "I can do that."

"Then do. Please."

All day long, Ian had been telling himself she was Lucas Chesney's whore. When he had seen her in Lisle's arms, a violent feeling had charged through him, a feeling that could easily have turned into a deep, fiery hurt.

He had buried himself in venomous thoughts. She was English. All the Sassenach women he knew were either harlots or cold fish. Since not even by the longest stretch of the imagination could he term Miranda a cold fish, he forced himself to conclude that she was a harlot.

Lucas Chesney's harlot. Perhaps the very day she had blown up the warehouse, the two of them had met and made love and laughed at the world. Lucas fooled no one with his claims of secret trysts, of keeping their treasured love chaste until he found the backbone to tell his family he had fallen in love with a woman whose blood was a shade less than aristocratic blue. A woman who might not be able to put several thousand pounds into the Chesney family coffers.

A woman who was as beautiful as the stars on a summer night.

She lay draped upon the chaise, watching him expectantly, defying him to dismiss her as another man's whore. Daring him to make her his own. His wife.

Never a great believer in self-denial, he took her in

his arms and pulled her against him, feeling the curves
of her body beneath the diaphanous layers of her gown.
The rhythm of her pulse invaded him as he dipped his
head to kiss her throat, slowly tracing his tongue along
the ivory flesh. He felt himself wanting, wanting with a
fierceness that was new and strange to him.

"Ah, love," he whispered. "There are things I wish
to do to you that you might find . . . shocking."

She merely nodded, raising no objection.

No missish airs. He liked that. Perhaps she had
been this way before, or perhaps she had forgotten
false modesty along with everything else. It didn't
matter now. Nothing mattered now.

He wanted her hair down. It was an unusual thing
for him to desire; in general he paid little heed to the
way a woman's hair was arranged when there were so
many more interesting things about her. But Miranda
was different. _Everything_ about Miranda interested
him.

His fingers found a pair of metal hairpins that held
her curls loosely on top of her head. He drew them
out and dropped them to the floor, his eyes never
leaving hers. The curls tumbled down past her shoulders, giving her beauty the pagan lushness of an
ancient goddess. She was Isis, Aphrodite. Or maybe
Persephone, about to lead him to a place he dared not
go. He paused to furrow his hand into her hair, feeling its satiny texture as he leaned forward to kiss her.

He untied the front of her robe and parted it. An
involuntary gasp hissed from between his lips.

"Is something wrong?" she asked.

"I assumed you had on a gown beneath this robe."

"Surprise," she said softly.

"Aye. You _are_ a surprise." He kissed and tasted her
throat, her smooth skin. She kept her hands resting

lightly on his shoulders and her eyes half closed, yet he sensed a wildness in her, a hunger, an eagerness.

Had she been anyone but Miranda, he would have stripped down and made short work of his own satisfaction. But this was Miranda. This was the wedding night they should have had in Scotland. He refused to look too closely at his reasons for wanting her pleasure even more than his own.

He cupped her breasts in his hands, marveling at the silken smoothness of her skin. Bending forward with exquisite restraint and care, he kissed one breast, then the other, his tongue fondling her until he felt her fingers dig into his shoulder, just above his healing wound. *Ah, harder, love,* he urged her silently. *Let out the wildness.*

His hand drifted down, parting her thighs and the dark nest of curls, and then her woman's flesh. He kissed her mouth and pulled back, watching while his hand caressed her, round and round. She wore a look of startlement, of anticipation, her lips moist and swollen from his kisses.

This was Lucas's whore, Ian told himself, trying to fix the idea in his mind. Yet even as he thought it, tried to use it to maintain his detachment, he knew he was wrong. He cupped her in his hand, his fingers finding a spot that made her catch her breath.

"Ian!"

"Aye, love, what is it?"

"I'm afraid. . . ."

He stopped immediately. The last thing he wanted was to scare her. "Afraid," he repeated.

"If I used to know how to do this before, it's one of the things I've forgotten."

He couldn't help smiling. God help him, he could not. She wasn't Lucas's whore; she never had been.

Innocence shone like a beacon from her velvety brown eyes.

"Do you want to go back to your room?" he asked.

"You're jesting, aren't you?"

His desire was growing painful by now. "Actually, I'm not. I won't make you do anything you don't want to do, Miranda."

"But you said once you started, you wouldn't be able to stop."

"That's my strutting male bravado talking." He kissed her lightly on the brow, though every movement was painful, every breath he took filled with the essence of her. "The truth is, I wouldna hurt you, Miranda. Nor even cause you discomfort."

"Well, you haven't done either."

Yet, he thought grimly.

"So go on," she said.

"Go on," he repeated, a slow burn rekindling in his loins.

"With what you were just doing."

His hand caressed her breasts, then slid downward. "With that?"

"Yes."

"And . . . that?"

She gasped. "Oh, yes."

He bit lightly at her earlobe and tried something else. "And what about that, love?"

"Yes, that, too."

He felt her wonderment as if it were his own. He took off his shirt and let her small, deft hands drift over him.

"You have a lot of scars," she whispered.

He skimmed one hand down her bare torso and cupped her hip. "You have none."

"You were in the wars."

He did not ask how she knew. He did not want to find out, not now. "Aye."

"Did you ever tell me about it?"

"Nay."

"Will you one day?"

"Perhaps. But not now." He had to stifle a groan in his throat. "Right now, we're busy."

"We are, aren't we?" She leaned forward, placed a soft, shy kiss on his throat, and let her mouth trail down his chest.

Lucas, you fool, Ian thought. How in God's name could you fail to hold her?

Then he banished all thoughts of his rival. It was as if the world had shrunk to the tiny area illuminated by the candle on the mantelpiece. Everything began with the woman in his arms and ended at the edge of light. There was nothing but the two of them, and he was filled with the need to bring her pleasure.

She was not bashful, but inquisitive and increasingly passionate. He had, Ian realized with a start, won her trust, at least in this arena. She wanted him and saw no point in being coy about it. When he took off the rest of his clothes and lowered himself to the chaise, hovering above her, she subjected him to a brief, frank assessment, then looked up into his face.

"Oh, my," was all she said.

Simple words, but delivered in that tone of voice, it was the most lavish compliment a man could receive.

"Aye, yours." He brought his arm around behind her and lifted her against him. She came willingly, arching with supple grace, her hand finding him and setting fire to the last reserves of his control.

"Put your legs around me, love," he whispered in her ear. "Aye, like that. Are you comfortable?" He almost trembled with the effort of holding himself back.

"Actually, yes," she said with a smile in her voice. She rocked her hips a little. "Yes."

He kissed her and parted her with his hand, his tongue in her mouth echoing the movements of his fingers until he could wait no longer. With excruciating slowness, he sank into her, making himself wait, terrified by the idea of hurting a woman who was supposed to mean nothing to him.

It was she who grew impatient. Her legs tightened and she tilted up, her hands pressing him closer, closer, and then a long sigh hissed from her when they were fully joined at last.

He was not surprised to find that she was a virgin. He had failed to fool himself into believing she was Lucas's harlot; that had simply been a way to keep himself from falling in love with her. Now what excuse would he use?

"Ah, Ian," she said in a quavering voice. "That is—" She broke off.

"What?" he prompted, thinking she would tell him it hurt, that she wanted to stop. He had suffered tortures in his life, but none so punishing as that.

"That is exactly what my body craves every time I look at you."

Her stark honesty torched his blood even as it broke his heart. He was stealing her virtue from her, stealing her past, making it into something it wasn't.

"I want you to like this, Miranda," he whispered, starting to move. "I want to bring you joy."

"Ian?"

"Aye?" He could barely speak now; their bodies were joined, and the very idea of being one with her consumed him utterly.

"It's working."

"What's working?"

"The joy."

He fused his mouth down upon hers then, silencing her so that her body could know the truth of what he felt for her, so his mouth would not have to utter any more lies. Like this, making love to her, making both of their bodies sing like violins—that was his truth. It was the only way he could be honest with her—here, in the bedchamber, speaking not in words but with his heart.

Sensation crescendoed, building inside him, filling his chest until he couldn't breathe. Beneath him, Miranda was flushed, her skin damp and silky, her hungry lips clinging to his as her legs tightened.

All at once she pulled her mouth back from his. Her eyes flew open, and she gasped out his name again and again. Her soft pulsations drew from Ian the most exquisite climax he had ever experienced. A soaring exultation engulfed him, and then he shuddered downward, wanting to cover her like a blanket.

She was still saying his name, but her gasps had subsided to a purr of contentment. Her mouth curved in a smile that was both sweet and knowing.

He settled beside her, stretching out full length on the narrow chaise and propping himself on one elbow so he could look at her. The warm summer breeze wafted in through an open window, bringing with it the flower scents from the garden.

"It's late," he said at last.

"Yes."

"Perhaps we should go to bed."

"Do you want me to go back to my room?"

He wanted to scream *No!*, to forbid her to leave his side, but he forced himself to say calmly, "The handfast marriage is legal. You've done nothing wrong, Miranda."

"It could be awkward if we suddenly started behaving like husband and wife," she said.

"So for now . . ."

"For now perhaps it is best we leave things as they are." She laughed softly. "Which is awkward enough, but there you are."

"You're off to your bed, then." He was curiously disappointed. It was a deliciously appealing idea, spending the night sleeping, curled around her.

"Am I?" she asked.

"You should be."

She stretched with a slow, indulgent moan, rubbing against him sensuously. "Oh, very well. I know when I'm not wanted."

"Minx. You're going to make me say it, aren't you?"

"Say what?" She regarded him with round-eyed innocence.

"That I want you here with me all night." *Every night,* said a voice in his head. *Until the end of time.*

"And do you?"

With a fierce laugh he turned so that he was above her once more, and he entered her with no preparation other than the love they had just made. Her eyes flew open wider than ever, then drifted half shut.

"I do, Miranda," he growled. "I do want you here."

He made love to her all over again. And again. At some point he realized he should send her away to her bed, but selfishly he stole the night from her, holding her there, watching her wonder and passion grow with each passing moment.

The most dangerous thing about her, Ian knew, was her innocence. It was her innocence that posed the greatest threat to a jaded heart like his.

14

Mad, bad, and dangerous to know.
—Lady Caroline Lamb

How did one pretend that one's life had not changed, when in fact a blossoming had occurred deep in her soul? Miranda wondered as she made her way to breakfast the next day. How would she act in front of Frances and Lucas? *Could* she ever again behave like a virgin?

She paused on the marble staircase, her hand resting lightly on the rail, and drew a deep breath. It was going to be awkward, just as she and Ian had predicted the night before. But the night before, they had laughed away their hesitation with the determined eagerness of two people engulfed by passion.

Engulfed. That was what he had done to her. He had not simply made her his. Had not simply made love to her, mated with her. He had engulfed her. Taken her entire being into himself, and she had emerged like a butterfly from a chrysalis.

It was the most wonderful, most frightening thing that had ever happened to her.

At least she *thought* so. Perhaps other delights lurked in her memory. Other kinds of pleasures. But if that were true, why did she still fear to recall the past?

She stood for a few more moments, wondering what remembrances hid inside her, waiting to leap out like ghosts. Why didn't she want to recall each separate precious moment she and Ian had spent together?

She shivered despite the warmth of the day. When she closed her eyes, she could still feel him engulfing her. Could still smell his scent, taste him, know the silky texture of his tanned flesh over firm muscle, hear the sound of his low laughter in her ear.

Her body responded as if he had caressed her; she caught her breath and felt a little flood of warmth that made her knees go weak. "Unbelievable," she whispered, infuriated by her lack of control over her thoughts or emotions. Determinedly she let go of the banister and walked down the stairs.

The moment she stepped into the dining room, her fears became real. Lucas looked up at her with the wounded bewilderment of an injured stag, while Frances regarded her with canny feminine understanding.

Miranda couldn't decide whether to bluff her way out of the situation or to concede defeat.

She blew out a sigh. "Lying takes too much energy," she said, seating herself and pouring coffee. She added a generous helping of cream to the cup and took a sip. "Was it Yvette who told you?"

She thought of the maid, pretty Yvette, who was so solicitous yet so oddly watchful.

Lucas steepled his fingers together over his untouched plate of eggs and rashers. "Thank you for not lying to me," he said. "Thank you, at least, for that."

The tone of his voice was like an arrow to her heart. She had hurt him. He had been nothing but kind and protective, patient and understanding. He maintained that he loved her. And she had hurt him.

"Lucas—"

"Oh, for heaven's sake." Frances dropped her napkin on the table. "She's married to MacVane, after all."

Lucas swallowed hard. His hand, icy cold, found Miranda's. "What disturbs me the most is that there is *nothing* in your eyes when you look at me. Not even the faintest echo of what I saw when you were . . . yourself. When you were mine. It's as if he's completely taken you over. Not just your heart and your mind, but your very soul."

Miranda shivered again. *Engulfed her.* She turned away and served herself rashers and eggs from the sideboard. "All I know is that I wed him willingly. If I discover I was wrong . . ." She could not finish.

"When you do, I pity you," he said softly. "For then it may be too late for us." He turned his gaze out the window. "It might already be too late."

"Come now, let's not get maudlin, at least not until I've had my coffee," Frances said. Yet there was a telltale brightness in her eyes.

Miranda had no appetite, but she picked up a spoon and reached for the crystal bowl of jam. Her hand shook, and her head began to throb. The cut crystal seemed to slice into her hand, and she flung the bowl away, shattering it on the floor.

An explosion detonated in her head. Thoughts

formed like the breaking of the crystal, but in reverse, the pieces coming back together, reshaping themselves into something familiar.

She was hit by wave after wave of images, memories of the past, all jumbled up, making no sense yet making perfect sense.

Try the plum preserves, sweetheart, said her father's kindly, distracted voice. *It was always your mother's favorite.*

Miranda's breath came quickly, urgently. She felt a hand on her shoulder, heard Frances snap out an order to a servant, heard the clink of glass as someone poured water and held the cup to her lips.

She drank and opened her eyes. Frances peered at her inquisitively. "Well?"

"My father. I remember . . ."

Lucas snatched up her hand again. "And me? Is it clear now, my darling? Do you remember me?"

His certainty that she should recall him after being with Ian all night disturbed her. She shook her head. "This is about my father. I know where he might have gone."

"Where?" Frances asked, an edge of urgency in her voice.

"I can see it, can picture it," Miranda said, "but I can't recall where it is." She removed her hand from Lucas's grip again and rubbed her temples. "An old building, some sort of tower. Ancient stone, crumbling mortar. A well sweep in the yard. Larkspur blooming at the gate. Rolling hills behind, grazing sheep, very few trees."

"You just described half of England," Frances said.

"Somewhere at the seaside?" Lucas asked.

"No, but there's a pond or lake or something—"

He jumped up. "I've got to go out."

Miranda stood, too, swaying. "Wait. If you know something about this—"

"I may. And I may not. But if I do, it'll prove once and for all that I am the man you knew before you lost your memory. Not Ian MacVane."

He dashed out as Ian walked in, his hair damp from his morning ablutions. He smelled of soap and clean laundry, and he was whistling a tune.

"Ladies," he said, bowing from the waist. "Where was Lord Unlucky going in such a hurry?"

"Oh, spare us, MacVane," Frances said.

He winked at Miranda. An intimate knowledge sparkled in that wink. "Cheerful, isn't she?"

"Spare us," Miranda echoed. By light of day, the deep intimacies they had shared made her cheeks flame. She had cried out his name in ecstasy, had begged him to touch her in places for which she had no name, had boldly explored his body with her hands and mouth. Worst of all, she wanted it again.

He went to the sideboard and loaded a plate with food. "I consider myself a learned man," he said over his shoulder. "There was a time in my life when I was confined for months on shipboard, and there was naught to do but read books." He seated himself, smiled his thanks to the maid who poured his coffee. "But not a single one of the books I read during that time or ever since managed to answer the most baffling question that has ever occurred to man." He paused and sipped his coffee. "What do women want?"

Miranda glared at him. "We are not amused."

"She remembered," said Frances.

Ian froze, his fork poised above his plate. Miranda thought she saw the color drain from his face, but she couldn't be certain, for the morning light was so bright that it formed a halo around his devilishly dark hair. Then he attacked his breakfast with great gusto.

"Indeed," he said. His charm was as smooth as new satin gliding over marble. "And can you tell us, darling, what it is you remember?"

She stared at him for a moment. What was he saying, between the charming smiles and the heated glances? That he expected her to recall that she was wildly and passionately in love with him? Or that before the explosion, she had never seen him in her life? If only she could be sure . . .

Then she pictured a kindly, distracted man with a face that was too handsome for his own good, and her stomach churned with urgency. She felt guilty thinking of her own romantic problems when her father might be in danger, when he needed help.

"It's about my father," she said in a rush. She closed her eyes and fought back tears. "I can picture him, every detail of his appearance. I can hear his voice. I can feel—" She broke off, bit her lip.

"Feel what?" Ian prodded.

She opened her eyes, forced herself to go on. "Feel . . . his love for me." Then the tears spilled out, and she made no move to check them. "Oh, God. I was so afraid that there was no one in the past, that no one loved me. But my father did. As imperfect as my recollection is, I know that much, at least."

"Is there anything more?" Ian asked. He exchanged a look with Frances.

Tears blurred Miranda's vision. She buried her face in her hands.

"Miranda." His voice, with its gentle burr, soothed her. His hands covered hers, and he brought their joined hands down, uncovering her face. "What more do you remember?"

"It wasn't about you." She was surprised to feel faint relief at the thought. Her grief faded to concern and a deep frustration. "But about a place that I know. A stone tower and a desolate moor."

At Ian's coaxing, she explained about the old building, the garden, and the well sweep. Frances called for paper and ink, and Miranda tried to sketch the images from her head.

Ian held out the drawing, turning it this way and that. "Thomas Lawrence has nothing to fear from you," he said with a gentle wink in her direction. "This looks to me like a peel tower. That would mean it's situated in the Borders of Scotland."

"Perhaps. No," she said, not pausing to question where her conviction came from. "It's like a peel tower, but it lacks the ground fortifications. And the hills are more like those of the Cotswolds, or the West Country. Gentler, perhaps."

He studied the picture. "What's this at the edge?"

She shrugged. "A signpost or a milestone."

Frances leaned her elbows on the table. "A signpost would tell us exactly what we wanted to know. Look, Miranda. Here's the beginnings of the letter *H*, and then you reached the edge of the paper."

Miranda looked and looked. She touched the nib of her pen to the letter. Think think think. *Where are you, Papa?*

"H. What begins with H? Hatfield," she said. "Hackforth, Hallifax, Hagworthingham."

"Hever, Humblestone," Frances guessed.

"Honeybourne," Ian added. "Horncastle, Hildersley. This is getting us nowhere."

Frustrated, Miranda twirled the tip of her quill in the ink and sketched idly while she sank deep into thought. *H. High.* Unwittingly she had finished the word, her writing drifting off the page and onto the snowy tablecloth. She stared at it, knowing she should apologize for ruining the linen but struck mute by the thoughts suddenly swirling in her head.

High. High Wybourne.

Miranda, he's a danger to you. He'll try to convince you otherwise, but you must not trust him. Must never, ever trust him. Her father's voice whispered in her mind.

She dropped the quill as if it had burned her and shot up from the table. In seconds Ian was at her side. "You've gone pale as whey. What is it?"

She nearly let the entire story tumble out, but then she stopped herself.

Perhaps her father had been warning her about Ian. The thought made her feel ill. Last night he had stolen her very soul, and he had not even had to win her trust in order to do it.

She kept thinking of Lucas's face when she had come down to breakfast. His bleak disappointment. His utter certainty that when she remembered, she would remember *him*.

"I feel quite unwell, all of a sudden," she said. "I think I'd like to go to my room and lie down."

"Of course, love." He escorted her to the stairs. "I'm not surprised you're worn out."

"I can manage on my own," she said.

He cradled her cheek in his hand, and she felt again the tenderness he seemed to reserve solely for her. And she remembered, vividly, everything he had done to her last night. Had done with her. All the emotion, all the ecstasy and passion he had coaxed from her. Had it been a lie, then? Was it possible to find such perfect joy in the arms of a man who could deceive her without blinking?

"Miranda," he said, "are you having regrets, lass?"

"Are you?"

"Nay."

She leaned her cheek into his palm, wishing his warmth were something she could believe in. "Ah, Ian. I won't lie to you, either. I don't know."

"Either?"

She forced herself to hold his gaze. "I didn't lie to Lucas."

"You *told* him?" Ian took his hand away and raked it through his hair. "Jesus—"

"Of course not." She put her foot on the first step. "I didn't have to."

He muttered something in Gaelic.

"I'm not ashamed of what we did," she declared. Then she added with tears thickening her throat, "I just don't know if I can trust you."

He grasped her shoulders. "What did you feel, lass? Can you trust that?"

She would not let herself answer. She pulled away from him and started up the stairs. "I must go to my room." She would not let herself look back at Ian, would not let herself see the shape of his beautiful mouth and remember his rough, evocative kisses.

Once she found the refuge of her chambers, she leaned back against the door.

"Mademoiselle needs something?" asked Yvette, bustling in and tilting her head to one side.

Miranda hesitated. She could not afford to trust anyone now. "I'm fine, Yvette. Perhaps you could take Macbeth to one of the footmen for a run, so that I can rest."

She waited for the maid to leave, and then she hastened down the back stairs. She had to make this all-important quest alone.

*   *   *

"Gone!" roared Lucas, startling the sweating horse beneath him. The animal sidled, and savagely he dragged back the reins to steady it. "What the hell do you mean, she's gone?"

Ian sat his own horse, regarding Lucas with an icy calm he did not feel. He had ridden hard to Blackfriars, where Miranda and her father had once shared a shabby flat, thinking to find a clue about Gideon's country place. Instead, in the roadway outside the house, he had encountered Lucas.

To make matters worse, Lucas was wearing a sword. A rapier, designed for dueling.

"To my knowledge," Ian said easily, "there is only one way to interpret the phrase. She's gone. Fled to parts unknown. Decamped."

Lucas, whose golden hair had blown askew from a fast and furious ride, struggled visibly for self-control. "And how, pray, did you manage to lose her?"

"Damn it, man, she's not a rabbit's foot I keep in my pocket."

"So she fled you." Grim satisfaction grated in Lucas's voice. "It's because her memory came back, isn't it?"

Ian refused to flinch. He refused to admit that Lucas might have guessed correctly. He said nothing.

Lucas plunged on. "She discovered that you've been lying to her all along, that she never knew you—"

"Positive, aren't we, my lord?" Ian asked with an ironic twist to his mouth.

Lucas held his reins in a death grip. "She never knew you. It was *me* she knew, *me* she loved."

"Indeed. Yet you claim you had no friends in

common. You did not even dare to tell your family about her." Ian watched the color drain from Lucas's face. He should pity the man, but instead he twisted the knife. "Perhaps you did know Miranda; I'll allow you that. But she spoke of you not at all, my lord."

"Not to you, she didn't. She never spoke of you either, MacVane."

Ian lifted one black eyebrow. "Are you quite sure? Were you with her every single waking moment?"

The question leeched the last of the color from Lucas's normally ruddy face.

Touché, MacVane, Ian said to himself. He had managed to plant a seed of uncertainty in Lucas's mind. "No doubt you amused her, Lisle," he said in a bland voice, "but which of us did she turn to last night?"

With an ominous whisper of steel, Lucas drew his sword. "I'll send you to hell for that, you philandering Scottish bastard."

Ian pretended to have no reaction to the blatant provocation, though his every sense went on alert. The blank windows and smoke-blackened façades of Blackfriars brooded indifferently at them. There was no foot traffic in the street. No one stood about to observe them.

"That I am Scottish, there is no doubt," he said easily. "That I am lying is likely, for men of our station lie constantly for our own purposes, do we not? That I am a bastard, my lord, is an insult I might decide I cannot tolerate." He stroked his chin, pretending to think hard, when in fact he was thinking of the throwing dagger concealed in his boot cuff. In seconds he could deliver a mortal wound to Lucas Chesney, could do it with the icy dispatch of a mercenary.

He knew this without vanity or even any sort of satisfaction. Life had taught him to be swift and ruthless. If he left His Lofty Lordship bleeding on the ground, he could explain his way out of it. Lord knew he had done so before.

"I've decided to let you live," he said at last, "but pray, put away your sword. Swaggering bravado annoys me."

Lucas looked nonplussed. "You're refusing my challenge?"

"Do you want to go through that again?"

Lucas swore and sheathed his rapier. Ian tried not to smile. Under different circumstances, he and the pretty viscount might be friends. It was easy to see why Frances was smitten with him. He had the perfect, chiseled looks so favored by the *ton,* manners courtly enough to please the most exacting *maman,* and a lithe grace of movement that could ruffle the petticoats of even the most demanding of debutantes.

He tried a different tack. "What are you doing here, Lisle?"

"The same thing you are. Trying to find answers."

"Do you know where Gideon Stonecypher's country residence is?"

Lisle sniffed. "If I knew, I would not be here." He dismounted and walked up the steps to the apartment.

Ian considered for a moment, then followed. "Your maid is playing informer," he said.

"Yvette? I haven't the faintest idea what you mean."

"Oh, do tell." Ian took out the note he had seized from the tearful maid earlier.

Lucas paused on the stair and studied it. "Gibberish. I haven't a clue what it says."

Ian believed him. It was a risk, aye, but he'd find out soon enough if Lucas was in on the conspiracy. "It's in cipher," he said. "And no, it does not say where Miranda went. She didn't tell the maid." Wise girl. What she lacked in memory she made up for in common sense. Yvette had pleaded ignorance about the origin of the note.

Methodically he and Lucas began to sort through the apartment. The place had barely been tidied up after the initial horrible discovery of Midge's body and the ransacking. Stacks of books and papers remained on every surface.

Miranda's needlework still lay on the arm of a chair. "One father is more than a hundred schoolmasters," read the stitching.

He felt a bitter twist of guilt. She was a woman—a frightened, confused woman—yet they had been treating her like a puzzle to be pieced together. Ah, she was so much more than that. So very much more.

He tried to picture her here, a homey scene, Miranda sitting bent over her needlework while she and her father debated—

Ian froze. His gaze locked on the needlework sample. The spray of forget-me-nots encircled a scene that was eerily familiar. A tower house. Hills rising behind it. The tribute to her father stitched in blue silk floss.

And in the bottom corner, in tiny letters formed with a single strand of black, she had stitched the words *H. Wybourne, 19 April 1814.*

High Wybourne. That was where she had gone.

Straight into the belly of the beast, if his instincts were correct.

Ian looked at Lucas, who was holding a blue knitted shawl, a look of melancholy on his face. Though hopeless against Ian in a duel of swords or pistols, he was still quick and skilled enough to be of some use.

"Come along, if you've a mind," Ian said simply. "But remember, I give the orders."

"Stop here, please." Miranda leaned forward and spoke to the driver of the tilbury gig.

"It's the middle of the woods, miss," he said, scowling beneath the brim of a rough brown cap.

She sighed and parted with yet another coin from the fast-dwindling supply in her reticule. A few days earlier, Frances had insisted on giving her a purse of coins, "just in case." In case of what, Lady Frances had not said, and Miranda had not been inclined to ask.

"Can you take the rig off the road, into that grove of trees?" She pointed.

He pocketed the coin and clucked to the horse. Evening sunlight slanted down between the leaves, creating a fiery beauty she had no will to admire.

"I need you to wait for me," she said. "Please. That's all I ask."

He eyed the reticule tied at her waist. She set her jaw but parted with another coin. He nodded grumpily and drew his hat down over his eyes. "Aye, then."

Though she didn't trust him, Miranda could delay no longer. She gathered her plain shawl around her shoulders, retied her bonnet, and climbed down. She had not told the driver what she had seen through a break in the trees.

A tall building of old stone and crumbling mortar. Larkspur blooming riotously along a low fence. A well sweep in the yard. A swift-flowing bourn and hills in the distance. A signpost at the head of the deeply rutted road.

It was exactly the place from her vision, right here on the outskirts of High Wybourne.

Which proved that it had not been a vision at all, but a memory.

She lifted her skirts away from the brambles that tore at the hem and hurried down through the woods. She stayed in the shadows, hanging back, uncertain how to proceed.

The place was strange to her, though she knew it had been a part of her life. She and her father used to come here to—

To what? She frowned, pressing her thumbs to her temples as if to squeeze out the memories.

And why would her father come here? If he was here at all. If someone had ransacked their flat in London, had murdered their servant, had left him for dead in the river, why would he come openly to a place where he might be caught again?

A coldness seized her stomach. To protect a secret. Or to protect *her*.

There was no reason, she reflected, that she should not march up to the door and walk in. No reason except a sense of caution she had learned from Ian. So she waited, shivering in the gloom, as the darkness deepened. A black shape swooped over her, and she started, then leaned limply against a tree trunk when she realized the shadow was only an owl.

A single window, low in the tower, was lit with a golden glow. Someone was there!

Dusk. It was time for her to go forward, to find her father. She put her hand on the top of the gate. She remembered a visitor, a dark-haired, smiling man stepping through, giving Papa a happy greeting. She had disliked the narrow-faced stranger on sight.

Why? *Why?*

Keeping to the deep shadows that fringed the garden, she made her way to the window. Voices drifted, muffled by the glass. She could not see inside, for the window was set too high. She pressed closer to hear.

"What does this mean here?" asked a weary, harassed-sounding voice. "These Greek squiggles."

"It has to do with the trajectory. I've explained it a dozen times."

Papa's voice! He was alive! She wanted to shout with gladness, but not yet. Not yet.

"I need to know just how to calculate it. Perhaps your pretty daughter can elaborate, Gideon."

Miranda's blood ran cold. In her mind, an equation blossomed like a sudden inspiration. Mathematical formulae often ran through her head, and she wasn't certain why.

"She knows nothing, I tell you," her father said.

He was lying. Lying in order to protect her.

"She is your soft spot, Gideon. If not for that sketch you placed in the *Times,* we never would have learned that you'd survived." His voice had an accent. Vaguely French, but with a different inflection.

Shaking, Miranda leaned against the building. The stones still held some of the sun's warmth, but she could not stop trembling. Her head throbbed with hammer blows of memory.

The foreigner was questioning him about the rocket. The Stonecypher missile, to be precise. What a lark it had been at first, she remembered, the memories rushing through her like a fever. To take the Congreve rocket, improve on it, make it useful for something more than noise. She had thought, naively, that a missile that could be aimed would prove a boon to miners, allowing them to blast from afar without endangering lives.

But of course, the men who wanted the plans for the rocket were not miners.

Suppressing a whimper of horror, she slid down the wall into the grass, where the dew was beginning to gather. Here was a piece of memory that came back to her almost whole, as if it had simply been waiting for her to bring it out.

You don't know this, her father had exhorted her, whispering in the dark on the night they had been taken. Dragged off to a dark place.

She stifled a hiccup of hysterical laughter. She had lost her memory because her father had ordered it. Now his life depended on her recalling the complicated formula.

Once he had unveiled the Stonecypher design, Gideon had at last gained notoriety as a natural philosopher. After years of inventions going awry, of being the laughingstock of the scientific community, he had come up with a design so singular that his name was bound to live in infamy.

Gideon's model had one asset that could change the face of war. The rockets could be aimed at a target.

Not simply pointed in a vague direction, but aimed along a trajectory. Congreve rockets had been used for a few years, but they were unpredictable, more useful in creating fear and confusion during battle than in destroying a given target.

Neither Gideon nor Miranda had thought much about the use of them. They had simply worked together on a puzzle, just as they had on the weather instruments and the aerial balloon designs. Oh, God, she thought. The balloon, too. There was something about the balloon. . . .

Military minds had seized upon their ideas. She remembered the day the first request had arrived—a parchment dotted with official stamps and signatures.

Characteristically, Gideon had ignored it. And all the ones that came after it. Then someone had come who had refused to take no for an answer.

Miranda heard a thud and a faint moan from her father. Anger rose up like a fountain of fire inside her. How many times would they try to pry the formula out of him?

How long before he died to protect her?

Yes, her. The design was her doing. Her invention, not Gideon's. She had guarded his secret because she loved him. She wanted him to have the prestige he craved.

But now her noble gesture was a threat to her father.

Miranda had come a long way from the frightened, confused creature in the midst of a warehouse fire. She had learned to confront danger squarely and unflinchingly. To embrace each moment, to live inside it, to come out whole on the other side of peril.

Fear knocked at her rib cage as she crept toward the door of the tower house. It was a strengthening fear. One that made her swifter. Smarter. Stronger.

She would find a way to recuse her father. At the moment, her only weapon was the element of surprise. But memories were returning quickly to her. She recalled another entrance to the tower house, a low door in the back.

She hesitated. The voices inside the house had fallen silent. It was too quiet, almost as if—

Too late, she heard the rustling footsteps and

harsh breath of the approaching man. Like a steel talon, a hand closed around her wrist. "I've been hoping you would pay us a visit," the foreigner said.

Miranda screamed as he dragged her into the house, but the scream died when she saw her father.

Gideon was slumped in a chair.

Miranda ran to him.

"No," Gideon moaned. "Ah, Mindy, no."

She forced herself to look at their captor—narrow face, dark hair, smirking mouth, deceptively slim build. A tall man, he was wearing black gloves worn through at the knuckles. "You're wasting your time," she told him. "He does not know the formula."

"How appropriate." The man's voice was surprisingly melodious, as if he were at a social gathering. "The inventor of the Stonecypher missile does not know the formula."

"On the contrary, she does," Miranda countered.

He lifted an eyebrow over a hard, assessing brown eye. "She. You mean you."

Gideon muttered, "She knows nothing. Nothing."

She fought a wave of forgetfulness. That was the phrase he had used to make her forget in the first place, and just hearing the words made her want to fall into a comfortable oblivion. Instead she said, "I know exactly what you're looking for. And I'm prepared to give it to you. But first, you must meet *my* demands."

With a graceful swoop of his lithe body, the man moved behind Gideon. He plunged his hand into Gideon's abundant white hair and pulled his head back, baring his neck.

A razor-sharp knife touched her father's neck.

"Your demands?" the man asked. "I'm sorry, my dear. Perhaps I didn't hear you correctly."

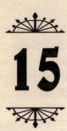

15

I remember, I remember
The house where I was born,
The little window where the sun
Came peeping in at morn.
                    —Thomas Hood,
                    I Remember, I Remember

A scream built in her throat. She ground her teeth together to keep the sound in. She prayed her terror was not etched on her face and remembered one of the most important lessons Ian had taught her: *Never show that you're afraid.*

The thin man seemed to expect her to know him. She must have known him in the past, possibly when she, too, was his prisoner.

"Miranda, get away, now!" Gideon said through chattering teeth. "Duchesne won't spare me no matter what you tell hi—"

The man called Duchesne backhanded Gideon across the mouth. Her father spat blood and slumped forward, coughing. It took all of her strength not to go to him, not to give vent to the scream clawing at her throat.

And inside her, something extraordinary was happening. Hate and fear and rage built like a volcano about to erupt. She did not remember this man, this Duchesne, but she remembered the hatred he inspired in her.

Use it, Miranda. Don't let the anger use you.

"When you stop tormenting a helpless man and start acting like an adult," she said, "I might be ready to talk to you." Her voice was as hard as coins dropped into an icy well.

Duchesne looked startled. Even Gideon blinked in surprise, seeming to forget the blood dripping from his mouth onto his shirt. Apparently the old Miranda had lacked the gift of cold command.

Duchesne's puzzlement lasted only seconds. "Let us see if we understand each other. You claim you have what I want. I have what you want." He glanced down at the knife at Gideon's throat. "Your father's life. So do we have a trade?"

"Absolutely." She still had utterly no idea what the formula was. Yet. She went to the table. When she looked down, years-old memories seized her.

I've met a most interesting man, poppet. He is an expert at ciphers and signaling. Monsieur Duchesne, lately arrived from Switzerland. . . .

So that was how Duchesne had insinuated himself into their lives. Perhaps he had, at one time, been the scholar he claimed to be and only recently had turned to the politics of empire.

Her hand was steady as she reached for a quill, dipped it in thick black ink, and began scribbling on a broad sheet of foolscap.

"Here you are," she said over her shoulder. "This is how you calculate the trajectory of a rocket." Her hand worked independently, as if her fingers, not her brain, held the knowledge. Before her eyes appeared long strings of equations, elegant and sophisticated, and she was astounded to realize they were products of her own mind. Oh, Lord, could she think her way out of this?

The figures on the page looked crisp and neat. "This *is* what you wanted, is it not?" she murmured.

"What mischief are you about?" Duchesne edged away from Gideon to peer over Miranda's shoulder.

The back of her neck tingled like the kiss of heat lightning. She watched her hand reach down as if to dip the quill. In one swift movement, she grabbed the inkpot and spun around, flinging the ink in his face, across his eyes.

The thick, midnight liquid blinded him. He stumbled and fell forward. He swore in French and flailed his arms, the knife catching in the fabric of her cloak.

She snatched up a stool and brought it down on his head, wincing when the wood splintered. He reached out, groping the air with his stained hands. The stool had barely slowed him. Damn! The Punch shows in Hyde Park made it look so easy to knock someone silly with a stick of wood.

Papa, can we stay? Can we stay and see the puppets? A memory flashed, his tall boots and her grubby hand clinging to his.

Ah, Mindy. I've not even ha'pence for admittance.
Are we poor, then, Papa?
Sometimes I think we are.
I'll take care of you, Papa. We'll not be poor when I'm big enough to take care of you.

Rage and fear came back, stirring up the well of strength and conviction inside her. With the cold-blooded aim of a soldier, she brought the leg of the stool down on his arm, hearing a dull snap as both wood and bone broke.

Duchesne screamed. The knife skittered across the floor, and Gideon stopped it with his foot. The foreigner lunged for her, roaring like a mad animal, and she jumped back. She could hear Gideon sawing at the ropes that bound him.

A moment later her father stumbled toward the door. "The key," he said, gasping.

Miranda remembered. Both she and her father were constantly misplacing their latchkeys. They always kept one over the lintel. She raced ahead of him, retrieved the key from the dusty shelf above the door, and pushed Gideon out into the night.

Duchesne stumbled toward them, still blinded and groping wildly. She slammed the door in his ink-blackened face and pulled on the handle with all her might while she twisted the key. Then, even as the sound of breaking glass shattered the night, she grabbed her father by the hand.

"Can you run?" she asked.

"Yes, by God, at least for a while."

A glance over her shoulder confirmed her fears. Duchesne had hurled the stool through the window and was climbing out. He moved clumsily, favoring his injured arm.

"I have a gig waiting in the woods," she said to her father. "Can you make it?"

"Aye." He walked with a limp. "Dear God, Miranda, I've never seen you like that. You were quite amazing. A Valkyrie. An Amazon! What's come over you?"

"You have no idea," she said between her chattering teeth. She pulled him up the dark slope toward the woods, praying they could outrun Duchesne. The forest was black; she could not see the branches that scratched her face and tore at her dress.

Moments later, she found the spot where she had left the driver. Empty. Ian's favorite word slipped out of her mouth.

"My, my," Gideon said. "I never realized you knew any curses but those in ancient Greek. What is the matter?"

Panic built in her chest. "Now we have no way to—" She broke off. There was a rustle somewhere in the underbrush.

Duchesne. He must be gaining on them.

She could not see her father, but she did not have to in order to know that he was too weak, too badly injured, to go farther. She would have to stand and fight. At least Duchesne had a broken arm.

He also had a dagger and a good, strong arm. And a cold-blooded mission.

The rustling grew louder. Then, even before she could scream, a shadow detached itself from the blackness and leaped. Miranda drew in a breath to scream.

A gloved hand clamped over her mouth.

Ian felt her soft, struggling body beneath him, and in the dark he gave a wolfish grin. What a sick mind he had, to think of bedding Miranda when they were out in the wilderness with God knew who after them.

"Steady now, lass," he whispered into her ear. "It's only me. It's Ian."

She fell still. He imagined a sweet smile of relief on her face, a word of gratitude on her lips. He lifted his hand from her mouth and his weight from her body.

"You bloody jackanapes," she said in a harsh whisper, hitting out at him, catching him on the chest. "You scared the last of my wits out of me!"

"I rather like you witless."

She made a sound of disgust. "I so admire your coolness while in peril. Father? Are you all right, Papa?"

"He is fine." Lucas's flat, aristocratic voice whispered across the clearing.

"Never better," said the weary voice of an older man.

Ian froze. The father. Would he be able to identify Lucas? Would Gideon Stonecypher point the finger of accusation at Ian and declare him an imposter?

He groped in the dark to help Miranda to her feet. She pulled away and staggered up.

A crashing sounded, an angry noise, like that made by a wounded stag or a wild boar. Ian saw a shadow in the dense trees, moving swiftly. The blood hummed in his veins, and his senses tingled with alertness.

There was an edge to mortal danger that sometimes felt oddly like pleasure.

He had already decided not to kill the assailant, for he would need to extract information from him.

He warned Lucas in a low whisper. "Don't shoot—"

There was a swift white flash followed by a thud and a groan. The stink of sulfur fogged the night air.

"Trigger-happy, aren't we?" Ian muttered. The brief illumination showed a cloaked figure fleeing on horseback. "So much for questioning that one."

"Perhaps he won't get far," Miranda said. "He's

got a broken arm, and I threw ink in his face." She sounded slightly dazed, yet more sure of herself than he had ever known her to be.

"His name is Duchesne," Gideon said. "Pierpont Duchesne."

"The shot didn't even faze him," Lucas said, sounding amazed.

Ian glowered in the dark. "You have much to learn about subtlety, my lord."

For Gideon's sake, they stopped at an inn for the night. Ian, who rarely went anywhere without a purse full of gold crowns, bought the best rooms in the house. Dressed in a long woolsey nightgown borrowed from the innkeeper, Gideon sat up in the bed, sipping mutton broth and looking bewildered.

"You lost your memory?" he asked Miranda.

She nodded. "That is the only way I know how to describe what happened. A few weeks ago, I found myself in an exploding warehouse along the Thames, and I had no idea who I was." She fished in her bodice, drew out the oval pendant. "The name 'Miranda' is engraved here. If not for that, I would not even have known my name."

"Then it worked!" Gideon said.

"What worked?"

"The mesmerism. It is more than a parlor trick. I was able to convince you to forget what you knew. Amazing."

"And do you know how to bring the memories back?" she asked.

He shook his head despondently. "Anton Mesmer was not a very good natural philosopher."

"What was it that I knew, Papa? What did you want me to forget?"

"You overheard them talking of their plan. They are in league with Bonaparte."

"Did you hear it, too?" Ian asked, tensing.

"They spoke in French." Gideon stared at Miranda. "Her French is fluent, and mine is not."

Ian watched the two of them, and his heart felt oddly small and tight. They were father and daughter. They should love each other. Instead she regarded Gideon as a polite stranger, and he looked back at her with the brightness of tears trembling in his eyes.

Lucas sat stiffly on a stool beside the bed. He'd had little to say. Ian guessed that he was still furious with himself for letting Duchesne escape.

Until Miranda remembered everything, they would never know Duchesne's role in recent events or even who his master was.

"They did not call each other by name," Gideon said. "Duchesne is the only one known to me. But . . ." He frowned, thinking hard.

"Any detail," Ian urged him. "The least matter could be important."

"One of them was known by a French moniker. Le Couleur. No, that's not right." Gideon set his jaw in concentration. "La Couleuvre."

The words seared into Ian like a heated brand. He moved not a muscle, but his gaze locked with Miranda's.

"La Couleuvre," she repeated, correcting Gideon's pronunciation. "The adder."

"Is that significant?" asked Lucas.

Red flashes of rage detonated in Ian's head, pounding at his temples. The adder. Mr. Adder. It was probably only coincidental, but it caused fifteen-year-old

wounds to reopen, to throb anew. After a long silence
he said, "We'll know more when we return to London."

Gideon nodded distractedly. He kept staring at
Miranda. "You are the same, yet different."

"What do you mean, Papa?"

"You used to hold yourself aloof, living more in
your mind than in the world. Now there's something
about you—a freshness, a vitality. You've changed so
much. Tell me everything. All that's befallen you."

In a quiet voice, Miranda told her father what had
happened. Or rather, she told him the least disturbing
version of what had happened. She left out the nightmare of Bedlam, the sea voyage to Scotland, the
handfast marriage.

Clever girl. Ian knew then exactly what was coming, and he braced himself. Miranda was going to ask
her father which man, Lucas or Ian, had been the one
she loved.

He heard a snapping sound and looked down. The
stoneware mug of ale he had been holding was broken. The pressure of his hand had crushed it. He
glanced up, saw the three of them staring at him.

"Clumsy of me," he muttered, bending to pick up
the pieces. "I'll just take these to the dustbin—"

"In a moment." Miranda spoke quietly, but with
conviction. "I want you"—she looked at Lucas—
"both of you present for this."

Lucas sat straighter on his stool. Ian's shoulders
tightened in defense, though he took pains to appear
relaxed, as if breaking a cup in his bare hands were an
everyday occurrence.

"Papa," Miranda said gently, "are you certain you
feel quite well enough to stay up and talk?"

Gideon gave a thin smile. "Believe me, Mindy,
after being Duchesne's prisoner, this is a pleasure."

She shifted nervously on the edge of the bed. "Papa, did I ever speak to you of a—of my personal life?"

He winked. "You pretended to have none. You pretended that your work was your life." His face sobered. "In truth, Miranda, you were never free with your feelings. There was . . . a coolness about you, a distance. My fault, of course, for dragging you across England like a piece of baggage. And I paid the price. I was never quite sure how you felt . . . about anything. Even about me."

She flushed and looked down at her fingers knotted in her lap. "What sort of person would be such a distant stranger to her own father?"

Ian felt her desperation. It was a struggle to sit by and watch her, knowing she hurt, wanting to comfort her. But he forced himself to wait while he pondered the changes in her. With him she had been unreserved, spontaneous, trusting. Too trusting.

"Oh," she said at last. "Then I suppose there's no point in pursuing this. It was a silly idea in the first place—"

"I said you never spoke to me of your personal affairs," Gideon cut in. "That doesn't mean I wasn't aware of them." With shaking hands, he set his soup bowl on the bedside table. "I lacked your mind for invention, for learning, Miranda. But not for the deep human understandings of the heart. That was *your* lack. And it was all my fault, God help me."

She gasped and stared at him. "What sort of person was I?"

Lucas started to say something, but Gideon waved him silent. "Forgive me," he said. "Miranda and I have private matters to discuss."

"Then you knew I was, er, involved?" she asked him.

"You were in love, my dear, and at great pains to hide it from me. I suppose you thought I'd be afraid you'd abandon me or some such nonsense. I was just waiting for you to tell me." Looking bleak, he shook back his long white hair. "I imagine I'd still be waiting. We simply didn't speak of matters of the heart. Ah, if only I'd paid more attention to you as a child."

She swallowed hard. "So I never told you who he was."

Ian felt like an intruder, watching father and daughter struggle through an estrangement that had clearly started long before she had lost her memory. He could tell Gideon was a man who revealed what was on his mind in his own time, and there would be no pushing him.

"You never did. Never told me a thing about him." Gideon glanced from Ian to Lucas, then back to Miranda. "So. Which one is he?"

Miranda's shoulders shook. At first Ian thought she had begun to weep, but then she threw back her head and laughed, long and loud. Lucas stiffened in shock, and Ian wanted to pound the disapproval from his face. No doubt the viscount did not believe a proper lady should show mirth so blatantly.

But it was laughter born of pain; Ian could see that. She was on the verge of hysteria.

"That's just the problem," she said to Gideon, wiping her face with her sleeve. "I've lost my memory. I have forgotten my one grand passion in life."

Gideon gazed at her in affectionate bewilderment. "You didn't ask them?"

Losing patience, Ian blew out his breath. "Lord Lisle and I both claim her."

"*He* is lying," Lucas stated.

Miranda giggled wildly again. "Perhaps you are

both telling the truth. Perhaps I was a wanton, flitting from one man to another. Did you ever consider that, hmm?"

Ian wanted to shake her. Instead he rested his fists on his knees and feigned a blasé sense of amusement. "Actually, the point is now beyond debating, since we're married."

"Married!" Gideon sat forward in bed, clutching the covers to his chest. "Who is this man? Can he provide for you? What sort of fam—"

"I took her to Scotland and married her." Ian felt an absurd sense of pride.

"Illegally. Against her will." Lucas reached for Miranda, grasping her arms. "Sweetheart, I beg of you. Think. Think very hard. I was the man you chose, and I am the man you must choose now. We loved each other. You're rising in society. Soon we'll be able to wed properly. You'll be the Viscountess Lisle." His voice broke with anguish. "We used to share a dream, Miranda. Don't let it go. Please, don't let it go."

The last vestiges of humor left her face. Her eyes blazed with fury, but also with frustration. "Perhaps what I've learned from this ordeal is to avoid *any* man."

Ian felt her eyes on him, felt Gideon's eyes, too. He knew they were waiting for him to make a similar impassioned speech, to try to outdo Lucas. He felt weary to the bone, exhausted by all the pretense, all the unaccustomed emotional turmoil.

"I have nothing to say." He rose from his chair and walked to the door, turning to fix Miranda with a piercing stare. He had to take this risk, or he was doomed. "Except that the truth is staring you in the face, if you'd only see it."

Impressed by the grandeur of his own bluff, he left the room and sought his chamber. It was small, with a dormer window and a roomy bed covered by a good feather tick. He took little pleasure in his surroundings, though, and even less in the fresh country breeze that blew in through the open window.

He doubted he would be able to sleep. Miranda was on the verge of having a breakthrough. Soon she would remember everything. She'd know he had been lying to her.

And then there was Gideon. What an odd, gentle old soul he was. Clearly he adored his daughter. Just as clearly, she baffled him. What must it have been like, raising a child like Miranda, trying to keep up with the demands of her hungry, brilliant mind? Trying to understand what lurked in her private heart?

No wonder the old fellow was befuddled.

Befuddlement or not, tomorrow Gideon would have a few things to answer for. He, at least, had not lost his memory. Though he seemed confused at present, perhaps after a good night's sleep he would be more forthcoming with information.

La Couleuvre. The Adder. The name chased itself round and round in his head until he envisioned a black snake, head and tail connected, forming an endless circle.

Ian set his candle on a wall shelf and went to the window, looking out over the gently rolling hills, glistening gray green in the moonlight. He loosened his cravat, then discarded it altogether, flinging it over the back of a chair.

Then he plunged his hands into his hair, raking with his fingers as if trying to comb his brain for answers. All the information was there, floating about like wind-borne seeds. But he could not gather them in, make sense of them.

Finally he lowered his hands and propped his shoulder against the side of the dormer. If that were the only thing troubling him, he would have been asleep already. To himself, in private, he could admit it. Miranda. He wanted her.

God, he *needed* her. And he was about to lose her.

Ian MacVane had never been more frightened in his life.

Miranda bent and kissed her father on the brow. The gesture felt awkward, rusty, as if she had never done it before. He slept deeply, peacefully, and she felt a surge of warmth when she held up a bowl lamp and watched him.

You are my father, she thought, feeling the truth bloom like a small miracle inside her. *My father.*

Here he was, living, breathing proof that she had been wanted, loved. Never mind that huge pieces of her past were still missing. She could remember the important things. He used to tie her bootlaces in sailor's knots. He brought treatises and textbooks to church so she could read if she got bored during the sermon. When they had no place to sleep at night, he made a bed for her in his arms.

With a lump in her throat, she backed away from the bed. Why had she kept secrets from her own father?

The thought raised prickles of apprehension on her skin. She remembered the man in black who had approached her at the Thomas Lawrence sitting, confident that she was part of his plot. Had she been living a double life? A traitor to England hiding behind the guise of a scholar's dutiful daughter?

What she hated the most was that she knew nothing for certain. And the three men in her life—Gideon, Lucas, and Ian—were no help to her at all.

One true thing had come out of the conversation tonight, though. She had learned to trust her instincts. So, strictly on instinct, she walked past her chamber door and went to another door, envisioning the man within. Was he pacing up and down? Wondering if she would come? Wondering what she had decided?

It was only fair to tell him. Now, before she lost her nerve. Before she started to doubt.

She rapped very lightly on the door. It opened a crack, and then farther, and he stood there, unsmiling, expectant, heartbreakingly handsome.

Her mouth went dry. She looked up at him, gathered her courage, and said, "Hello, Lucas. May I come in?"

16

Every room is a masquerade.
—Miss Mitford,
Our Village

Carefully Ian closed the door to his room, though he longed to smash it out of its frame.

He stood, feeling a shock that rocked the very foundations of his pride. Hearing a sound outside, he had gone to his door and looked out in time to witness his wife going into Lucas Chesney's room. He saw the scene over and over in his head. He was inside a bad dream from which there was no waking.

He managed to reach down and take a small silver flagon from his boot. The whiskey burned, but even though he drained the bottle, he could tell drinking wasn't going to work.

She'd gone to Lucas. Even after all that had happened, after he'd made love to her as if his very life had depended on it, after he had started to care about her with an intensity that terrified him, Miranda had gone to Lucas.

She had remembered.

"The charade's over," he muttered, prowling the room restlessly, then stopping to glare out the window. *"Over."*

He told himself all was happening for the best. He'd known the risk he was taking the moment he had decided to spirit her away to Scotland. He'd known that one day she would remember, would learn he had played her false.

He just wasn't prepared for how much losing her would hurt.

And it wasn't like Miranda to accept what he had done to her. Why wasn't she here, in this room, confronting him, accusing him?

He wondered if he should be feeling guilty. Hadn't he, after all, robbed her of a future with a titled nobleman? Worse, hadn't he endangered her chance to be with the man she truly loved?

Aye, he had done both, but the odd thing was, he did not regret a single moment. Perhaps because her nobleman was on the verge of ruin and forced to enter into shady dealings to stay afloat. As to Lucas being the man she truly loved—

Ian sucked in a breath between clenched teeth. As a stowaway on a merchantman long ago, he had been under the lash more than once, and that pain returned now, searing him and flashing out along his limbs to the very tips of his fingers. Only this pain was worse, for it wouldn't go away. He could not stop thinking about their night together, the way they had touched, the things they had said to one another. He had seen and felt things that not even words could express. Joy and brightness and possibility . . .

Enough, he told himself. She'd had no memories of the past then, save the false ones he had planted in her mind and in her heart. He had not played fair, and now he would pay the price of his cheating.

It was no more than he deserved.

He yanked his frock coat from its hook on the back of the door. He should have gotten out of this mess long before. He should have gone back to his life of routine espionage, watching people from afar, laughing cynically and secretly at their posturing, holding himself aloof. Treating ladies like whores and making them beg for his favors. Winning fortunes from drunken gentlemen at the clubs. And every once in a while, providing some critical bit of information to the British government.

It was an empty existence. He wondered why he had never noticed that before.

No matter. It was preferable to the torment he had found with Miranda Stonecypher in his arms. In his bed. In his life. In his heart.

A faint tapping sounded at his door. "Now what?" he grumbled. With his cravat untied and his frock coat hanging askew, he yanked open the door.

And froze where he stood.

Several seconds passed, and then he found his voice. "Miranda?"

She took a deep breath for courage and stepped into Ian's room, closing the door behind her and then leaning against it with her hands behind her back.

"I have no idea if I've done the right thing," she said. "But it's done, and there you are, and I feel ever so much better."

He had only a single candle burning. His face was half in shadow, but she noticed a tension about him. Taut lines pulled at his mouth and around his eyes.

"You'll have to explain, Miranda." His voice was chilly. "I have no idea what you mean."

She had hoped for some measure of compassion from him. But he was an unpredictable man, moody and hard to know. Perhaps he had always been that way. She drew a deep breath. "I went to Lucas's room just now."

He propped an elbow on the mantelpiece and crossed one ankle over the other. Though his stance appeared casual, she sensed a restrained violence in him, and she stayed by the door.

"Indeed?" was all he said.

"I went to tell him that I could not possibly have been in love with him before the accident, because—" Her mouth felt dry as dust. She licked her lips, but it didn't seem to help. "Because I love you."

"Christ," he muttered, his breath causing the candle flame to waver.

She lifted her chin even as her pride plummeted. She had been so certain it was the right thing to do. "Is that all you have to say?"

"How did Lucas take the news?"

She swallowed hard, remembering the stricken look on his face, the glitter of anger and hurt in his eyes. "He insisted that I was making the biggest mistake of my life. That you are a stranger who means me harm." She pushed away from the door and went to stand before him, fearlessly facing his hooded suspicion and his volatile mood. "But I knew that couldn't be. Not after the night we shared."

In one swift movement, he caught her against him. "Why do you trust me, Miranda? Why?"

He frightened her, but it was an exhilarating fear, a

challenging one. She glided her hands up over his chest, glorying in the hard sculpture of muscles beneath his broadcloth shirt. "I trust what I feel when you hold me in your arms."

He said something in Gaelic, another swear word, probably. Then he crushed his mouth down on hers. Gladness rose like a fountain inside her. She had made the right choice. She had to believe that. Lucas was simply a decent man who thought she needed protecting. Ian was her love, her life, her past and her future.

"What did you say?" she whispered against his mouth, hungry for more kisses. "What did you just say to me in Gaelic?"

"Never trust a moment of lust."

She laughed and went up on tiptoe to nip his earlobe.

"You think I'm joking?" he asked.

"I never know when you're joking."

"I never joke."

"Ah. Then I shall be deadly serious." She stepped back and pulled at the fastenings of her dress.

"Miranda—"

She ignored the warning note in his voice and disrobed. When he looked at her with hungry yearning, she felt a delicious sense of power and an answering longing so intense it held the keen edge of anguish.

Was it always like this with us? she wondered as he swept her up and carried her to the bed. He set her down, not gently, but then again, she did not want him to be gentle. He all but ripped off his own clothing and then covered her like a stallion on a mare in season, dominating and consuming her, yet at the same time remaining uncommonly sensitive to her merest want, her smallest vagary of mood.

He was an unpredictable lover, taking her swiftly

one moment, slowly the next, bringing her to a high, trembling state of ecstasy until she was certain she would shatter. And of course she did, shattering in his arms, her inner being exploding, set off by the touch of his hands and mouth and body. The passion was almost frightening in its intensity, dark with an edge of fire.

She wondered vaguely, in some distant part of her mind, if there might be danger in feeling this strongly, this sharply. The love burning inside her was no gentle sentiment, but a madness, one that brought to mind the chained prisoners of Bedlam.

He plunged down, engulfing her in that all-consuming way, thrusting his tongue into her mouth and making her want him with a need that was nothing short of madness. He seemed to want to brand her with himself, his teeth nipping her vulnerable flesh, leaving a trail of tiny marks on her throat and breasts. He ran his hands and then his tongue down between her legs, finding a spot of such searing sensitivity that she nearly cried out with the pain and the pleasure of it. His passion was like a whirlwind around her, and though part of her wished it would go on forever, she understood that every storm must spend itself into silence.

"Ian," she whispered after they had made love. "Ian, I'm afraid."

"Shh." He kissed her, leaning over as if to shield her from the world. The menace she had sensed in him earlier was gone now; he seemed to have spent his unexplained anger along with his lust, and what remained was simply tenderness. "What are you afraid of?"

"That this can't last. That something is going to happen to change what we've found together." She waited, expecting him to deny it, to reassure her.

Instead he kissed her again, very gently, his lips feathering across hers and his hand skimming down her torso. "Then we had best enjoy the moment while we may," he said.

"That wasn't what I wanted to hear, Ian MacVane."

He twined a lock of her hair around his finger and studied it. "I can't make the world go away, Miranda, much as I'd like to. I can't stop things from happening. And I canna help it that I've got a duty to do."

"Why?" she asked. "Why you?" She traced her hand through the fine hair on his chest. "Perhaps you've told me before and I've forgotten. But I want to understand."

"Understand what, lass?"

"Why you are the way you are."

He laughed without humor. "I daresay you've never asked me that before. No one has."

"Then tell me, Ian." She pressed her ear against his chest, smiling when she heard the surge of his beating heart. "I want to know."

"It's not very interesting. I was like thousands of others—a poor boy forced to work in Glasgow."

"That's where you were sent after the English raided your family's croft." She still had trouble picturing it—the peaceful dales of Crough na Muir aflame and overrun with marauders.

"I worked as a climbing boy," he said with slow deliberation, "indentured to a chimney sweep. But climbing boys must be small in order to fit into tight spaces. My brother and I were fast to outgrow the job."

His heart beat more quickly now, though his voice remained matter-of-fact. She wondered what memories haunted him, to make his heart pound in fear or dread all these years later. Perhaps there was some small advantage to not remembering the past.

"And after you grew too big to fit in small spaces?" she asked.

"We were forced to work anyway. Accidents were common." He held up his hand. In the shadowy candle glow, she studied the last finger, cut off at the first joint. "I lost this. My brother, Gordon, lost his life."

She pressed her palm to his, and his hand was stiff for a moment; then he tried to take it away. "No," she whispered. "You're always covering it up with a glove. It's not necessary. I swear it's not." She closed her hand so that their fingers were laced. "How?" she made herself ask. "Your brother, that is."

The heartbeat went even faster. "He fell. Three stories to his death. I saw it happen."

She couldn't stand it. Could not stand to think of all he had endured. Her tears began then, flowing down her chin onto his chest.

"'Tis past," he reminded her, cupping her head in his hand. "Forgotten a very long time ago."

She dried her face with the sheets. "I hurt for you, Ian. I do. When I think what it must have been like for you, I can scarcely bear it."

"It all turned me into a manly little lad," he said with a dark chuckle. "I vowed, of course, to punish the man who had brought about Gordie's fate."

"And did you? Punish him?"

All mirth died in his throat. "Nay. I lost track of Mr. Adder, and eventually all the lands of Crough na Muir were sold. Though it would be sweet indeed to find him if he still lives, to make him pay for what he did."

"Is it only happenstance that one of the Bonapartistes is called the Adder?"

"I don't know . . . yet." He hissed out a sigh. "I dream of it, you know. Of finding him. Killing him."

The chained violence she heard in his voice disturbed her. "You're no murderer, Ian."

He chuckled, a mirthless rumble in his chest. "Some would say it's what I'm best at."

Feeling reckless, she touched him intimately, smiling in the dark at his response. "I know what you're best at, MacVane. And it isn't killing people."

"Wench." He pressed her back against the soft mattress and filled her yet again, robbing her breath, her will, her very self as he lifted her up to a sweet, piercing rapture. This time he was swift and silent until the very end, when shudders pulsed through him and he spat her name like a curse.

She lay quietly for a long time. "You're angry."

"Nay. . . . Aye, perhaps. You consume me, Miranda. Sometimes with you I feel powerless. Adrift. You have glimpsed more deeply into my soul than anyone ever has."

"And I still don't understand you. Finish what you were saying . . . before."

He curled a big hand around her breast. "I forgot where I was."

She grew solemn and moved his hand. "After . . . Gordie. How did you survive alone, then, without even your brother?"

"I ran away to sea. Stowed away, to be precise. It proved to be a better education than you'd suspect. The first vessel, a merchantman, had a vast library. Out of boredom on a voyage around the horn of Africa, I read the noted philosophers."

She smiled, picturing a young Ian studiously bent over a book. "I never thought of a ship as a place of learning."

"Oh, aye, it was that. But the books were only part of my education. To stay alive, I had to learn a steady hand with a sword and a dead-on aim with a pistol."

She shivered. "It is a wonder that you survived, Ian. And became such a fine man."

"Dinna make more of me than I am. It's the human will to live, plain and simple. We all have it."

She turned so that she was on her side, looking at him, watching shadows flicker across his rugged face. "I suspect you have it in greater measure than most. But I worry, Ian."

He propped himself on one elbow. For a moment, his heated gaze flared over her bare breasts. "Worry? About what?"

"You take joy in danger. I've seen that in you. It's as if you're amused or distracted by it, as one is in a sporting game. You take refuge in danger and risk."

"Ah. And why would I do that, lass?"

"You'll get angry if I tell you."

"Tell me anyway."

"Well . . ." She forced herself to ignore what his hand was doing, circling and caressing her breasts. "I think there is one problem you will not admit even to yourself. I believe you hunger for peace. For an abatement of the grief you carry with you through every moment of every day."

He stopped touching her. She studied his face. "See? I've made you angry."

"Nay, lass."

She held her breath. He claimed he loved her, but could she trust what he said? "Do you know how to love, Ian?"

Candle glow and silence bathed the room for a long time. She could hear the gentle thud of his pulse and her own, could hear them both breathing. The tangled bed linens, smelling of strong soap and sex, were warm beneath them.

"Ian?"

"I know the limits of passion," he said. And before she could demand an explanation, he turned her on her back and showed her what he meant.

In the morning, Gideon declared himself well enough to travel by hired coach to the country estate of Lady Frances Higgenbottom. Miranda was somewhat relieved to ride with him while Ian and Lucas went on horseback. She felt intensely private about what she had shared by dark of night with Ian. Not because she was ashamed, but because the searing intimacy was almost hurtful in its poignancy.

She thought of Lucas, too, who had stood in the dark last night and listened to her with a look of numb incredulity on his face. This morning he was angry; she could see that in his cold eyes and abrupt movements, the way he snapped the bit to and fro in his horse's mouth. He had little to say to her, virtually nothing to say to Ian.

Ian, for his part, had inquired politely after Gideon's health. Gideon had appeared reluctant to speak of his suffering.

Miranda was in a half-dreaming state while her father slumbered comfortably across from her. She leaned her head against the side of the coach and moved the leather curtain aside to look out the window. The day was overcast, the hills rolling past in long, undulating waves that seemed to go on forever.

Remember, she told herself. *Remember.*

But she couldn't. Still she couldn't. Even having her father with her did not bring back the forgotten past. She knew he was her father. She could look at him and experience the sense of love and exasperation she had always felt for him, but she had no specific recollection of their relationship.

He had told her, somewhat sheepishly, of her peripatetic childhood. He had dragged her from shabby salon to shabby salon, letting her run wild in between visits for scholarly debate. He had loved many women, but none of them well enough. Her education was both unconventional and incomplete, of that she was already aware. She was probably the only young lady in England who could converse in Greek and apply Newtonian principles, yet remain ignorant of which fork to use for fish.

In the late afternoon, they went directly to greet their hostess. With her usual unflappable hospitality, Lady Frances welcomed Gideon to the vast country house, built by her father as a hunting retreat. Within minutes she had him situated in a bedroom, a blanket wrapped around his legs and a cup of tea warming his hands.

"Now," she said pleasantly, patting her bouncy yellow curls. "I understand you've had quite an adventure, Mr. Stonecypher."

He sipped his tea. Miranda was pleased to see a bit of color returning to his cheeks. "Indeed I have, my lady."

"Then why don't you just take a few moments and tell us all about it? Exactly who attacked you, and what did they want?"

After three hours of listening to the old man's ramblings, Lucas Chesney was ready for a drink. Gideon Stonecypher, it turned out, could tell them no more than they already knew. Miranda had found out something she shouldn't, and because of that, half of England seemed to be after her.

Lucas withdrew to his quarters with a decanter of brandy and a crystal glass, sat down at the desk, and began to drink with the quiet, steady determination of a condemned man.

There was a horrible sort of justice in all of this. He had insisted that he and Miranda must live a lie. Now that he was ready to tell the truth, she didn't believe him.

It had taken all his self-control to keep from groveling at her feet the night before. How confident she had sounded, coming to his room to tell him baldly that she could not possibly have loved him in the past.

There was one tiny glimmer of hope, he told himself. Miranda was a natural philosopher and a scholar. She believed in that which could be seen and touched. Concrete proof. It wasn't enough that he knew about her birthmark, and God help him if she ever did remember the occasion on which he had seen it.

She needed something she could hold in her hand, see with her eyes.

Adder. Addingham. Silas had let something slip one night at Watier's, when he'd been in his cups. Adder. Addingham.

Lucas drank some more and took out a sheaf of papers from his valise. The writing on the papers stacked on the desk blurred. He didn't have to see them to know what they were. Bills. Duns for payment. Entreaties from his family for more funds.

Lucas smiled crookedly and lifted his glass. "You are all as good as paid," he declared. "Here's to you, Mr. Addingham, and to our lasting friendship." He drained his glass and covered his face with hands that suddenly shook. "Thank God," he muttered brokenly. "Thank God you came along, Silas."

If not for Silas, it would have been disgrace and debtor's prison for Lucas Chesney. All those who loved him, who copied his manner of dress and admired his wit and his golden good looks, would know him for a fraud.

Silas understood him. When Lucas had despaired of regaining Miranda's affection, it had been Silas's idea to shower her with gifts. Silas had even procured Yvette, the lady's maid. That was an elegant touch.

There was one thing Silas's riches could not buy for Lucas. Miranda's love. All Lucas wanted, all he had ever wanted, was for society to approve of the woman he loved. Instead he had walked into murder and mayhem and a pair of doe-soft eyes that gazed at him without recognition.

Lucas refilled his glass and drank again, neatly, not letting a single drop of the brandy touch his snowy cravat. It was a trick he had learned in his unlamented secret pauper days. Keep the clothes clean. Save on laundering costs.

A door closed softly behind him. He knew who it was. He felt her stare boring through him. She stood silent for a moment; then, in her most cutting voice, she said, "Oh, please. This is too pathetic."

He looked at her reflection in the mirror above the desk. "That is what I love about you, Frances. Your endearing sense of compassion."

Her gown whispered as she crossed the room. "You don't need pity, Lisle, but a cuff on the ear."

"You're too much of a lady to strike me." He held out his glass. "Brandy?"

She tossed it back in one gulp, a gesture that would have scandalized half of society. The other half would have wanted to applaud. Lucas himself wanted to, but he didn't.

"Did the old addlepate say anything of use?" Lucas asked.

"Heavens," Frances said. "How would I have any idea?"

He laughed at her. "You had me believing for years that you were nothing but a vacant blond head. In the past few days, I've realized it was all an act. So you don't have to pretend anymore. You are in the secret service of the Foreign Office. It's amazing." When she opened her mouth to protest, he waved a hand to silence her. "Your secret's safe with me, Frances. On my honor, it is."

She held out the glass for more brandy. "Oh. Are you terribly disgusted with me?"

"No. Fascinated." He watched her drink again. She really was a pretty little piece, and knowing now what he did about her gave her unexpected depth and an air of mystery that intrigued him.

"So fascinated," she said, "that you had to withdraw to your rooms to get quietly drunk?"

To his horror, hot tears burned his eyes. He didn't look away from her in time. She saw, and her slim arms went around him, and she drew him against her bosom, her fingers curling into his hair. "Ah, Lucas. If only I could take your pain away."

"You can," he said brokenly, then swallowed hard, trying to regain control. There was something particularly comforting about the softness and the scent of her. Odd that before today, he had always seen her as a bit of fluffy female ambition. Now he knew better, knew the keen mind beneath the golden ringlets, the steely strength beneath the frothy dress.

"You can, Frances. All you have to do is prove to Miranda that MacVane has been lying to her. That he never knew her. That he is only using her to learn what she knows."

She stiffened, and the arm around his back held him tighter. "I've never been Ian MacVane's keeper. How do I know he wasn't swiving Miranda on the sly?"

The suggestion knifed through him. He wrenched away from her. "God. When did you become such a bitch, Frances?"

"I just can't bear to see you make a fool of yourself because of her."

He grasped her hands. "Then help me. Help me convince Miranda that Ian MacVane is no part of her past."

"And you think by doing that, you'll win her love?" Her eyes rounded in incredulity. "Are all men as simple as you, or are you just special?"

"I won't deceive myself. But at least with MacVane exposed as a liar, I'd have a chance."

"And that's all you want," she said. "A chance."

"Yes."

"Why in heaven's name would you expect me to give it to you?"

He brought her hands to his mouth and kissed them both. Fleeting pain twisted her face, but just for a moment; then she became her usual smiling self once again.

"Because you care about me, Frances," he said starkly. "And because if I fail, you'll get to be the first to say I told you so."

She stripped her hands out of his and pivoted on her heel. At first he thought she was walking out on him, but instead she stopped at the door and turned. "Well? Are you coming?"

He shot up from the desk, swaying only slightly. "Where are we going?"

"To get—" Her voice broke. She cleared her throat, squared her shoulders, and faced him with rock-solid conviction. "To get the evidence you need."

17

Psychology cannot experiment with men, and there is no apparatus for this purpose. So much the more carefully must we make use of mathematics.
—Johann Friedrich Herbart, 1816

Supper was served late that night, and Gideon sought his bed almost immediately after. Miranda bade him a fond good night and bent to kiss his silky white hair.

"I'm so glad I found you again, Papa," she said.

For a moment, he seemed completely stunned by the gesture of affection. Was it unusual? she wondered. Had the old Miranda never kissed her father good night? The suspicion made her feel small and cold inside.

He patted her hand. "All will be well, Mindy my girl. One day, all will be well." He drew a long breath, then exhaled slowly. "I could wish . . . "

She frowned. "Wish what?"

"That you would simply remember what you overheard and tell them."

She sat heavily on the edge of the bed. "I cannot remember."

"Somehow I managed—or your own terror managed—to employ Mesmer's techniques and convince you to forget everything." He squeezed her hand; sweetness and melancholy tinged his smile. "It's quite odd."

"What, Papa?"

"I know I'm a stranger to you because of the aphasia, but from my perspective, we've not been this close in a very long time."

She blinked rapidly, and her throat felt full. "Was I that awful, Papa?"

"Just . . . busy. Distracted. Absorbed by your work. Sometimes I think you did that on purpose. To escape."

"Escape what?" she asked, frustrated.

He regarded her with placid wisdom. "Feeling anything deeply. Fully. I blame myself. You had a shallow existence with me, a haphazard upbringing. I never taught you the meaning of commitment, of family. But now . . ." His voice trailed off, and he looked about the room.

"Now what?"

"You've learned it, somehow. I see the way you care for the people around you, and I realize that in one brief summer you've learned things I couldn't teach you in a lifetime."

"You taught them, Papa." She sensed that he was getting tired, and she kissed his brow again. "Apparently I just didn't catch on until recently. I've been meaning to ask you—"

"Aye?" He stifled another yawn.

"I had a fleeting memory of you warning me not to trust him. Have you any idea who that was?"

Gideon's brow knit above his sleepy eyes. "Never saw him. When we were captured, he promised you our lives if only you would agree to help him."

"Help him what?"

He flinched as if the memory hurt. "I think I was unconscious by then."

"Oh, Papa. They hurt you so."

He patted her hand. "I'm fine, now, Mindy. Just fine."

Feeling wistful, she returned to the withdrawing room, where Frances was halfheartedly trying to amuse the gentlemen with a game of cards. Desperate to lighten her spirits, Miranda smiled and entered the room.

"Ian's cheating," she remarked. "I saw him nick a card from his lap." She met his smoldering look with a teasing smile, but a thrill went through her body. She prayed her father was right—no matter what she had been in the past, now she knew how to care, how to love. Ian was the key that had unlocked her passion. In just a short time they would be in one another's arms, the taste of him flowing through her, the forgetfulness of desire lifting away her cares. What a blessed thing it was, to be in love with a man like Ian.

His mysteries were as deep as the night itself. His slightest touch, even a look sent across the room, had the power to set off a heated yearning inside her. Had it always been this way with them? Or was their love growing, invading every aspect of her life? It was almost frightening the way he seemed to enter her every pore, her mind, her soul. Frightening and wonderful.

"MacVane is a born cheater," Lucas said, throwing his cards down in the middle of the table.

His fury drew a taut, thick band of tension across the moment. Frances trilled with laughter, an earnest effort to ease the strain. "Cheaters are made by hard work and necessity, Lisle," she declared. "You of all people should know that." She moved to the pianoforte and began to play a merry waltz.

Wordlessly, showing no sign of anger at Lucas's words, Ian crossed the room and dipped a formal bow. "May I have this dance?"

Dazzled by his smile, his courtliness, Miranda held out her hand. Ian took her into his arms and they danced, light as air, swirling across the carpet, past a glowering Lucas, and out through the tall open glass doors.

They waltzed across a flagstone terrace bordered by a carved stone fence with marble benches and ivy flowing down the walls. With the stars wheeling overhead and the full moon bathing them in a blue glow, she fancied it was the most romantic spot on earth.

And she was in the arms of the man she adored with a fervor that made her memory loss seem less a tragedy and more an opportunity to rediscover him. Whether he knew it or not, he possessed a power that called across her damaged mind and promised to heal it.

"Ian, I love you so much," she whispered.

He stopped dancing. "Miranda—"

"You're uncomfortable hearing it. I don't know why. Perhaps it's something I'll understand when I regain my memory. But I thought that here, in the dark, I could say it." She gazed up at the sky, frosted by a cool bluish glow. "Maybe in moonlight I can say anything."

He shook his head, regarding her with exasperation and undisguised affection. "God, you are . . . I want—" He stopped himself and cursed, then kissed her swiftly, his mouth warm and searching. She arched her back, welcoming the painful ecstasy of loving him.

"Part of me wants never to remember," she admitted.

"Why not?" he whispered.

"Because no memory could be this sweet."

"Then don't," he said in a low, rough voice. "Don't remember. Ever."

She thought it an odd thing to say, but before she could ask him what he meant, she heard footfalls ringing on the flagstones.

They broke apart to see Lucas stalking toward them. Looking alarmed and helpless, Lady Frances hurried along behind him. The viscount, Miranda observed, wore a look of haughty disdain that was so perfect, she wondered if he had practiced in front of a mirror. Perhaps it was something he had learned at Eton.

Eton. She frowned. Why was she so certain that Lucas had attended Eton?

Darling, if the masters at Eton had one-tenth of your learning, England would indeed rule the world.

Lucas had said that to her once, long ago.

She swayed, encountering Ian's solid length behind her. His hands came up and cupped her shoulders. "Are you all right?" he asked.

"I'd hoped you wouldn't let things go this far," Lucas said. His voice was abnormally calm, as if he had struggled for control and was hanging on by a thread. "I'd hoped you wouldn't make me hurt Miranda by showing her proof of the truth about you."

Ian's hands tightened. Miranda held her breath. She felt disoriented, confused. A moment ago she had been dancing in the arms of the man she loved. Now she was almost drowning in a flood of disjointed memories and staring like an idiot at a piece of paper Lucas held in his hand.

Take my hand, sweet Miranda, there's my girl. Before you know it, you'll learn to greet a roomful of people like the most dainty of ladies.

But Lucas, why would I want to be dainty? Or even a lady, for that matter?

Ah, my exasperating sweet. Because when the time comes for us to declare our love to the world, they'll all expect it of us.

A part of Miranda held herself detached, as if the moment were happening to someone else. Lucas and Ian might have been a pair of actors on a stage. Ian reached for the paper and Lucas snatched it away, thrusting it instead into Miranda's hands.

"Let her read it, MacVane. Let her read it, and she'll be the judge of how badly you treated her."

She pulled away from Ian. She felt an inner recoiling, as if she knew she was going to be hurt and would not be able to stop it. She lowered herself to the stone ledge that bordered the patio and angled the paper so that the moonlight illuminated it.

At first the words made no sense, as if they were in another language. But then she recognized, with a jolt, that the message was written in her father's own cipher—though not his handwriting. Creating cipher codes was the one thing Gideon did perfectly.

The message was penned by Frances; Miranda recognized the dainty script and glanced quizically at her friend. How did she know Gideon's cipher?

Miranda's mind did the swift calculations necessary to break the code. Her fierce gaze riveted on the last bit: " . . . sleep with the girl. It is the best way to—dare I be so tasteless?—get her to reveal herself to you. . . ."

At the bottom, the scribbled reply was in Ian's bold hand: "When I bed a woman, my dear, it's for my own reasons, not because anyone orders me to. . . ."

She made herself read the message over and over again. Each time her mind searched frantically for some explanation other than the truth.

There was none. She finally held the real story right here in her hands. Ian had never known her. His goal had been to find her and to learn what she knew. To dispose of her once the truth was known. She had no idea where she found the strength to look up, to stare Ian square in the eye.

"You never knew me," she said slowly. "You never saw me before the night of the explosion, and yet you had me convinced we were in love." She prayed he would interrupt, but he stood silent. "You wed me," she went on, dying inside, "in order to control me. To learn my secrets."

Please deny it, her heart pleaded. *Please tell me I'm wrong.*

Instead he watched her without expression. That, perhaps, was the cruelest blow of all. That he could face her accusations without so much as a flicker of guilt or regret.

It was Lucas who went to her, who held out his arms. "Come, my love. I'm sorry you've had such a shock. I simply didn't know any other way to prove to you that MacVane is a fraud."

She clutched at the stone railing. "We did know each other, you and I," she said.

"Darling!" Joy lit his face. "You remember?"

She could feel no answering joy inside her. How could she, when her heart was breaking?

"We quarreled that night, didn't we?"

Lucas's smile disappeared. Behind him, Ian moved like a shadow, dark and vaguely threatening. Miranda wanted to scream at him to go away, but for some reason she did not.

"A lovers' tiff," Lucas declared. "Hardly worth remembering. In fact, I've forgotten the entire af—"

"You tore my dress." Her hands came up and covered her bosom as if he had bared her right there in the moonlight. "That is how you saw my—the birthmark."

Both men were liars. Her judgment was pitiful. Why couldn't she find some stable clerk to fall in love with, or better yet, why couldn't she stop herself from falling in love at all?

"That was an accident," Lucas said. "Really, darling, it was nothing. You and I were so deeply in l—"

"Let her finish." Ian's voice, thick with his brogue, interrupted Lucas. "It's what you wanted, isn't it? You wanted her to remember. So let her."

She couldn't have stopped herself if she had tried. Wave after wave of memory washed over her. The strength of them was almost physical, staggering in intensity. Yet the memories made no sense. In her mind's eye she simply saw herself and Lucas, nose to nose, furious with each other, flinging angry words.

"We were quarreling about an acquaintance of yours," she said, trying to fit the fragments of memory together like pieces in an intricate puzzle. "I demanded to know who he was to you, and all you would tell me was that he had promised to save you from losing everything and landing in debtors' prison."

His face scarlet, Lucas glanced over his shoulder at Ian as if horrified that the secret was out. "That is a private arrangement, and you were angry because you didn't understand the nature of—"

"Good God," she snapped. "I don't know where the truth ends and the lies begin." She walked up and down, feeling the coolness of the summer night rippling over her skin. If she stopped walking, stopped talking, she was certain she would start to weep and never cease.

My love, all I ask is this one small thing. One small thing, and Silas will take care of the rest.

Lucas, I would hardly call seventeen kegs of gunpowder one small thing.

Silas. The charming Mr. Addingham. She clutched at a vine pergola growing up the side of the house and swung around to face him. "It was Silas Addingham all along, wasn't it? He was hiding something at the warehouse. That's why I set off the explosions." Horror blossomed like noxious smoke in her mind.

Lucas plunged to his knees before her. "I beg you, Miranda. Forgive me. I had no idea what Silas's plans were. He said he was going to create an evening of fireworks for the visiting dignitaries. It's not unusual. He's a wealthy man. He wanted to impress people. I saw no harm in that. All I knew is that I was about to break under the pressure of my family, my ambitions, my own weakness." He hung his head. "Silas exploited that weakness. But that is all I'm guilty of."

Ian stalked toward the house, his strides long with deadly purpose. Seeming to forget all about Miranda, Lucas shot up and blocked his way.

"Where the hell are you going, MacVane?" he demanded.

"I think you know, my lord. You've solved quite a puzzle for us. It's time we brought Silas Addingham to justice."

"No!" Lucas planted his feet.

"I don't blame you for being afraid, Lisle. Because

Addingham is certain to drag you down with him. Treason is a dirty business, and this is a little dirtier than treason."

"Treason! I saw service in the wars, was cited for bravery!"

"I dinna question your bravery, only your judgment. Did you ever wonder about the source of the money pouring into your bank account?"

"The source was Silas, and it was supposed to remain a private matter between us."

"Silas is flat broke," Frances said quietly. "I've investigated his affairs."

"The money came through him," Ian went on, "but it originated in Corsica."

Bonaparte's homeland, Miranda thought, reeling.

Ian started to turn away.

"Wait." Lucas was breathing heavily, as if he had run a great distance.

Miranda stared at them both in horrified fascination. How beautiful they were, tall and strong, one fair, one dark, both as corrupt as fallen angels.

"There's something more about Addingham that I think you'd like to know."

"Lucas, no—" Frances broke in, but they ignored her.

"I'm listening."

"Addingham is not his real name. He took it because it sounded less bourgeois. I found out the truth when I happened to see some of his personal papers, and later he had a bit too much to drink and explained it all to me. As it happens, he was willing to part with a tidy sum to keep it quiet. His real name is Adder."

Adder.

Miranda watched the realization slam into Ian. It was like seeing a man at an execution the moment he was shot. At first he showed no sign of pain, only shock. Utter, numb shock. Then came the anguish, a fleeting shadow across his face. Finally, his face hardened into a mask of anger. A mask like a corpse.

"No," she whispered, then forced herself to speak up. "Ian, no. What Lucas said might or might not be true, but surely you see what he's doing. He's forcing you to act in reckless haste. He wants you to murder Silas Addingham so he'll take all his secrets to the grave."

"I can't imagine that you would care in the least," Ian said. His coldness clung like a frost around her heart. It was hard to believe that only a few minutes had passed since they'd been dancing. A few minutes had changed the course of her life.

Ian reached the door to the drawing room. Miranda caught up with him, touched his sleeve. He turned and stared at her hand until, feeling awkward, she let go. "There is no reason I should care at all about you," she said. "But I have to say this." She looked up into his dark, rugged face, and fresh agony ripped through her.

"You could do so much more than hate," she said brokenly. "You could be so much more than a bloody mercenary—if only you'd let yourself."

One side of his mouth slashed upward in a parody of a smile. "I canna think why you would believe that now, lass," he said. Though his voice was heavy with self-mockery, she detected a deep sadness, too. He glanced at the crumpled letter in her hand. "I wouldna think you cared if I went to the devil."

Knowing the identity of Adder filled Ian with new resolve, but the taste of it was bitter. As he rode west-

ward to the tower on the hill, he felt no satisfaction at
having made a breakthrough into the plot.

He didn't care.

At the base of the semaphore tower, he hesitated.
His chest tightened, and his hands became clammy.
The ground beneath his feet blurred and seemed full
of motion, as if it would rise up to meet him. Acrid as
the taste of blood, fear flooded his mouth. The platform rose to a dizzying height above the rolling hills.
His stomach churned, and he felt sick simply contem-
plating the climb. He should wait until full noon,
when the regular signalman would come to receive
any message that might be arriving from the south.

Too long a wait, he told himself, still shuddering
but determined. He had to send a warning to London.
He placed one hand on a wooden rung of the jointed
ladder that clung to the side of the tower. Then a
foot. The other hand. The other foot.

Don't think, he told himself. Don't feel. Don't
look down. Don't watch the ground disappear
below, don't remember Gordie falling and falling,
spiraling fast, his mouth a black O of horror. . . . Ian
was bathed in sweat by the time he reached the platform of the tower. Panting, he sat down to await the
dawn. As soon as it was light, he would start his
transmission.

His every instinct told him to race to London, to
confront the murdering bastard face-to-face, to kill
him in cold blood.

He forced himself to choose a more reasoned
approach. He took out his silver whiskey flask and
drank it dry. A semaphore transmission to Duffie in
London would take a few hours or less.

It was too risky to wait. Adder might act any moment;
perhaps he already had. Ian's plan was to transmit the

warning, ordering Angus McDuff to detain Mr. Silas Addingham by whatever means necessary.

A taut, humorless smile tugged at Ian's mouth. To most people, Duffie appeared to be a harmless old retainer. But Ian knew that deep down Angus McDuff was a wild Celt, with the warlike wiles of an ancient champion wielding a claymore.

Addingham, with all his wealth and dearly bought airs of gentility, didn't have a prayer against Duffie.

Ian wondered why he had not recognized the man who had butchered his family. He had been young, that was the answer, and in those days Adder was crude and gaunt and hungry for gold. Apparently his yearning for respectability had come later, after Ian had escaped Glasgow. The years had added girth to Adder; a gifted tailor gave him the silhouette of a man of fashion.

But no amount of money could cleanse the soul of a murderer. Ian wondered what Adder thought about each night as he lay in his bed and went to sleep. Did he remember the shock and fury on Fergus MacVane's face when the soldiers shot the crofter down like a dog? Did he still hear the unearthly shrieks of Mary MacVane as man after man took his turn plunging into her? Did the wails of a baby girl, left to die in her cradle, still haunt the Englishman? Did he have any recollection at all of a pair of small boys, marched away like slaves to Glasgow? Did he even know that the forced servitude had caused the death of one boy and had destroyed the soul of the other?

As he watched the night fade, Ian tried to piece together the rest of the puzzle. Adder, in his guise of Addingham, was paying a high price for respectability. So why would he jeopardize his newfound status by embroiling himself in an assassination plot?

Frances had found the answer to that. Men like Adder

had no master save greed. Having lost his fortune, he had sold his soul to the fanatics who supported Bonaparte.

Adder had been after Miranda. Why? Just what was the plan he had in mind? Why did he need her knowledge and expertise?

Ian told himself he'd find out soon enough. The task at hand was to transmit the message. The sun crept up on the eastern horizon; then a blaze of summer light leaped like fire into the sky. A perfect day. Not a wisp of fog to mask his signal.

He stood and grasped the levers of the flags, opening the dialogue of signals. When the next signalman indicated that he was on alert, Ian sent the message. If the semaphore system worked as planned, the message would be relayed from one tower to another, all the way to London.

Addingham was as good as caught.

The knowledge should have brought Ian some measure of satisfaction. Of comfort. A sense that an old wrong was about to be righted. Instead the ghostly echo of a feminine voice came back to haunt him.

You could do so much more than hate. . . . You could be so much more than a bloody mercenary—if only you'd let yourself.

Ian felt a sense of dizziness, of disorientation, that was even worse than his fear of heights. He had already allowed himself to do too much, feel too much, where Miranda was concerned. His business here was nearly at an end.

The sooner the better, he told himself, wishing he could believe it.

*　　*　　*

"Brace yourself," Frances warned Miranda as the coach lumbered past the outskirts of the village. "We're on the open road now."

Almost as soon as she spoke, the coachman whistled to the team, and the whip cracked through the early morning air. The coach bolted forward at a speed that took Miranda's breath away. Gideon, who was dozing, muttered in his sleep. His chin bobbed down to his chest.

"I have no idea if we'll catch up with Ian," Frances said, "but it would be better for all involved if we did."

She looked paler than usual, and her customary sauciness was missing this morning. She had not met Miranda's eyes except by accident.

"You provided the note for Lucas, didn't you?" Miranda said, her words not so much a question as a statement. "Why? I thought you loved him."

A bitter smile thinned Frances's lips. "Why else would I unveil my true self? I love Lucas. He loves you. If my love is as constant and selfless as I like to believe it is, then I want to see him happy. Even if it means losing him."

"After last night, I can't see how any of us will be happy again."

Frances gave a snort of disgust. "Would you prefer to keep living a lie?"

"No. Of course not." Miranda sank back against the cushions. She had not slept at all the previous night. It had seemed impossible to close her eyes against the revelations that had barreled at her from out of the dark. Her father's muddled statements. Ian's betrayal. Lucas's greed. Her own part as an arsonist. Where did it end? Where in God's name did it end?

And more, where had it begun?

She held a leather strap attached to the roof of the

coach, leaning her cheek against her fist. "Where do you fit in, Frances? What's your part in all this?"

Frances let out a long, pretty sigh. "It started with my father, God rest his soul. He was the greatest spymaster in England before his death. But he had a secret weapon."

"He did?"

"He had me." Frances fluttered an imaginary fan against her lacy pink bosom. "I've always looked like this. Like a confection from a candy shop. As lacking in substance as spun sugar. When I was very young, it was a curse. People were always fussing over me, treating me like a poppet doll who had no thought in her head. Then one day I heard two men gossiping, and they were spelling out secrets because they thought I was too s-t-u-p-i-d to understand. You can't imagine how convenient I found it. I was able to report the entire plot—it had to do with Admiral Nelson's battle plans—to my father, and no one was the wiser. Since his death, I've taken on the role myself."

Miranda stared at her. "So you are involved in the business of spying."

"I am. And if we don't stop Ian from charging down to London, leaping upon Addingham, and making fools of us all, I'll be forced to retire in disgrace." Frances leaned back against the cushion. "I wish I could retire anyway. Some days all I want to do is grow flowers and have babies. Do you find that odd?"

Miranda swallowed a sudden lump in her throat. "No." Her thoughts flitted to a moment she remembered from the past. Her father was in the yard, standing over the charred remains of yet another experiment gone awry. When she had run to him and flung her arms around his waist, he had picked her up, twirled her around, and laughed.

He had laughed in the midst of his greatest failure. She remembered thinking what a gift that was.

"It's all in knowing the importance of things," Gideon had declared. "My experiment failed. But that means I get to spend the rest of this glorious summer day with my daughter. So where's the failure in that?"

"You're not at all odd, Frances," Miranda said. "In fact, I think you should retire."

"What's the use now? I've lost Lucas—not that I ever had him in the first place."

"How can you say that? Whatever it is that Lucas and I shared is gone now. My memory is incomplete, but I do know that much. We had a terrible row the night of the fire. It was over between us."

"He still pines for you." Frances looked at her with anger but, surprisingly, no resentment. "And who can blame him? You're everything I'm not. You're beautiful—"

"And you're not?" Miranda stared at her incredulously.

"Pretty. In a few years I shall be plump and matronly, while you'll only grow more alluring and elegant. But it's not simply looks, Miranda. You're brilliant. Fascinating. No wonder half of the *ton* and most of the visiting princes and generals are in love with you."

"And the other half with you," Miranda reminded her. "If ever I've met a brilliant, fascinating woman, it's got to be Lady Frances Higgenbottom."

"That's the trap I've set for myself. I've gotten so accustomed to playing the role of brainless beauty that everyone believes that's all I am."

"Then show them otherwise," Miranda said. "Take the credit that's yours. For heaven's sake, you've stopped conspiracies that could have brought about the ruin of England. In your own way, you're as vital as the duke of Wellington."

Frances shook her head. "The moment I reveal my role in these things, I make myself a pariah. No one will ever trust me again."

"Lucas wants to love you," Miranda said, remembering the way he looked at Frances when he thought no one was watching. "He refused to let himself because his family tried to force you two together. And I think, deep down, he had a horror of taking your fortune for his own when he himself was on the brink of poverty."

"Instead he turned to that slimewort Silas Addingham," Frances said. "What could he be thinking?"

"When male pride is involved, there seems to be very little thinking." Miranda's thoughts returned to Ian. The last time she'd seen him, he had been frozen with rage.

That was the only way to describe it. He was standing there, still breathing, still looking the same, yet one by one, each cell of his body and soul had seemed to freeze, to grow rock hard with cold, resolute fury.

"Do you suppose Lucas will stay loyal to Addingham?" she asked Frances.

Frances's eyes were overly bright. "If he does, he's not the man I've been pining my life away for. And that will mean he's sold his soul to a murderer."

"Then what do you suppose he'll do when he catches up with Ian?"

"I'm afraid he doesn't mean to catch up with him. Think of how simple things will be if Ian simply murders Addingham out of pure revenge. Then there will be no one to point the finger of accusation at Lucas."

Miranda looked down at her hands. She remembered Lucas gripping them tight that last night before the accident. He had covered her hands with kisses and begged her to—to what?

"Are you all right?" Frances asked.

"No."

"What is it, Miranda? You must tell me."

"There's something more to this plot. I can't recall what it was. Lucas wanted something from me. Even more than the gunpowder."

"The information about your rockets."

"That, yes. For Silas Addingham. But there was something more." She scowled, racking her brain. "Addingham planned something so atrocious that I actually felt sick. I recall the feeling, if not the details. I was physically ill."

"Lord in heaven. What is it? A bombardment of Carlton House?"

Her head pounded with frustration. "I don't know. Let me think awhile, and perhaps it will come to me." She pushed aside the flapping curtain. In a few more hours they would be in London. Maybe by then she would remember.

At first she paid little attention to the faint dark thread that rose in a wispy column above the hills in the distance. She merely saw it as part of the landscape, the rippling hills with their neat hedgerows and stone terraces, the flocks of sheep pale clumps grazing in the sun.

Then the coach crested a rise in the road, and Miranda realized what she was looking at. "Oh, dear God," she said.

Frances joined her at the window. "Oh, no. Miranda, it can't be."

"It is. Tell the coach to stop. That semaphore tower is on fire."

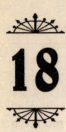

18

I have something more to do than feel.
—Charles Lamb

Ian heard the thunder of hooves and the creak of coach wheels, but he didn't turn to see who had arrived. It was too late in any case.

In the blaze of the afternoon sun, he raised a hand to shade his brow, looking up. Smoke and ash stung his eyes and seared his nostrils. The flames had consumed the tower, and now it resembled a gaunt black scaffold with great clouds of smoke billowing from the signal-man's platform. Miles to the north, Ian had sent a message. But clearly the transmission had been interrupted.

"Ian!" Miranda's voice came from the road.

He had been quite certain he would never see her again. Frances, ever efficient, would see to the dissolution of the handfast marriage and to setting up Miranda and Gideon in comfortable circumstances. Perhaps Miranda would fall in love with the Viscount Lisle again. At any rate, none of it was Ian's affair.

So why, when he turned to greet her, did his heart turn over in his chest? Why, when he looked at her shining face and sparkling eyes, did he feel a leap of joy inside himself? Why did the very sight of her, the sound of her voice, remind him of the deepest bliss he had ever known?

Lucas rode up on his horse, glared at Ian for a moment, then turned to Miranda. "Looks like there's danger hereabouts. You'd best wait in the coach with your father."

"She'll do nothing of the sort," Frances said, walking briskly across the field. "She and I are perfectly capable of investigating this problem."

Lucas looked baffled, no doubt because he had never seen Frances take charge.

She turned to Ian. "You sent a message by semaphore."

"Yes. This morning."

"Do you think it got through before this tower burned?"

"It's doubtful." He strode toward the tower, feeling the hot breath of the fire on his face. From the tall grass at the base of the wooden structure came the sound of a faint groan.

"Sweet Jesus." Ignoring the heat, Ian ran to the fallen man and scooped him into his arms. The smells of burned fabric and blood seared Ian's nostrils. The man's mouth worked in silence, then fell still. His slitted eyes were already glazing over.

The moment propelled Ian back to the days of war, to battlefields littered with bodies. When men knew they were going to die, they wanted it over quickly. He saw that same plea for mercy frozen in the signalman's unseeing eyes; he felt that same sense of hopelessness, of futility, of rage.

As he bore the flagman to the edge of the field, he knew that he was carrying a corpse. He laid him down in the tall summer grasses and knelt on the ground. Ian set his jaw. He felt responsible, since the message had originated with him at dawn, in the north.

Lucas was the first to speak. "Was it an accident, do you suppose?"

"Even you couldna be that daft, Lisle," Ian said, opening his eyes. "This was a deliberate act of murder in order to interrupt the transmission."

"How can you be sure?" Lucas persisted. "It hasn't rained in weeks, and—"

"Oh, Lord, Lucas, spare us," Frances snapped. "You'll say anything to try to protect your benefactor, even when the facts are staring you in the face. I simply can't believe that you would align yourself with a murderer rather than marry me for money."

Ian was stunned to see tears running down her face. Poor Fanny. She had everything money could buy—except the one thing she truly wanted.

Lucas was quiet for long moments. Unexpectedly Ian felt a wave of compassion for the English viscount. Faced by pressure from his family, from society, from his own sense of honor, Lucas had done a foolish thing. He wouldn't be the first.

"When I first met Silas," he said, "I knew nothing about his past. I simply thought he was a cit with plenty of money and plenty of ambition. I had no idea he was a murderer."

"Not even," Ian said with cold fury, "when you learned that his former name was Adder?"

"Not even then." Genuine shame flooded Lucas's face. He looked utterly miserable, a man whose honor had not been able to withstand an onslaught of greed.

Under different circumstances, Ian realized, they could have been friends.

"There is too much evidence to ignore," Lucas admitted, his conviction sounding harder with each word he spoke. "Nothing is worth selling my soul to a murderer." He lifted his gaze to Ian. "I'll help you. I'll join forces with you to stop this assassination, if indeed you think that is what Addingham plans."

Ian considered for a moment, wishing Lisle were not so transparent. Even now he thought not of atonement, but of saving face. Ian saw straight through Lucas's plan. To keep from being implicated in the plot, he meant to kill Adder.

Which made him no different from Ian.

A pair of local men arrived, farmers by the look of them, wearing leather jackets and tall hobnail boots. "Jesus," one of them cried, sinking to the ground beside the signalman. "'Tis Tomkin Blackwell."

"He were a local lad," the other man explained, leaning on a cane and shaking his head. "A fine one, too. Read and spoke like a scholar. Loved the tall tower messages, he did."

"Did you notice anyone suspicious about?" Ian asked.

"Oh, aye. There was that bloke with his arm in splints. We thought he were a tinker or Gypsy."

"Pierpont Duchesne," Miranda whispered.

"So where is he now?" asked Ian.

"Long gone, make no mistake," the man said mournfully.

"He is surely Silas Addingham's minion," Frances said, tugging Miranda's hand and leading her toward the coach.

"Where do you think you're going?" Lucas asked.

"To London," Miranda answered over her shoulder. "Ian's message didn't get there, so we'd best make haste."

Ian walked back toward the coach with her. "Do you understand now, Miranda? There are lives at stake. Recovering your memory might have saved them. Might save more still. I had to be with you, be . . . close to you. To get you to remember."

She regarded him coldly. "But did you have to break my heart to do it?" She turned on her heel and went back to the coach.

"I'm feeling ever so much better, dear," Gideon Stonecypher said to Frances the next morning. They had returned late to Biddle House. To no one's surprise, Yvette had gone, probably fleeing like a thief for the wharves.

Gideon smiled across the table at Miranda, who was swirling a spoon uninterestedly in a dish of hot chocolate. "Indeed, I could conquer the world."

"Save your good efforts, sir," Frances said. She was seated in front of a silver tray heaped with invitations that had arrived during her absence. "Napoleon Bonaparte has already tried that." Idly she opened an invitation, scanned it, and set it aside. "Thank heaven he's in exile where he can do no more harm."

Miranda froze. The spoon in her cup stilled completely. Do no harm. Do no harm.

Surely, darling, it can do no harm. Lucas's voice, charming and sunny as a summer morn. *I should think you'd be flattered by Mr. Addingham's interest.*

Interest in what? What, what, what?

Miranda pushed back from the table and went to

the window, where the morning sun blazed over the gardens. It was yet another perfect day.

What an extraordinary time to be in England, she reflected, and it was a thought she had had *before.*

She reached down to run her fingers idly through Macbeth's coarse fur. She heard Ian and Lucas come into the dining room.

"Silas is nowhere to be found," Lucas was saying.

"You inquired at all his usual haunts?" Ian asked.

"The usual haunts are empty. The prince regent ordered the bishop of Chichester to hold a mass of thanksgiving to celebrate Bonaparte's defeat. All of London's on holiday."

Frances took up a broadsheet and read from it: "The little Corsican is gone; he shall be forgotten as quickly as a summer rose after its petals fade and disperse on the autumn winds."

Il reviendra au printemps. He will come back in the spring.

Miranda turned swiftly from the window. "Lucas, I must know. What was it Silas Addingham wanted on the day before the explosion?"

"He was curious about your work with wind power and navigation. Something nautical, I assumed."

Wind power. Navigation.

She and her father stared at each other. More pieces of the puzzle clicked into place.

"It was my one great endeavor," Gideon said. He looked around the table at the others. "Balloon flight. Miranda had been doing navigational experiments. We'd hoped to learn to use the winds that flowed like currents in the sky."

"We tried it only twice," Miranda said, memories and feelings filling her mind. "Both times it was a success."

Gideon frowned. "Not . . . exactly."

"What do you mean?"

He waved his hand. "It's not important now."

With growing agitation, she recalled her reams of copious notes. Where were they?

Frances was still busy opening her invitations. She found a large cream envelope sealed with ruby wax and opened it. The scent of violets wafted through the room.

It was a light, floral odor, yet Miranda felt nauseated, ready to retch then and there.

"Good Lord." Frances shot to her feet.

"What is it?" Ian asked.

"An invitation."

"Oh?"

"To a balloon ascension."

The estate was half a day's travel south of London. In the almost frantic scramble to provide the most original, most enthralling entertainments for visiting dignitaries, Addingham had clearly scored a coup.

Everyone was present, prepared to be dazzled by the sight of the silk balloon sailing through the summer sky.

Sailing was the key. Miranda had predicted that the sea winds could govern the path of the balloon.

"Papa," she asked as the coach rolled to a stop in the graveled drive, "how do you suppose Addingham found out about the balloon?"

Gideon ran a hand through his hair. "Ah, Mindy sweet. My impatience. It'll be the end of me yet. I'm afraid I published the results of the experiments. Sent them in to the Royal Aeronautical Society."

"So anyone could have read of your endeavor," Frances said.

"And did indeed," Gideon admitted. "How could I have known a madman would find an evil use for something as harmless as a balloon?"

"It's not the balloon," Miranda said, half to herself. The last memory embedded like an arrow in her brain. She winced with the agony of it. "Or at least, the balloon is only part of our worries." She scanned the grand stone-and-wrought-iron gateway. The black iron fence seemed to march on forever, disappearing into thick woodlands, the sharp-spiked tips of the poles thrusting skyward.

"What do you mean?" Frances asked.

Miranda spared no time to explain. Even before the coach creaked to a halt, she had opened the door and scrambled out, hitching up her skirts. She ran in search of Ian.

He was pleading before the prince of Wales and not having much luck.

"So let me be certain I understand, MacVane," said Prinny, waddling along a verandah of the grand mansion. "You want me to cancel this event. Send each and every guest packing. Insult our host with a wild accusation. All on the strength of information from a madwoman with no memory?"

Exactly, you ignorant toad, Ian wanted to reply. But he did not. The prince of Wales was a misguided and desperate man. His popularity was at a low ebb. The last thing in the world he wanted to do was bring to light a threat to people's lives, making the British look careless or, worse, conspiratorial.

"On the strength, Your Highness," Ian said, trying to keep his impatience and contempt at bay, "of my word. The same word that saved a regiment at Busaco."

"I don't question your competence in battle. All that proves is that you're damned fortunate, and a busybody to boot," said Prinny, fingering his pocket watch. "All summer long, I have put up with your worrying like a mother hen over a clutch of eggs. Excuse me. I have an event to preside over."

You great ignorant prick, Ian thought, glowering after him. Then he looked out at the broad lawn and saw a couple hurrying across the garden, a small child in blue silk breeches between them, holding their hands and swinging his feet. The moment hung suspended in Ian's mind, a tableau of streaming sunshine and laughing people in beautiful clothes.

Prinny's life wasn't the only one in jeopardy.

Behind the house, in the middle of a broad greensward, in a billow of smoke, a blue-and-yellow silk balloon was nearly inflated but still anchored to the ground. The dignitaries and their friends and families and children were all maneuvering into place, crowded into a great reviewing stand, eagerly awaiting the launch.

In the gondola of the balloon, wearing a tall silk hat and a smile of pure triumph, was Silas Addingham. Adder.

Ian's reaction was a swift, visceral hatred that burned like a fire in his gut. The old craving for revenge seared his throat, almost closing off his air. He knew he would commit murder right here, right now, before all the crowned heads of Europe.

But he never made it as far as the smoke-filled area. Far on the opposite side of the garden, with her skirts hiked up over her knees, running as if the very devil were after her, was Miranda.

Mounted Cossacks trotted their horses up and down behind the pavilion where the dignitaries waited. The presence of soldiers should have made Ian feel better, but somehow he suspected Adder's plan would include a way around the Russian bodyguards.

Instinctively he kept his presence unknown and hoped Adder had not noticed Miranda racing across the green. Ian intercepted her behind the pavilion, clutching her shoulders and holding her steady as she tried to catch her breath.

She was more beautiful to him each time he saw her. Perhaps one day . . .

He forced himself to release the thought. Why on earth would she ever forgive him? He had lied to her. Stolen her innocence. Broken her heart. It was a wonder she would even look at him now.

Yet she did, with eyes wide and worried. And abundantly clear and knowing. "I overheard the plan," she said in a rough, gasping voice. "That's why they were all after me. I think I've finally put everything together."

"Tell me, Miranda. Hurry!"

"Addingham built rockets equipped with navigating devices I designed. They're aimed at this reviewing stand." She wrung her hands. "Now I understand why I went to the munitions warehouse that night. I was trying to destroy them—but he must have saved them, or moved them, perhaps built more."

Laughter and chatter erupted from the crowd. How festive they all looked, garbed in their finest for this event. They were lifting glasses and drinking toasts.

"Where would they be?" Ian asked. With every fiber of his being he wanted to leave her here, to sprint across the green and seize Adder. Wanted to throttle the life out of a man he had hated for all of his life.

She must have sensed his struggle, for she put her hand on his arm. "Addingham will escape. The balloon is designed for that. He will try to reach the coast, perhaps cross the Channel and join with the Violettes. The Bonapartistes."

"No—" Ian gave a strangled denial.

"If he sees you come near that balloon, he'll shoot you on sight," she warned Ian. "We must find the missiles. They're more important than your blood feud."

You could do so much more than hate, she had said to him that night, tears streaming down her face. *You could be so much more than a bloody mercenary.*

If he would let himself.

But how could he? Not now. Not after so many years of this hate. The moment he had found out Addingham was actually Adder, he had been certain his fate was to confront the man who had destroyed his life. Find him and take his revenge. Aye, his dearest wish, something he wanted more than food, more than life itself. More than . . . ?

He glanced down at Miranda, and his thoughts slammed to a halt. More than Miranda? Was there anything in the world he wanted more than Miranda?

She was speaking, moving her lips, but he could not hear her. Somewhere in the depths of his heart he found the conviction to let go of his need for revenge. Because of Miranda, he had found a higher purpose. He would leave Adder to whatever fate found him.

He felt a lightness inside as his heart relinquished

its darkest wish. He took Miranda's hand. "Come, my love."

She looked startled. "Where are we going?"

"To dismantle the rockets."

She did something most unexpected then. She leaped into his arms and kissed him hard on the mouth. "First we need to find them," she said.

"You mean you don't know where—"

The bone-jarring tones of a tolling bell drowned out his voice. He recognized the sluggish dissonance of "The Day Is Done." Miranda stumbled back, her eyes haunted, her face pale, as she looked at the crowd on the lawn. She turned and started to run. Between tolls of the bell, she said, "I know where they'll have to be in order to hit their target."

How remarkable she was, Ian thought. All of Miranda's beliefs—about herself, her world, and the nature of love and trust—had been tested to their limits. Even with her spirit hobbled by a devastating loss, she had emerged stronger than any woman he had ever known.

He had always regarded Englishwomen with contempt and superiority. Little had he known he was destined to be humbled by one of those ladies.

The tolling of the church bell faded just as they reached a remote area of the garden. Fountains hissed gently into the summer air, cascading into lily ponds. With geometric precision, box hedge and geraniums bordered the walkways leading to three Grecian gazebos.

At first the rockets looked harmless, almost a part of the landscape ensconced in the little arbors surrounded by columns. Then a thread of gray yellow smoke betrayed the lethal weapons. The fuses were already lit.

Ian picked up his pace.

Too late, he realized that if the rockets were lit, someone might likely be tending them.

"Miranda!" he yelled hoarsely.

Too late.

Events unfolded with dreamlike lethargy. She reached the gazebo in the middle, holding her skirts away from the burning fuse. Ian had his foot on the bottom step of the rotunda and was reaching for her, to drag her away. A swift shadow descended, slamming her against a stone column.

"Stop, or the woman dies." The man spoke with an accent. The arm with which he restrained Miranda wore a splint. Pierpont Duchesne.

Miranda's white throat, where the skin was so delicate that he could see a bluish tracery of veins beneath the flesh, moved as she swallowed. "Do it, Ian," she said. Though her voice trembled with fear, her conviction shone through, glittering like a steel blade in sunlight. "Call his bluff."

"Ah, she is brave, *non?*" the stranger said. "She breaks a man's heart. Yet even the brave can die."

Ian MacVane, who had the soul of a mercenary, knew the man wasn't bluffing.

Miranda's gaze flicked to the sizzling fuse on the floor. "He'll cut my throat whether or not you stop this. Do it, Ian. I beg you."

He tamped back a roar of fury. To trade the life of the woman he loved for the lives of the strangers who ruled the world. To take that risk—

Tears streamed down her face. "Ian," she begged. "The fuse!"

"Enough," Duchesne snapped. "I grow weary of—" A round red dot appeared in the very center of his forehead. At the same moment, Ian heard the sharp report.

Duchesne's eyes went wide and then blank. He sagged back. The knife blade hovered at Miranda's neck, then fell from the man's slackened hand.

She shrieked and leaped away from her captor, who slithered down the side of the column, leaving a smear of blood on the white plaster. In a single stride Ian was upon the fuse, grinding it beneath his boot heel. "Get the other one," he told Miranda.

She lifted her skirts to run, but before she could move, a pleasant voice said, "We've already seen to it."

Miranda's fists clenched into the fabric of her dress. Ian felt a cold thud of disbelief inside him as he turned to face the man who had just saved both his and Miranda's lives.

"Lisle," he said.

With them were two of the men who had ridden into the Scottish village with Lucas. That firelit night seemed ages ago. The men held two others—Yvette, her face white with fear, and a man in black.

"He's the one who approached me at the portrait sitting," Miranda whispered. "The one who spoke to me so cryptically."

Lucas handed a smoking pistol to Duffie, who set it in its case. "It was a risky shot, but I didn't have time to make a better plan."

Ian studied the fallen man. "You're a keener shot than you let on at our duel, my lord."

Lucas looked sheepish. "I was angry with you that night, MacVane, but not angry enough to kill you."

Miranda stumbled toward him, clearly shaken by having a knife at her throat one moment, a man shot before her eyes the next. "Lucas, thank you. From the bottom of my heart, I thank you."

He bent forward a bit stiffly and kissed her brow.

The world stood still. Ian could not believe his eyes.

"Do that again," Miranda whispered.

Duffie opened his mouth as if to protest. Ian waved a hand to keep him silent.

Lucas kissed her again, his mouth tender and affectionate on her smooth, pale forehead. "Like that?" he asked with a smile.

She touched her brow where his lips had brushed her. "Yes. Like that. Like you used to." She laughed briefly. "When you did that just now, I remembered the rest. Everything."

"Everything?" Lucas asked.

"Everything we were to one another," she said. "The good times and the bad. Lucas, I remember that at one time, all I wanted in the world was to be with you."

Ian strode away. He could not bear to see the scene play itself out. He'd heard enough. *Everything.*

The real Miranda, the stranger he didn't know and who didn't know him, was back now. He could not simply stand there and watch her take on her old life, her old memories, falling back into her role as Lucas's long-suffering secret love.

He could hear shouting as he loped across the garden, back toward the main yard. But he ignored the noise.

In the distance, he could see the swaying silken top of the aerial balloon.

Adder had not yet made his escape. There was still time for Ian to take his revenge.

"Where is he going?" Miranda asked, feeling bereft and abandoned as Ian raced away from them. She put her hand to her throat, still feeling the cold ghost of

Duchesne's knife. The memory made her shudder. But she nearly forgot the incident as she watched Ian leaving without a word of good-bye.

"Think a wee minute, lassie," Duffie said. "Clearly, he didna understand what happened between you and His Lairdship."

"He heard what I said." She gazed calmly up at Lucas, knowing that he, too, had changed. "I remembered my past with Lord Lisle. I remembered that at one time, all I wanted was to be with him."

Lucas shoved a hand through his blond hair. But she could tell that he was strong enough to hear this now. Things had changed for him, too.

"I also remembered that on the last night we were together, we quarreled. Not just over your arrangement with Mr. Addingham. We simply did not suit. You needed a wife who would be an ornament to your position—well behaved, well spoken, and well born. I am none of those things and never will be."

"I did love you, Miranda," he said. "But—"

"But I'm correct. I'm also correct when I say the proper match has been right in front of your nose for years. She's the most well-spoken, well-born woman in England."

"Frances?" He chuckled. "I'd hardly call her well behaved."

Duffie tucked the pistol case under his arm. "Two out of three is better than most men get."

"I know," Lucas said. "I only pray she'll give me a chance to— Good God!"

Miranda and Duffie followed his astonished gaze. "The balloon!" she said, and started to run.

19

*Better to die sword in hand than in an unworthy
retirement.*

—Letizia Bonaparte,
mother of Napoleon

Miranda reached the reviewing grounds in
time to see Silas Addingham casting off the anchor
ropes that moored the balloon to the ground and then
heaving sandbag ballasts overboard. It was a reckless
launch, the act of a desperate man.

The ascent began slowly, clumsily, but inevitably.
A vigorous breeze blew the craft sideways. The
crowd, baffled by Addingham's frantic manner,
gasped in chorus.

As soon as the balloon's gondola cleared the top of
the reviewing stand, Miranda understood what all the
excitement was about.

"Glory be to the saints and send me to hell and
back," Duffie said.

Miranda was speechless. For there, dangling high

above the earth from one of the balloon's tether ropes, was Ian.

The balloon swayed awkwardly, the silken bag lolling like a drunken man's cap. Addingham was using a knife of some sort to saw at the rope Ian held.

He swung back and forth like a pendulum, and Miranda's heart turned over in her chest. This was hell, she thought. This was the very meaning of the word *terror*.

"Dear Lord, keep him safe," she whispered, oblivious of the people rushing around the quadrangle near her.

It was the sharpest, most unbearable irony she could imagine. Ian, who possessed more courage than an army of trained warriors, feared one thing in the world. "He's so afraid. He's so afraid of high places."

He climbed toward the gondola, his legs swinging this way and that as his powerful arms pulled him, hand over hand, up the stout length.

Could he make it before Silas hacked through the rope?

She had a sudden, piercing vision of Ian leaving her only moments ago. He thought she was remembering Lucas. He thought she was remembering love.

If he only knew. Please God, if he only knew. She'd had no notion of the true meaning of love and faith and trust until she had met Ian MacVane.

Now he was in danger of dying, and he would never know how much she loved him, how much he meant to her. What she wanted to mean to him.

A sob tore from her throat. The wind swept the balloon higher. Ian's weight made it sag. Miranda dared to hope he might bring it down. But then Addingham—or Adder, she forced herself to call him—cast off more ballast.

The lightened balloon soared, bobbing like a buoy in an invisible body of water.

Hand over hand Ian climbed while Adder sawed away. A babble of voices rose like the tide around Miranda, but they sounded distant, like the swish of the ocean heard through the curling caverns of a seashell.

Adder raised his arm and brought it down hard, giving the rope a final chop.

The severed rope dropped away from the basket.

Someone screamed. Miranda faintly recognized her own voice.

The gondola dipped and swayed. Ian had hold of the wicker edge with one hand.

Adder raised the knife again.

Gordie, take my hand!

Ian heard his own voice in the far reaches of memory. Suspended in the sky over England, he could clearly hear the desperation of the boy he had been.

In a flash, he saw his brother's terrified face, his mouth opened wide in a scream as he fell, leaving Ian with one hand empty.

A low growl of fury sounded above him. Adder.

Even as Ian grappled for purchase on the curved sides of the gondola, the knife came down toward his hand. Ian moved quickly enough to avoid the blow.

Fear was a powerful ally. He would do anything, *anything*, to keep from dying that way.

He made the mistake of glancing down. There was a certain terrible beauty in the estate below, the formal gardens perfect in their symmetry and the lawn an eye-smarting green. The people swarmed about like colorful ants. The curving wrought-iron gates embraced the front of the estate, with the finials of the iron thrusting skyward like great teeth.

And everywhere else the forest loomed, layer upon layer of deep emerald blazing in the sun. A lake, like a distant mirror, sparkled in its nest of summer trees.

Farther off lay the Channel. Adder's intended escape route.

Even as he took in a sight most men would never see, Ian swung his legs up. His foot caught the top edge of the basket. Silas's blade slashed cold fire across the back of Ian's hand. But Ian had something much more powerful than a knife. He had utter terror—and some twenty years of fury.

With a final heave, he tumbled into the gondola. It swayed and danced on the wind. Silas shrieked and grabbed the sides of the churning basket. But he recovered himself quickly, his powerful form reeling toward Ian.

The years fell away. Silas had changed so little that Ian was amazed he had not recognized him on sight. The bearded creature who had not flinched at butchering Scottish crofters so long ago still had the same icy gaze, the same ruthless mouth, the same greed-driven strength.

The blade drove straight for Ian's heart. He rolled to one side. The apparatus above their heads, the source of the coal gas keeping the balloon aloft, hissed in protest. The silk flapped like a ship's luffing sails.

Ian grabbed a rope, his hand dripping blood and growing numb. He slashed a humorless grin at Silas. "Could you not put that thing away, Mr. Adder, and let the two of us die in peace?"

"Count yerself dead already." In his agitation,

Adder forgot to affect his cultured accent. "I have work to do and a pretty reward waiting for me in France."

Wary, his gaze trained on the knife, Ian recalled what it was like to be driven by work alone. Miranda was lost to him now. Even if she never forgot the nights she had spent in his arms, she had made her choice. To Ian, it was yet another death. Another fatal wound to the soul.

He let out a curse and caught Silas's wrist on the next downward thrust of the knife. The sharp blade trembled between them.

Silas's face grew bright red with effort. He gritted his teeth. "Should've made short work of you up at Crough na Muir."

Ian's surprise must have shown, for Adder wheezed out a chuckle. "Aye, I've known for a long time that you were one of the clan MacVane. Filthy crofters, all, and you got no better than you deserved."

"Your name is a curse on the lips of Highlanders," Ian said between his teeth. The blood pulsed out of the wound on his hand, and his grip on Adder's wrist slipped. Ian recaptured it, eliciting a yelp of pain from Silas.

The man was desperate, Ian thought, looking deep into the chilly depths of his eyes. He kept watching the blade, waiting for a chance.

"They should thank me for clearing the district of useless human rubble. I should've been more thorough. Tell me, MacVane," said the big Englishman, his voice soft and cunning, "how is your mother these days?"

*   *   *

In some small, still-functioning region of Miranda's brain, she became aware that the entire military elite and blue-blooded nobility of Europe were watching Ian's struggle, high above.

"For the love of God, *do* something, Arthur!" shrieked Wellington's wife. The duke of Wellington paused in his pacing to stare skyward, his mouth tight, his face ashen. He was a man whose humanity had not been tarnished by the horrors of war, a man who could still look upon a terrible death and be moved by it.

"I didn't even know MacVane and Addingham were acquainted," the prince of Wales mused. "And here they're behaving like mortal enemies. It's all a bit of a puzzle to me."

"*Comme d'habitude,* Your Highness," Frances said with a blasé matter-of-factness that went right past him.

Miranda neither moved nor spoke. It was like being in the middle of a hideous, vivid dream, the blue-and-gold silk balloon bobbing in the crystal clear summer sky, each gust of wind sweeping it farther and farther away.

Then Lucas appeared, but he did not approach Miranda. It was as if he knew that to touch her now would cause her to shatter. She stood like a statue, her face tilted toward the sky, her chest so full of dread she thought she would burst.

Lucas went to Frances and took her in his arms, and she clung to him.

Miranda remained in the middle of the green, surrounded by jabbering, shouting people. She felt cold despite the heat of the summer sun. Alone despite the crowd.

Her father came to her then, aided by a bentwood

cane. "Miranda, I'm so sorry," he said. "I'm so sorry it's ending this way. If only I had been able to get away sooner, if only I had understood what Addingham was after, perhaps I could have stopped this."

"There are too many if-onlys, Papa," she whispered, then winced as the balloon took a drunken dip and the wind dragged it in the direction of the thick forest. "They do not console me."

"I know, my love."

A small boy in blue silk breeches stood nearby, shading his eyes. He reminded Miranda poignantly of Robbie, back in Scotland. Dear God, someone would have to break the news to Robbie. "That man is going to die, isn't he?" the child asked.

"We must pray for a miracle," Miranda heard herself say. She felt her father's surprised gaze and realized the old Miranda had not believed in miracles. The old Miranda had clung to hard scientific principles, believing only in that which could be proven. Now she knew better. Now she knew that the most important things in life were invisible and could never be touched—yet they were more real than Newton's apple.

"Do you think he's praying?" the little boy asked.

She thought of Ian, her dark angel, and wondered if he knew how to pray. Yes, she thought. Yes, he does. When he had taken her to the top of Crough na Muir, they had looked out over the soaring landscape, and the expression on his face had been spiritual, peaceful.

"We must pray with him," a woman said. "Come along, dear."

Miranda refused to blink for fear of missing something. She wondered if Ian was thinking of her. She wondered if, in his last moments, he would remember all she had been to him and know that she had loved him.

Love. Once she'd discovered it, she had been convinced that it was the most powerful force in the universe. Powerful enough to heal her wounded mind, to heal Ian's shattered soul. Because of her, because he believed he'd lost her love, Ian had flung himself into peril.

The men in the balloon went back and forth, tearing at each other's throats in a deadly dance. It was impossible to tell which was which. They both wore black clothing, and they were so far away, and drifting farther by the second.

"Ian's strong," Miranda said, her hands twisting together until her knuckles ached. "He'll overpower Silas and then find a way to land the balloon safely."

"Ah, Miranda." Gideon's voice was broken, defeated. "I didn't want to have to tell you, but I've failed you once again. It can't happen like that."

"But why not?" she demanded. "I don't know what you mean—"

"He's going to fall!" a voice in the crowd shrieked.

"To the gates!" someone else bellowed. "They're above the front gates."

One of the men in the balloon was leaning out over the edge of the basket, the other's hands at his throat. He teetered precariously, and the balloon dipped. Ian or Silas? she wondered frantically, even as she began to run toward the gate.

Gideon bellowed an order to a pair of slack-jawed footmen. They made a seat of their arms and bore him like a Roman centurion along with the surging crowd.

The struggle high above went on, but clearly one

man was about to go over the side. Still Miranda could not tell which was Ian. The bottom of the gondola wavered perilously, then careened and snapped like the tail of a kite. She stopped running when she neared the front gates. The footmen carrying Gideon stopped, too.

A black-clad man fell from the sky.

There was silence while he fell, as if every part of the world had stopped except for the plummeting body.

The body. The body that struck the wrought-iron bars of the gate. The body pierced through by black iron finials. It had a sound all its own, a wet thud and then a rush of air like steam hissing from a kettle.

The silence reigned a moment longer.

Then the screams started. Men and women alike covered their eyes, wept with horror.

Feeling as if she were in the middle of a waking nightmare, Miranda went to the gate. The air felt thick, like water, slowing her, but she forced herself onward. Toward the motionless body bowed across the fence.

She took one look at the lifeless face, hanging upside down, the eyes staring, and rushed back to her father. Sobs racked her body, and tears streamed down her face. "Oh, my God, Papa," she said, crumpling into his arms. "My God, it's *him.*"

"Damn me, who? Which one?"

She shuddered, almost unable to bring herself to say the name. Then she dredged it up past her aching throat. "It's Silas Addingham. Adder is dead."

Gideon closed his eyes a moment, his nostrils thinning as he inhaled. "Come, sweet," he said, turning away. "Let us go back to the house. You need a draft of brandy, or—"

She pulled away from him. "Papa! Ian is still up there!"

The balloon, lightened of Silas's weight, bobbled and pitched even higher, scudding above the thickest part of the forest.

"I must watch him land. He doesn't know what he's doing, so we'd best be ready." She studied Gideon's face, and a chill streaked up her spine. "You said something a moment ago, Papa. When I told you that Ian could overpower Silas and land the balloon, you said it couldn't happen like that."

"Did I?" Gideon's shoulders narrowed in defeat. "I did."

"What did you mean?" She grasped his hands, held them desperately. "Tell me, Papa. Tell me what you meant."

"I've failed you too many times to count, Miranda. But this time will be the last, for after today, I won't expect you to speak to me ever again."

"It's the balloon, isn't it?" she said, watching its almost comical dance through the summer sky. "There's something wrong with the balloon."

He nodded in misery and shame. "I discovered a flaw in the design. The copper fuel tubes tend to rub against the gold-beater lining of the silk. After a while, it creates sparks."

"Oh, God," Miranda said. "No, please God . . ." She forced herself to watch the balloon, forced herself to ask one final question of her father. Her well-meaning father, whose folly was going to kill Ian MacVane. "What's going to happen?" she asked.

The balloon caught fire. Ian felt nothing more than a dull, hollow surprise when it happened. After heaving Adder over the side, he had experienced a single rush of elation, a sense of justice, as quickly gone as a stroke of summer lightning.

For what did it mean, after all?

Silas's death would not bring back Ian's father, or Gordon, or the baby. It would not make his mother whole again.

It would not make Miranda love him.

And why should she, anyway? He had lied to her. Placed her directly in the path of danger. Stolen her innocence. Worse, shattered her fragile trust.

So when Silas went over the side and the lightened balloon swooped dizzily upward, Ian merely felt battle shocked, like a soldier who had just lost a limb and still felt the tingle of its presence.

In his mind, Miranda lingered like fine perfume. The magic of her was strong, as if she were very near, caressing him, calling to him, whispering his name.

Except that the whisper was an angry splutter and a hiss. He glanced up in time to see an orange flame leap up, lick at the gold-lined silk of the balloon.

At first, he could not bring himself to react. No force in creation was stronger than his terror of heights; if he stood in the gondola, he would be compelled to look down, to see the toy houses and tiny trees below.

He inhaled deeply. The air was frigid, and the breath did not seem to feed his starving lungs. How odd, he thought, realizing he was growing lightheaded from the altitude.

Wrong. What was wrong? Oh. The idea that there was no force stronger than his fear. But there was. There had to be. He tried to take another breath. Remember that one time . . . ?

Remember.

How often he had urged Miranda to remember,

only to seize her memories and use them for his own cold purpose.

Remember.

A fire. A dizzying height. And he had overcome his fear. He had defeated his darkest enemy. Because . . .

He shook his head, listening to the crackle of the fire, watching without comprehending as the edges of the silk blackened and curled.

Because of Robbie. The answer flared in his head. That was it. He'd held the lad in his arms and known that if the fear conquered him, they would both perish.

There. You've proven it, he told himself, grasping the sides of the gondola, hauling himself up. You've found something stronger than fear. The need to survive. For Robbie. For Miranda. For the memories he held in his heart. For the days he had shared with her, the nights of being her lover.

He drew himself to his full height. He had flown higher than ever and sailed over the woods now, the green woods and the winking blue lake and the endless sky stretching out into eternity.

Suffocating, shivering with cold, his thoughts muddled, he tried to concentrate. He could not reach the flaming silk to douse the fire. He could not cut off the supply of gas, for then he would simply plummet to the ground.

He touched one of the cords that anchored the gondola to the silk bag. The balloon teetered.

And once again, he remembered Miranda. Something she'd said. *One day, we'll be able to sail a balloon much like a ship sails the seas.*

"Avast!" he shouted, laughing with the hideous irony and hopelessness of it all. "Blow me to the bounds of buggery!" Cackling like a crazed pirate and drunk from lack of oxygen, Ian MacVane began to work the controls. The balloon responded feebly, wavering down and to the left. "Heave to, and no more five-water grog!" he bellowed.

And he was laughing. Laughing, because his fear was gone. Laughing, because this was the ride of his life. Laughing, because he was about to fall from the sky in a burning silk balloon, and there wasn't a damned thing he could do about it.

Exit laughing, he told himself, tugging on the ropes, pretending he could steer the balloon like a seasoned helmsman. Aye, laddie, there's the spirit. Exit laughing.

20

When flying machines begin to fly
We shall never stay at home,
Away we'll skip on a half-day trip
To Paris, perhaps, or Rome.
　　　　—The Musical Comedy
　　　　　　The Bride of Bath

    The crowned heads of Europe bowed in regret as the flaming balloon plummeted into the forest. Chroniclers and reporters would swear, when their hands stopped shaking and they wrote their accounts of the extraordinary day, that everyone heard laughter—eerie, joyous laughter—as the balloon went down.

The duke of Wellington organized a detachment of men to comb the smoke-filled woods for wreckage.

Miranda knew that her heart was still beating in her breast, because when she put her hand there, she could feel it. But she was a dead woman. Her spirit had died. Her soul had died.

She had never really lived until she'd met Ian MacVane. She had been a woman half alive, sustained by the meager satisfaction of scholarship and invention. No wonder Lucas Chesney had seemed to her the very epitome of romance and excitement.

But that was before Ian. Before she had looked across a roomful of madwomen and seen his astonished face, his fiery blue eyes. Before he had whisked her away on a sea voyage and danced with her on the deck of a ship. Before he had stood before all the people of Crough na Muir and pledged to wed her.

Before Ian, she'd had no notion of her own capacity for passion and joy. And for pain.

Oh, God, Ian, what happened to us?

Brutal reality was what had happened, she told herself.

She was barely aware that she was following the men into the forest, walking doggedly toward a gray billow of smoke.

Even at his most deceptive, Ian had managed to convey a sense of caring and tenderness that made his duplicity irrelevant. She remembered his gifts—a small pony of a dog and a sprig of heather. They weren't the gifts of a hardened spymaster, but those of a man who loved with a reluctant heart.

He *had* loved her; she knew it with the diamond-hard certainty of perfect hindsight. He had loved her until it hurt, and he had kept on loving her, long after he should have let her go.

"You let me go at last, my love, my Ian," she said, the heat of the tears like flames on her face. "Ah, love, you let me go."

Men fanned out through the woods, some of them stopping to beat out bits of burning debris in the dry wood and underbrush. Someone yelled that he had reached the lake, and that the men should bring buckets and barrels from the estate.

Near Miranda, a tall dead tree flared up, the flames decking its branches like fiery autumn leaves. There was a great *whoosh* as the fire sucked at the air.

She fell back into the past, back to that night when she had caused the explosions in London. She used to fear trusting her own judgment, yet now she felt strangely calm as she walked toward a wall of fire.

Someone shouted at her to stay away, but she went closer and closer, mesmerized by the hot, strong beauty of the burning woods.

She saw him then, a shadow man like the one she had glimpsed that night long ago, an image out a dream. Aye, a dream, it had to be, for he walked through the golden veil of flames and emerged unscathed.

He could not be real, but still she ran to him, thinking that his ghost was a gift from God, a last chance to tell him good-bye, to tell him of the love that wrenched her heart.

"Ian!" she screamed, knowing they would think her mad. "Ian!"

He swooped her up in his arms and spun her around, and her face was streaked with tears, her dress wet by his sodden clothing—

She stumbled back. "You're alive!"

He spread his arms wide, showing her the drenched rags of his shirt and trousers, the tall black boots squelching on the forest floor. "I fell into the lake. I came back down because I had to tell you something."

She shook her head in shock and disbelief. "You have to tell me . . . something," she repeated stupidly.

He took her hand and she saw that his was cut and

bleeding. "Never mind that," he muttered, and hurried her out of the woods to the fringe of the green, where a cool breeze swept over them. Already the fire was dying as a small army of men brought it under control.

Miranda heard a buzzing sound in her ears like a swarm of bees. The sensation of utter joy and relief. Too powerful for words.

"I conquered my fear of high places," he said, speaking matter-of-factly, as if he had not just fallen out of the clear blue sky. "That was one thing I wanted to tell you."

"There's more?" she squeaked, unable to form a coherent thought.

"I thought you might want to know that. The navigating ropes on the balloon need work, though the idea has promise. I remembered what you said about wind currents. I sailed through the sky like a ship on the seas, Miranda, just like you said. A bit faster than I would have liked—"

"*That* is your big announcement?"

"I aimed myself for the lake. The water broke my fall. Not the smoothest of landings, but there you are. And here I am."

"Here you are," she echoed dully. *Here you are here you are here you are.* Her mind reeled and bobbed crazily, as the balloon had, thousands of feet in the sky.

"There's something else I need to say to you, Miranda," Ian went on, quite calm, seemingly oblivious to her shock and confusion. "The most important thing of all. The very reason I fought so hard to stay alive."

"I'm . . . listening."

His arms slipped around her, and she began to

believe. The feeling unfurled inside her like a blossom opening to the sun. At last, she could believe he was real, he was alive, he had survived. He was actually here, holding her in his arms.

"Ian, I thought you—"

"Weesht, lass, and listen." He pressed a finger to her lips, then removed it, leaving the taste of soot on her mouth and apologizing with a grin. "I was given a second chance. Like you, love. You had the answer all along."

His hand burrowed into her hair, cradling her head. "You are the one who taught me to fly, my beautiful Miranda. You taught me to fly, but more than that."

"I should hope so," she said, beginning to feel peeved.

"I know I don't have to leave the ground in order to soar."

A sob ripped from her throat. She wasn't sure why his words darted into the very softest part of her heart, but they did.

He let her go. "Ah, my love, I am so sorry. You chose Lucas, and I'm prepared to accept that."

Yet another shock jolted her. *"Lucas?"*

"I think in future he'll be more discriminating about the company he keeps. He's a decent sort and one hell of a sharpshooter. He'll probably get a handsome reward for stopping the rockets and apprehending Yvette and the Austrian. You'll be well heeled enough too—"

"You think I chose Lucas." The words dropped like dull thuds of disbelief from her. Then, abruptly, she threw back her head and shrieked with laughter. She coughed, realizing she was close to hysterics and even closer to tears. "You are the most thickheaded of idiotic males, Ian MacVane. You went stalking off after revenge before you realized what was happening between Lucas and me."

"And what was that?"

"I *did* remember. The moment he kissed me, I remembered. Whatever Lucas and I shared in the past is gone. We could not have been in love, because it didn't last. Couldn't last."

"How," he asked, a cautious optimism lighting his blue, fierce eyes, "did you come to be such an expert in love, Miss Miranda Stonecypher?"

"It's Miranda Stonecypher *MacVane*, and that's one thing I'll not be forgetting," she told him, trying to laugh through her tears and failing miserably. "I love you, Ian. Even when I didn't know anything else in the world, I loved you. Even when I had every right to despise you, I loved you. And I always, always will."

She expected him to gather her into his arms then. She wanted it. She ached with wanting it.

Instead, he sank down on one knee, almost reverently carrying her hands to his lips, covering her fingers and palms with kisses that seared her very soul. "And I love you, Miranda. Right from the start, I knew I would. I told myself I was after your secrets. But deep inside, I knew it was more than that. I was after your heart."

She yanked him to his feet. "Then kiss me, for heaven's sake, MacVane."

And he did, at last giving her the kiss she had been waiting for, the kiss she would have waited for all of her life. When it was over, she looked up into Ian's face and smiled.

"Well?" she asked.

"Duty discharged," he murmured, and kissed her again.

pilogue

We live by admiration, hope, and love;
And even as these are well and wisely fixed,
In dignity of being we ascend.
                              —Wordsworth

Crough na Muir, Scotland
April 1815

   "You look," Miranda said, "like the very essence of Scotland." Her bright-eyed gaze swept unabashedly over her husband's tall form as he entered the morning room of Innes Manor, the newly renovated house on the hill.

The butter yellow sunshine of early morning streamed in through brand new casements, and the view outside was of abundant gardens splashed with color. Against a perfect sky, the mountain called Ben Innes brooded over the midnight blue sea.

"How does it feel to be the laird?" she asked in a

teasing voice. "You certainly wear the position well. What did you do this morning? Collect rents? Settle disputes? Dispense justice?"

He laughed, the color high in his cheeks. His hair had grown longer, thick and curling over the collar of his blousy shirt. In a kilt made of the MacVane tartan, he seemed to come from another time, a simpler time, when a man was measured by the deeds he did, not by the company he kept or the wealth he accumulated.

With long strides, he crossed the room and snatched her up off the chaise where she was reclining. "I spent the morning getting Callum's pig out of the Scobies' potato patch."

She recoiled, but he caught her, chuckling as he bent to nuzzle her neck. "I washed before I came in, love, and parked my mucky boots at the stable door."

She skimmed her arms up over his shoulders, glorying in the feel of him, his nearness, the sense of safety she felt with him. Nearly a year had passed since he had walked out of a burning forest and declared his love for her. A blessed, amazing year.

In recognition of his heroism, Ian MacVane had been designated a knight of the realm and granted full possession in perpetuity of the estate overlooking Crough na Muir. But more than that, he had been given a second chance to live. That was exactly what he had said that day, and even now, just remembering his words made her eyes fill with tears.

He shook his head, sympathy pulling at the tender edges of his smile. "Ah, Miranda. Weepy again?"

"You make me so, Ian MacVane," she said, trying to conquer the quaver in her voice. "You and no other have that power."

His hand drifted down, shaped itself around the

gentle, prominent curve of her belly. "I alone, sweet-heart? That I canna believe. Someone else is tugging at your heart— Jesus!" He snatched his hand away as if it had been burned and stared goggle-eyed at her belly. "The bairn! He—he—"

Her tears evaporated on gales of laughter. "Aye, my love, the bairn. He moves constantly these days. Agnes says it's a good sign."

A loud popping noise, followed by a shriek, came from the gardens. Ian and Miranda hurried out through the tall double doors to see what had happened.

Gideon Stonecypher stood glaring at a smoldering black circle on the lawn. Robbie was nearby, hugging himself across the stomach and screaming with laughter. Mary MacVane, looking frail but self-possessed in a tidy linsey-woolsey gown, had her hand over her mouth. Her blue eyes, so like her son's, danced. She still had her melancholy days, but having Ian near and Robbie to visit her were a tonic. And she took a certain delight in teasing Gideon about his numerous experiments.

"Now what?" Ian asked with mock severity.

Gideon put a hand to his abundant white hair, staring in puzzlement at the ground. "The savages of America send signals with puffs of smoke. If we could perfect that, we'd no longer have to build towers for the semaphore flags."

Miranda cleared her throat. "I thought we were going to turn our attention to practical matters, Papa. A spring-powered cradle that keeps rocking. A tread-mill for the sheep shearing."

She still had her thirst for invention, but after last summer she'd had her fill of weapons of war. She far preferred Crough na Muir. It was a little world unto itself, a place where they had no need to concern themselves with the destruction and mayhem that used to consume Ian and had nearly killed him.

A moment later, as if to contradict her thoughts, Duffie rode up, bearing a sack of mail. "The post arrived by packet," he declared, doffing his cap to the ladies. He held out a parcel bound in twine. "From Lady Frances. And you"—he winked at Robbie—"have a job to do in the stable."

Duffie offered Mary his arm and started toward the stableyard. Robbie led the horse off, with Macbeth, the deerhound, trotting behind them.

Miranda felt a fluttering of abject fear in her chest. Her happiness was too perfect to last. She knew it. Frances was summoning him back to London, or hatching some counterplot, since Napoleon had escaped from Elba in the spring and was marching northward through France, conquering as he went.

"No," she whispered, and Ian seemed not to hear her as he used a penknife to slit open the twine that bound the parcel.

The first item was a letter written on thick cream stock. The seal was that of the Viscount Lisle. Frances had married Lucas after all. It was either that, she had said, only half teasing, or bring him up on charges and deport him to Australia along with Yvette.

The pair proved to be amazingly compatible. "My dear MacVane," Ian read aloud, cocking a grin at Frances's form of address, "I know you are bound to tease me about this, but I have been stricken with an irresistible urge to grow flowers and have babies. Such happy pursuits must wait, however. It looks as though Bonaparte is entrenched at Les Invalides. Troops are deserting King Louis by the score; there are so many that Bonaparte is telling them, 'Thanks, truly, but I have enough now.' So annoying. Lucas has promised to join the effort to dislodge the little Corsican."

Miranda watched her husband closely. What was he thinking? Did he wish to be back in London, in the middle of things?

He read on. "I enclose an etching which is a copy of the portrait done by Thomas Lawrence last summer. I don't believe we'll ever see the like of such extraordinary company in one place again. You'll note the artist added a Very Fashionable Pair to the picture." Ian unfurled an engraving printed on heavy paper. It was a facsimile of the portrait begun the day Miranda had remembered her father.

The famous crowned heads and military heroes of the age graced the picture. As Frances had promised, Lord and Lady Lisle were present, hands clasped, two halves of a very happy whole.

"So there you are," Ian said brusquely. He looked thoughtful for a moment and walked to the edge of the garden above a steep hill that plunged down toward the glen.

Miranda went to join her husband, wondering what was going through his mind. Something stopped her from asking.

She was afraid to hear the answer.

Gideon, it seemed, had no such compunction. "Do you miss it, then?" he demanded, striding to Ian's side and glaring out at the hurling sea. "The intrigue? The subterfuge? The danger? Does rusticating up here bore you when you hear about all the excitement in London?"

Miranda felt a chill. "Papa, leave it alone."

"I'll answer," Ian said, his eyes wintry. "'Tis a fair

question." He lifted his face to the wind and sun. "I feel as if I've been on a journey all of my life." He closed his eyes briefly, then opened them and stared at his hand, braced upon the stone wall of the garden. He never wore a glove anymore, never sought to mask the stump of his finger. "It was like being on a voyage with no end in sight. And I hated it. God, I hated it."

He drew a deep breath between his teeth, and Miranda realized that this was hard for him, describing the life he had lived. It was like putting words to a melody that kept changing. "Finally, I was able to release the past and embrace the future, Gideon. And I knew where my journey had to end."

His blue-eyed gaze swept the vast expanse of Crough na Muir. She wondered if he could still picture the little croft, hear the voices of his long-dead family.

"Here," Miranda said with sudden understanding. "Right here, where it began."

"When did you know, Ian?" Gideon's voice broke. His meddling had almost brought about the demise of innocents, and the idea still haunted him. He was still on his own quest for peace. "When did you discover you could come home, start a new life, and put the past behind you?" he persisted. "Was it after you learned who Addingham was and sent him to his death?"

"No," Ian replied, turning swiftly and gathering his wife close to his chest. A wave of gratitude and tenderness washed through her. He looked down, his eyes brimming with all the fullness of his love. "It was after Miranda."

Escape to Romance
and
WIN A YEAR OF ROMANCE!

Ten lucky winners will receive a free year of romance—*more than 30 free books*. Every book HarperMonogram publishes in 1997 will be delivered directly to your doorstep if you are one of the ten winners drawn at random.

Harper
Monogram

Let HarperMonogram Sweep You Away

MISBEGOTTEN by Tamara Leigh

Only $3.99

No one can stop baseborn knight Liam Fawke from gaining his rightful inheritance—not even the beautiful Lady Joslyn. Yet Liam's strong resolve is no match for the temptress whose spirit and passion cannot be denied.

COURTNEY'S COWBOY by Susan Macias
Time Travel Romance

Only $3.99

Married couple Courtney and Matt have little time for each other until they are transported back to 1873 Wyoming. Under the wide western sky they discover how to fall truly in love for the first time.

SOULS AFLAME by Patricia Hagan
New York Times Bestselling Author

Only $3.99

with Over Ten Million Copies of Her Books in Print

Julie Marshal's duty to save her family's Georgia plantation gives way to desire in the arms of Derek Arnhardt. With a passion to match her own, the ship's captain will settle for nothing less than possessing Julie, body and soul.

Harper Monogram